The
Magdalene
Woman

The Magdalene Woman

by
MARGARET ROGERS

St. Martin's Press
New York

Copyright © 1980 by Margaret Rogers
All rights reserved. For information, write:
St. Martin's Press, Inc., 175 Fifth Avenue, New York, N.Y. 10010.
Manufactured in the United States of America

Library of Congress Cataloging in Publication Data
Rogers, Margaret, 1943–
 The Magdalene woman.

 1. Mary Magdalene, Saint—Fiction. I. Title.
PZ4.R7273Mag 1980 [PR6068.O35] 823'.914 79-28420
ISBN 0-312-50405-5

Permission to reprint excerpts from THE PSALMS: A NEW
TRANSLATION granted by William Collins Sons & Co., Ltd. and
the Grail, England.

For invaluable information, acknowledgement is hereby made to
DAILY LIFE IN PALESTINE AT THE TIME OF CHRIST by
Henry Daniel-Rops, translated by P. O'Brien.

To Pat, with love

I promise you, in whatever part of the world this gospel is preached, the story of what she has done shall be told in its place to preserve her memory.

• Matt. 26:13.

CHAPTER
• ONE •

IN THE END THEY starved them out. But it took one
hundred days to do it and fifteen thousand Roman soldiers
finally to raze the walls of Sion—those impregnable walls.
The trees too are felled. Not one oak or terebinth stands where
the great forests once flourished, for they crucified my countrymen until there was no wood left for the rough-hewn crosses. So
the rest were massacred along with the women, the children
and the old. These were the fortunate. They did not live to
endure the long voyage crushed in the fetid holds of the prison
ships or experience the horror of the Roman slave markets at
the end of it.

They say that ninety thousand Israelites were dispersed
throughout the empire—young women bound to patrician
mistresses who envied the beauty of these foreign maidservants;
young men fettered to the galley oars until death released them
to the sharks. Others provided sport in the games arenas or
built the Colosseum with their blood and tears. Countless
numbers died in their chains in the marble quarries of Phrygia.

A day to be marked with a white stone. A day of vengeance
for Titus and the long line of emperors who had impotently

1

cursed these ungovernable people, who would not bow their heads to the Roman yoke.

They came back from their hideouts in the mountains and found Jerusalem a smoking ruin, a graveyard of unburied dead. Through the smoldering holocaust of the Temple they wandered like shadows, and by Siloam's waters and not Babylon's they sat down and wept for the Holy City, the apple of Yahweh's eyes, Sion their Mother.

"Let us depart from this place."

On the night of Pentecost the Temple priests heard the voice that was everywhere and nowhere say these words, and the whole great edifice trembled. The first among many signs of pending disaster—and the high priest ignored it. No penance was done, no reparation made, for Yahweh could never desert his people nor give Israel, his dove, to the hawk.

But Jerusalem is leveled to the ground. The Temple sacrifice is abandoned and the Israel I knew is gone forever—as he said would happen.

"Behold, your house is left to you desolate."

It does not seem forty years since I came here, but old age with all its infirmities tells me it is so. I forget things now—faces, names, even the days of the week—but the past is always with me. The need has gone to slip back down the years seeking out those I knew, for my time, it seems, has come full circle and I am reunited with those I love, and they in turn assure me it is always thus as life draws to a close. But, looking up, I catch the young ones smiling and then I know that I am a foolish old woman who speaks her thoughts aloud and falls asleep twenty times a day. Foolish I may be, but not senile. Not by any means.

They call me mother now, acknowledging my years, and strangers refer to "the hermit woman" because I choose to live alone on the desert fringe, but my family and all my long-dead friends laugh when I tell them this.

"To us, you are Mary," they say. "Mary of Mejdel."

Then I remember. The door swings open and it all comes flooding back.

I was born in Mejdel or Magdala in the northern province of Galilee. It was a small village on the western shore of the Lake of Gennesaret or, as some of us called it, the Sea of Galilee. A quick glance would reveal that such a name was a gross exaggeration, but overstatement was a common failing in us. Even our surrounding hills we called mountains. But it was without doubt a lovely part of the country. Israel was our Promised Land, but Galilee in the springtime was Eden. Even the south conceded this, but there the praise ended, for the average Galilean had never been regarded as an outstanding example of the perfect Israelite. That prize went to the Judeans, an austere, orthodox people claiming pure descent from the tribes of Benjamin and Judah. From this stemmed their contempt for the northerner who, nurtured in a softer climate, was too tolerant for their liking, too afraid of hard work and far too liberal in interpreting the Law to suit himself. Above all, living in such a backwater, he knew nothing of the social, political and religious questions fermenting in Jerusalem until they were long out of date. He was a real country cousin. Even his accent was a cause for derision. Was he saying "immar" or "hamor?"—his lamb or his ass? The way he slurred his vowels made it impossible to know. It might even be "hamar"—his wine! Not by any yardstick did he belong to the elite tribes of Israel.

But strangely enough, none of this perturbed the average Galilean going on his tolerant way, and neither did it trouble us in our lakeside village. Indeed, we had only one cause for resentment. Forty years before I was born, Pompey marched his army across our borders and took Jerusalem. For the past five hundred years, we had been subject to foreign overlords and we found the role humiliating, for we were a proud people used to, and glorying in, weapons and warfare. Now, once again, we were unarmed and our country was occupied by a heathen rabble who came, they said, as peaceful intermediaries in the bloody dissensions which tore Israel apart and made civil war a fearful reality. It was natural, therefore, that many welcomed this protectorate, but the warring factions fiercely resented their presence and frequent uprisings brought Roman retribution and much bloodshed. But we seemed indestructible in those days, and as fast as they bludgeoned us down in one quarter we reappeared in another till orders came from Rome that the bulk of troops was to withdraw so as not to provoke us. But this singular concession from the ruler of the civilized world made small difference to our hostile attitude. Whether we saw the soldiers or not, we knew they were there, stationed in Syria and ready to pour down from the north at the first hint of trouble. Our men, of course, were exempt from conscription, for their religious duties made military service impossible. Besides, no Israelite would fight alongside a pagan.

We were good haters then. I suppose there was reason to be, but I do not like to think of it now. This same hatred we reserved for our tetrarch, a semi-Israelite giving partial observance to the Law and loyalty to the emperor who appointed him, a vassal-prince greedy for power and ruthless in retaining it while reaching out for more. During my years in Galilee our overlord was Herod Antipas, son of the infamous Idumaen, Herod the Great.

If the stranger could not guess that Magdala meant "the fish-tower," then the all-pervading smell would soon have enlightened him. Indeed, our pickled fish was renowned even as far as Rome but, this apart, Magdala had nothing of note to recommend it and was no different from the other villages scattered along the shore. But to us it was home and we loved it—my brother Lazarus, my sister Martha, and I the youngest. There were two other children who died at birth.

My father was originally a small textiles shopkeeper, but after inheriting a small sum of money, he decided to venture into wholesale trade, having one or two contacts in that field willing to help him start his new enterprise. He had been moderately successful over the years and could now rely on a small nucleus of regular customers to form the core of his trade. Father was basically a simple man and not greatly interested in a wide margin of profit so long as we had sufficient for our needs. Good-natured and tolerant, he was not at all the distant figure most Hebrew fathers seemed in those days.

But his wife was completely different. How often it occurs that a man will choose his exact opposite when marrying, and mother, industrious and orthodox, was no exception. I confess that I was never really close to her. I knew Martha to be her favorite daughter and never resented it. But even father was wary of her tongue, for she constantly urged him to be more efficient in his dealings with clients or less dilatory in gathering overdue debts, and nothing annoyed father more than to be told by a woman how to run his business. Actually mother was right in many ways about his methods, but when it came to tendering advice, she possessed little tact and never knew when she had said enough.

Only Martha, who neither idled nor argued, had mother's full approval, for my sister was amply endowed with common sense and humored everyone's foibles on the basis that we must all live together and so tolerance was a necessary virtue. Brimful of energy, Martha began each day with the chivvying out of father along with the odd incumbent hen, for none of the many tasks that faced us the moment the sun rose could be tackled with a man occupying our limited space. But father was always glad to

5

flee the daily bustle and willingly vanished till evening. How often I wished that I might go with him.

"If you would only go to your work with a will, Mary, you would not find it nearly so difficult," Martha observed as she rolled back her sleeves prior to plunging her arms into the bowl of greasy water where the cooking pots were soaking. But my will deserted me each morning as I gloomily contemplated the first task of the day—cleaning and trimming our ornate, old-fashioned lamp inherited from mother's family and the pride of her heart, and obviously designed to last for generations, unlike the simple earthenware vessel that others used.

". . . and it also needs a new wick. There's some hemp over there you can use." And Martha nodded across to one of the chests.

Ignoring her words, I gazed listlessly round our little garden, still cool in the early morning, and sighed. My sister looked up impatiently.

"Come, Mary, decide what you will do, for mother will soon be back and she'll not be pleased to find you idling."

Frankly, I did not know what I wanted, but one thing I did *not* want was to remain in the house trimming lamps on a glorious morning with the birds singing and the tamarisks nodding in pink sprays under the wall. I should like to go walking high in the hills above the lake. No one should be indoors with the dew still wet on the ground and the air . . . but at this point Martha, who detested slackness, interrupted my reverie by briskly stepping over me in the doorway to throw out the dirty water.

"I don't think you know yourself," she said, echoing my own thoughts. "You waste so much time daydreaming of what you would *like* to do and not what you *should* be doing that in the end your work is either badly done or not finished at all."

Coming back into the house, she gathered up the bedding. "Your fault lies in too much imagination. I should never achieve anything if I spent a goodly portion of the day thinking about it. It's your pair of hands we need in this house, not your imagination. Mother and I can manage without that."

Martha's lecture irritated me. That phrase "Mother and I" was typical of my sister—Voice and Echo, I called them privately. Roused from my torpor, I decided to retaliate, squabbles being a common domestic feature in our country where the women are herded together the entire day.

"And your fault, Martha, lies in not thinking at all! Your only aim and interest is to finish as much work as possible before the sun goes down—and to what avail? You must begin it all again the next day. I sometimes wish I'd been born a goat," I concluded peevishly as my desire for a quarrel faded with the sun's increasing heat. "Then no one would trouble or vex me." And I peered around at Sheba tethered nearby.

Martha, pausing in her work, looked at me in surprise, for my opinion of her had not been flattering. "Well!" she began in flustered, good-natured tones, "I don't think there's any cause to speak like that, Mary. After all, you don't need imagination to grind the barley or ret the flax, and I know," she continued earnestly with the bed rolls still clutched in her arms, "that every week I try to understand the homily so I can think about it during the sabbath, although it's true," she concluded honestly and apologetically, "that mainly I think about the washing and other household tasks."

My sister plucked absently at the loose threads of her bed roll and sighed over her shortcomings. "Perhaps you're right, Mary. I don't think enough of the important things. I should try and see your viewpoint sometimes. However," glancing down the road, "here's mother back and nothing done yet. Run and grind the barley while I finish the lamp."

Dear Martha. She was too good-natured to hold resentment, though I must have hurt and puzzled her often with my behavior. Years later it was painful to recall how I vented my

7

moods on my sister, leaving her to wonder what she had done to prompt such ill feeling. For like all humble people, she was willing to believe herself in the wrong. I would remember, too, how she acted as a constant buffer between mother and me, smoothing my path as much as she could. Then I would grieve to recall her beside me in the synagogue, her scrubbed red hands folded in her lap and her plain, solemn face a mask of concentration as she listened intently to the reader. I knew with a sudden pang how truly good she was, and that she had left me miles behind on a journey I had not even begun.

If father had one disappointment in life, it was my brother Lazarus. He was a year older than Martha and as slim and delicate as she was sturdy and robust. Having already lost two boys, our parents thought they were destined never to have a son as they nursed this sickly infant night and day, but Lazarus survived and slowly gained strength, though he was always prone to the fever common in our climate with its fluctuating temperatures. In many ways he was forced to lead a more restricted life than the other boys, but he had several friends as fishing companions, and their greatest joy was to go out with the boats while it was still dark and help with the nets. But this was a rare treat that only occurred when the fishermen were short of skilled help because of illness.

Despite his quiet voice and gentle ways, Lazarus was very popular among his friends, for he knew a wealth of fascinating things and, more important, helped them memorize those parts of the Torah to be repeated at school next day. My brother in fact was about the only boy in Magdala who was not virtually driven up the hill to his lessons each morning, and when ill health prevented his attendance, he was bitterly disappointed. But his favorite occupation was to slip into a backseat of the synagogue and listen to the readers expounding various portions of the Law. One day he would take his place there!

My brother's special friends were John, son of the *hazzan*— an important man in the community for he was the minister at the synagogue, custodian of the sacred scrolls and a great influence in our village affairs. He was the schoolmaster, too. John was a sober lad because of his father's position among us. Next came the twins, Josue and Jude, two of Susan's large clutch who lived across from us, and when father spoke of "those two young demons" we knew exactly whom he meant. Then there was Andrew, a sunny-natured boy whose burning ambition was to be the best fisherman in Galilee and who was drowned a few years later. One day he celebrated his bar mitzvah and the next his father carried his body up the shore still entangled in the nets. I remember as though it were yesterday.

Then, of course, there was always the other Josue down at Nazareth, who was one of our closest friends, for we knew him not only through our cousins in Cana, where his mother, Mariam, also had relatives, but through Joseph, her husband, who was one of father's oldest friends. The two men had known each other since they were children in Judea, and it was only when our grandparents moved back to their old home in Galilee that the two boys lost contact for a while. But a few years later great was father's joy to meet with Joseph again. Passing through Nazareth one day on his way home and absorbed in plans for his forthcoming marriage, father suddenly recognized his old friend in the *naggar*'s workshop that opened onto the main street. At the same moment Joseph looked up and for a few moments remained rooted to the ground with surprise and delight. Then, throwing down his hammer and thrusting the square into his belt, he rushed out into the road and the two men fell into each other's arms. Joseph, married by now and with a young son, had only recently moved into Nazareth, his wife's birthplace—hence father's ignorance of his presence in Galilee. However, celebrations were announced in the form of an immediate invitation to father's own wedding later that month.

It was inevitable therefore that any visit to our cousins was always extended to include Nazareth. Mother loved staying at Mariam's and it was the greatest treat for us girls to go abroad with them. Sometimes Mary, Mariam's sister-in-law, also accompanied us. We might visit the local bazaar, but it was better still to go farther afield to Sepphoris, the capital of Galilee, and spend a whole day there. It was full of Greeks, and mother had the gratifying experience of viewing all its pagan aspects about which she would regale the neighbors at home.

Meanwhile Lazarus and Josue stayed behind in the workshop to play their games in the sawdust or, when Joseph was concentrating on his planing, to touch his sharp knives and put a tentative finger on the hatchet's razor edge. But Joseph, with his back to them and with his jaws clamped round a dozen bronze-headed nails, could nevertheless see, hear and give vent to disapproval from the corner of his mouth.

"Josue, your mother has warned you those knives are dangerous and now *I* tell you that you must not touch them. You'll be taught how to use them soon enough. Now go outside with Lazarus and play while you can."

As they grew older, Josue sometimes traveled back with us for a few days, and father, delighted, encouraged their friendship. Indeed, whenever my brother fell ill of the low fever, Josue immediately came over to cheer him. When Lazarus was recovered they would go off together to their favorite haunt, the synagogue, for Josue was also well versed in the Scriptures. Father gloomily remarked that it was akin to having Hillel and Shammai, the great doctors of the Law, debating all day in his house.

"But they were rivals," protested Lazarus, "and we're friends."

"Bosom friends or sworn enemies," retorted father, "there's still too much talk beyond my poor brain. I'll go and unload Sarah" (our ass). "She believes everything I tell her and never argues."

Needless to say, the word went swiftly round when Lazarus fell ill, and the house was soon full of boys relating all the events the rabbi (as they called Lazarus) had missed during the past week. Then, spitting pomegranate seeds at Martha and me, they eventually ran off, promising to call the following day.

"God forbid!" said father devoutly.

But as Lazarus and Josue grew older, we did not see so much of Josue, for his father needed him at the workshop for the serious business of learning his trade. However, we always arranged to meet up for the feasts, and once a year Joseph came to do our household repairs, which father diligently saved for him. Even if Joseph could not come for several weeks, we still waited till he was free. The roof beams might need replacing. The walls could fall in about our ears. Father would have no one else. So we moved cautiously about in dangerous conditions till word came up from Nazareth that Joseph was on his way.

But whenever father looked at Josue or at Susan's sturdy little twins and then at Lazarus, he sighed. Like all Israelite fathers, he needed a strong, ambitious son capable of carrying on a thriving family business, and this, I knew, went against all my brother's natural inclinations. But I also knew of the innate sense of duty that would make him strive to succeed in a job that did not remotely appeal to him. His great desire was to teach, and I recall when I was a child his quoting simple words to me from the Torah, inscribing the shape of each letter and guiding my hand as I copied it. Father had insisted that we girls learn to read and write, although mother strongly objected, citing several daughters in the neighborhood who had made excellent marriages though they were barely literate.

"After all, you married me without either accomplishment," she said.

"That is a different matter entirely," father replied, adding unflatteringly, "Besides, your tongue compensates for the lack of both."

So father's word being law, we learned to read and write, but neither Martha nor myself enjoyed the latter, seeing no use for it in the future, and the practice was slowly abandoned. Today I can write my name and those of my family as Lazarus taught me years ago, but little else.

But as Lazarus grew older, heavier duties took him away from the house. He still attended the local school, and because of his exceptional ability, the *hazzan* urged that he stay a few months more. Father reluctantly agreed, knowing how much Lazarus loved his studies. In return for this recommendation my brother volunteered to milk the herd of goats the *hazzan* had recently inherited from a brother, and this extra task encroached even more on his time. At first I missed his company but I was growing older too, with new duties allotted me, and gradually these increased until the daily routine took me in its grip at dawn, not to release me till sunset.

Each morning there was a fresh batch of barley loaves to bake and spinning to be done while I tended the baking, or Martha might bring down the sun-dried flax for me to sort and comb ready for weaving. But other tasks we shared—pickling the cucumbers and salting the fish, which made my hands red and sore but mother said it was cheaper than buying them ready-preserved locally; crushing the olives we gathered each year from our tree in the neighboring grove; and making the white goat's cheese, for there was usually a surplus of milk from the *hazzan*'s herd and he gave this to Lazarus. Another shared task was the cultivation of our tiny garden packed full with herbs and vegetables. The soil was poor and stony but at least we had a strip of land, which many others did not possess. At right angles to the house stood the garden hut—a cool place in the summer heat—where the wine and provisions were stored and outside which Sheba was tied at a safe distance from the vegetables.

Two tasks from which I was exempt and which I should most have enjoyed, for they would have taken me from the house, were collecting the water and washing the linen down at the spring. But the latter was refused on the basis of my general incompetence in properly cleaning *anything*, which I suppose was true enough. I was sorry to miss fetching the water twice a day, but Martha, the moment the sluices were opened, hurried out with the gourd, assuring me over her shoulder that it was too heavy for me to carry and I should only spill it. I watched her departure with a cynical eye for I knew the real reason for her haste—apart from a gossip with her friends on the wet steps.

The young man, Matthias, whose father kept the *naggar's* shop across from the well, was sometimes standing in the doorway as the women came past, and father had focused on him as a potential son-in-law. Matthias did not speak to Martha, of course, for in our country a man will never publicly acknowledge a woman—not even his wife unless she falls dead at his feet—but Matthias could look, and I always knew when he had, for Martha returned very flustered and spilling water over the floor. But as she was obviously reluctant to yield me her place, I tried not to begrudge her these outings, for she often helped me in tasks I was particularly clumsy over.

There were the blessed occasions when I was left alone in the house with some simple job like swinging back and forth a skin of curds to make the clarified butter mother loved. She felt that even I could manage that, and furthermore it kept me in one spot, so, her conscience eased, mother lingered at the well with the other women. Left in peace, I stole a drink of sour milk or pomegranate juice and, curled up on the floor, I sipped and savored my leisure and solitude.

I wish that I could say that although I was reluctant and stupid over many of my tasks, I nevertheless looked forward to the day when I should have a home of my own, but I cannot recall ever wishing for this. I seem to have been born dissatisfied with my lot. I disliked my work, and the knowledge that I must pass my life in such an unrelenting, drab routine appalled me. At least I think this was the reason for my inner demon of restlessness, which reared its hydralike head, multiplying my discontent as I grew older. I recall my aunt's comment at a wedding feast over at Bethsaida, when I returned to the family group from flying round in the wild circle dance usual at such events: "I advise you to watch your youngest daughter, Levi, or she'll disgrace our family one day. I've seen it happen in others, so I know what I'm talking about."

"Indeed?" father queried dubiously, for he was not very fond of his wife's sisters and particularly this one. "Mary is simply enjoying herself and there is nothing harmful in that. I know some folk who would refuse to enjoy themselves in paradise."

Aunt shot him a sour look and turned to her sister for support. "Mark my words, Miriam, for they'll bear me out in the future. Your daughter is either lost in a daydream or running wild—and that is *not* a safe temperament to encourage. People who go to extremes are of no use to anyone. The best advice I can give you is to have her married as soon as you can."

"Perhaps you would give me leave to marry my eldest daughter first," father intervened irritably, knowing that his wife would take her sister's words seriously. "Mary is *not* your responsibility," he added, firmly closing the debate on my merits or lack of them.

But aunt, undaunted, simply gave mother a meaningful look over his head to imply that there was little use in talking sensibly with a man present, and I felt mother's troubled eyes

14

on my back. As the youngest sister, she had a great respect for my aunt's opinions, and my heart sank. My careless ways caused trouble enough without another member of the family finding something sinister in my behavior.

But as time went on, aunt's gloomy prophecies proved right. I seemed to lack the same equable temperament the others possessed, and when a group of girls came in to see Martha, I found myself constantly comparing and wondering if there was indeed something wrong that I could not enjoy and look forward to achieving the same goals. They were all so placidly content and only interested in quickly acquiring a husband and home, whereas I found myself more and more frustrated at the restraint surrounding me. I should so like some temporary relief from the pressure of people and perpetual noise.

That was really the difference between the other girls and myself. All I desired was a little peace when I wished it, but this commodity was unavailable in Magdala, in our home or any house I was likely to inhabit in the future. This wish to be sometimes apart from my family made me feel guilty—it seemed an unnatural desire—and coupled with this, I also transgressed in feeling entrapped, suffocated almost, by the strict laws of our enclosed society. All the things our ancestors had accepted unquestioningly for generations seemed to me so pointless and wearisome, and yet this was required of us by God. But though I knew that everything outside the Law was forbidden, this did not prevent my thinking that I moved in a narrow way and that many Gentile women enjoyed a far greater freedom than I ever would. How I envied them.

None of my family knew, but I had once met such a woman— to all intents she was virtually a Gentile—when I was about nine years old. I had been ill with some childish complaint, and to aid my recovery father had taken me with him on one of his visits, he leading Sarah and I jogging happily along on the bales of cloth. Our route took us away from the village and up the

15

winding road to a house high above the lake. This property belonged to a certain type of landowner whom father disliked intensely, though he was glad to call one or two of them his clients, even if it was only for the simpler household stuffs, since their linens and silks were imported. Possessing some capital, these astute people had acquired enormous amounts of land by simply buying farms, vineyards and other properties wherever they could, at the lowest possible price. They hired stewards to supervise these investments while their masters retired to live sleekly on this accumulating wealth.

Now having climbed the hill, we approached this particular house through a side gate and along a track that ran through a small orchard to finally merge with the flagged path that skirted the house. I doubt now if its size and architecture would have warranted more than a cursory glance from Herod but it stopped my excited chatter and awed me into silence, and while father was untying his bales, I peeped round the corner to view its frontage. I could not have been more impressed if it were Solomon's Temple.

It was a long, low, white-walled building flanking a central courtyard. A shady colonnade encompassed its three sides paved with colored tiles which I thought to be mosaics. At that moment father vanished through a cedarwood door after calling me to return and watch Sarah. But she was already occupied in nuzzling about, so instead of retracing my steps, I turned my attention to the stepped gardens sloping down to a sunken pool and—enchanting sight to a child—a miniature fountain flinging its spray into the air. I longed with all my heart to go down to it but did not dare move from my place. I felt as if I had somehow strayed into a different world.

Suddenly a noise startled me and I jumped around. From one of the low windows along the colonnade came the sound of discordant cheeping. I hesitated for a moment, but seeing that the shutters lay back against the wall inviting inspection, I stole forward, fascinated, to investigate.

It was the most beautiful room I had ever seen. The furnishings were spare, but it was so spacious, so airy, so *quiet* . . . The polished wood floor stretched away, dappled with pools of sunshine. I gazed and gazed, absorbing it all. There was a sofa lined with cushions opposite the window—one could lie there and look out over the garden to the fountain. Before it stood a low table of veined marble—it would be cool to the touch. My gaze wandered round, and there on a carved chest by the window was the answer to the noise I heard—a cage full of canaries and other singing birds of such varied plumage that I cried out in delight and, forgetting father's injunction, leaned over the sill to view them more closely. Suddenly—

"You! Come here," rapped a woman's voice farther along the colonnade. I leaped back in fright, noticing for the first time the figure seated in the shadowed recess behind the pillars. For a few moments I was rooted to the spot; then, as the order was impatiently repeated, I went slowly down toward the seat, feeling sick with apprehension. I felt sure I had committed some heinous crime of trespass and wondered fearfully if I would be allowed to return home with father and Sarah or if some dire penalty would be exacted instead. But before I had time to wonder how mother would manage without me, my dragging feet halted before her.

In my short life I had sometimes seen these women borne in litters through the streets of Jerusalem when we were all up for the feasts. I had seen them in the Temple in the Court of Women and gorgeously arrayed among the great gatherings in the synagogues. I often envied them their leisure and freedom from humdrum tasks, and hoped that I might one day encounter such a woman so as to enquire how she occupied all her unlimited time. My ambition was now realized, but as her cool gaze traveled from my face down to my dust-covered toes and up again I began feeling distinctly uncomfortable, grubby and disheveled. Looking up through my lashes, I studied her covertly.

Her face, almost on a level with mine, was pale, with glittering black eyes and rather thin lips, while her thick, glossy hair was dressed in the Roman style. Her garments were similar to mine—but the difference! Her white tunic was spotless, and its skirt consisted entirely of dozens of tiny pleats gathered under an embroidered belt. Feet like alabaster peeped out onto the seat where lay a dainty pair of leather sandals totally unlike my own ill-fitting ones, which chafed and cut between my toes. Her veil, fine-spun as gossamer, floated like a cloud about her.

Having completed my inspection, I stood miserably awaiting her wrath to fall in the same way mother's did, only worse; but she was silent, and when I raised my eyes again, she smiled thinly at me.

"What is your name?"

"Mary," I whispered.

"And did you like my birds?"

"Yes, madam," I whispered again, ashamed that she had witnessed my presumption.

"Are you waiting for your father?"

I nodded.

She looked away from me over the garden, absently twisting the gold bangle on her arm. From beneath the tendrils of her hair, I saw that her ears were pierced with tiny gold studs and I knew then that she could not be a nice person, for our Law forbids such disfigurement. Mother would say that she had forsaken her people's ways and gone over to the Gentiles.

But she seemed to have forgotten my presence beside her, and I did not know whether I was dismissed or not. Twisting my fingers, I pondered my position. Did she want me to remain there or to return to the side door and await father? Or perhaps I was expected to compliment her on the birds. So accustomed was I to being told what I must do each hour of the day that this sudden lack of direction bewildered me. But my dilemma was resolved by her calm statement.

"Your ass is trespassing in my orchard. She'll be trampling my flowers next."

I whirled round in dismay. Sarah, left untethered and unwatched, had pushed open the orchard gate and was now roaming hopefully around the currant bushes. Backing away, I fled up the colonnade, and after much scolding and belaboring finally drove out the poor beast and closed the gate. At that moment father reappeared—and not in the best of moods—so I was relieved that he had missed this little episode. Since he had distinctly told me not to stray, I never mentioned my meeting with the lady of the house and mother never had the opportunity to comment acidly on her pierced ears. In time I completely forgot her but one thing I always remembered—her freedom to sit undisturbed while time flowed past—and I wondered if she knew how blessed she was. Perhaps not, for she had not looked particularly content that day.

But the memory of that quiet room stayed with me always, and as I grew older, I hungered after it more and more till, in my mind, it became my own personal retreat from the noise and troubles and squabbles that filled my day, the one place where no one could follow me. But if, as I found, I could not seek it out during the daily routine, then I had only to close my eyes at night and I was there—leaning across the sill, looking down into *my* room, savoring the peace that lapped its walls like the lake on a summer day, the bird song so sweet in the stillness and the sunbeams moving across the floor.

Despite my increasing dissatisfaction, I was not so foolish as to make others aware of it, for the family bond is a very strong one in our country and one conformed to automatically. So I obeyed my parents, performed my household tasks, attended the synagogue and observed the feasts, not looking for any change or expecting a miracle to alter my way of life. Being ignorant and uneducated, I could not reason clearly or express my feelings to myself or others, but I sensed in a clouded way how much I should like to be someone else—someone who need not account for where she was and what she was doing each moment, someone who might go out alone for a while each day and not with a group of other women ceaselessly chattering on their way to the bazaar or synagogue. There indeed lay the root cause of all my discontent. If only I might be allowed to wander around the lake in the springtime or climb up into the hills and be alone for a while—to have a little freedom, a little time to think—then I could return to my hated tasks and their accompanying noise refreshed by the contrast.

But I did not have these things and never would. Indeed, if anyone had asked me what I wished to think about, I could not have answered. It was simply an idea I yearned after that would have received short shrift from mother, for my meditations carried out over my domestic tasks often ended in a burnt meal and a sharp slap for wasting time daydreaming when I should have been attending to more pressing matters. Then I felt misunderstood and pitied myself, envying father and Lazarus loudly thanking God in their daily prayers for not having made them women. Well you might, I thought. You would not endure my enclosed life for a moment. At these times my lips only grudgingly formed my thanks to God for making me according to his will. It seemed so wrong. Father could come in at any hour—and walk out too. We three women, being constantly together, were always wrangling over something and as there was but one room in the house, there was no escaping each other. But father could just exclaim, "Women!" which lumped us as a collective nuisance, and stroll out to sit under the eucalyptus tree, talk with a crony or throw dice. Mother was always in agreement with him and blamed us accordingly.

"I'm ashamed to have you as daughters—quarreling the whole day and driving your father from his own house! Mary, go and fetch some wine from the hut. It will help him relax in this heat."

Crouched over the fire, stirring the lentil stew, my tunic adhering to my back and my veil sticking against my wet forehead, I was speechless, wondering not for the first time if I was indeed an unreasonable, undutiful daughter or, like the madman, sane and all others crazy. How could mother deceive herself that father had a hard life and needed cosseting?

"And don't linger in the garden. Martha and I have the washing to do before noon."

"Ah," said a friend when I first recounted my tale, "but at least you can find peace and solitude on your rooftop, away from everyone?"

But I had to disillusion her. After all, our houses were single-storied and so not far removed from the street below. They were also built very close to each other. Once up there one could scarcely move, for the flax and wet garments drying there and the bedding left to air. Susan's daughters were calling to another girl to join them in tossing a ball across the alleyways between the houses. Someone was rolling his roof flat again after a recent shower. Our neighbor, a garrulous old man, was droning his lengthy prayers inside the folds of his *tallith*, while a group of women gossiped across to each other, exchanging confidences in tones audible on the lakeshore.

The noise! From dawn to dusk it never ended. But lying on the rooftop during the long summer nights, I dreamed wistfully of a room of my own where I might enter and close the door and be alone in a pool of silence. Somehow it always resembled the room in the house above the lake. I had only to think of it and my mind was flooded with its sunlight. So it was not surprising that my main reason for loving the sabbath was the peace it brought with it. I never minded the inevitable rush of the day of preparation, for it heralded in twenty-four hours of complete rest.

Two days' work was hurried through and then, when all was ready, I ran out through the gap in the hedge to see the groups of women, mother and Martha among them, returning up the winding road, gracefully balancing their gourds, their white veils fluttering in the blue shadows. I heard the low, musical murmur of their voices as they rested under the pepper tree with its rich clusters of scarlet berries. A fresh breeze swayed the dusty purple bougainvillea as I wandered back and climbed the outside steps to watch the sunset flame across the parched hills where the goats still cropped the patchy terraces and the gnarled olive trees twisted their ancient roots in the stony ground. The sun was setting over the Plain of Esdraelon as the *hazzan* blew the trumpet warning those still in the fields to leave their work now—and then again for all trading to cease down in the bazaar. The children were called in and the streets were deserted. Thrice the trumpet sounded, and below me and all around the lamps were lit in the houses and the sabbath began to shine. Magdala was hushed. No work, no cooking, no quarreling. The one day when I sat in the garden in my best veil and tunic, undisturbed by the usual weekday cry—"Come and sit with us, Mary!"—as happened at noon when it was too hot to do anything but sit indoors and gossip, slap away the flies and scream irritably at the children.

On this day friends might come for a quiet hour after the service in the synagogue, but they were only neighbors, for, of course, no traveling was permitted on the sabbath. But after greeting our visitors I was free to go into the garden, sometimes with a sleeping baby to relieve its mother for an hour.

Martha was happy sitting in the doorway with a friend who was recently betrothed and full of her new status. Sometimes

22

Josue stayed with us to complete various household jobs, thus freeing Joseph to attend the rush of commissions usual at harvest, when all the reaping equipment required a thorough overhaul. After the service he and Lazarus walked down together from the synagogue and continued their discussion squatting comfortably in the shade with their backs to the house wall. Sitting unobserved near the hut, I listened lazily, amused when Lazarus disagreed and grew mildly heated in the process. Then Josue's laugh rang out, clearing the air, and my brother shrugged, smiled and, conceding defeat, threw a handful of dirt at the hens.

Josue was still an apprentice-carpenter, and father told Joseph, "Let the lad come and practice on our house. It won't matter if at first it's ill-done. It's old and in need of constant repair, so he'll get plenty of experience."

But Josue had been trained well and was as steady a worker as his father, and we reaped the benefit. So well did he blend in with us that I felt as much at home with him as with my brother. When Lazarus was called away from these sabbath conversations, Josue and I chatted across to each other till he returned. I always endeavored to make the most of this recreation, for I spoke to few people outside the family circle, but when Josue answered abstractedly and lapsed into silence, then I retreated into myself again, fearing he was bored. I was painfully aware how little I knew compared to Lazarus, who spent hours animatedly discussing things. I wanted to ask Josue what he thought my brother should do now that his schooling was almost finished, for he was well over the leaving age. He still spent a great deal of time in the synagogue listening to the sermons and debates, and the name Rabbi still clung to him. I suspected that my brother longed to have it applied more seriously, and this opened up exciting prospects about which I knew nothing. I should have liked to ask if Josue might also use his knowledge to instruct others, but there again, if Lazarus wanted me to know their plans, he would tell me in his own time. That was one comfort. He sometimes entrusted me with secrets he never told Martha, but I knew he would be very angry if he discovered I had plagued Josue in his absence. Anyway, they both must learn a trade first—Lazarus in textiles and his friend as a carpenter.

Josue still sat opposite, keeping his own counsel, and to break the silence I asked the first question that came into my head. "Have you become accustomed yet to all the noise in the workshop? I could never bear that hammering all day. I should want to do something different."

But he just smiled a little, and immediately I was sorry to have asked such a fatuous question and twisted the ends of my veil with vexation. Oh, it was awful being so ignorant and unable to talk with people when one had the chance. Suddenly a happy thought occurred and, throwing caution to the winds, I told him the only important secret I had. I told him about my room, my little kingdom where all went well for me and which I often visited—not to enter it of course; I never dared do that or seemed able to—it was only to see that it remained unchanged, only to contemplate it in silence, and to wait. I never knew for whom or what I waited; but I knew I was content. "Sometimes," I concluded, "it seems so real, as if it were a part of me and—somehow—it is always the sabbath in there."

Then my voice trailed off lamely. That sounded ridiculous. That was what always happened when I tried to explain things to others. I felt my face turn crimson and wished fervently that Lazarus might soon come out or Josue go and find him. But even as I thought this my conscience smote me. I had forgotten that Joseph had been unwell lately. Small wonder Josue sat there, silent and withdrawn, while I babbled on about rooms and sabbaths. But just as I reproached myself, I heard Lazarus call his friend from the house, and I guessed they were off to visit John, the *hazzan's* son.

24

All the time I talked, Josue had been studying the ground intently. Now he rose immediately to join my brother, only pausing for a moment to say, "You have found the perfect place, Mary. Visit it often and then you'll always have the sabbath in your soul."

He went away leaving me comforted, for he had not smiled as though he had been humoring me or inwardly ridiculing my words.

The olives rustled like water in the lengthening shadows as I went up onto the roof to watch the end of the day. If only it might always be like this, I thought, but tomorrow life would return to normal—nothing would ever change but all would go on in the same, unalterable routine—and I did not know how to bear it. But even as I looked out over the rooftops, the sun set in a crimson lake behind Carmel, and soon Thabor loomed a shadowy mass on my left. Behind me Gennesaret receded into the darkness which fell as suddenly as a blanket, and the first stars came pricking out in the black vault above. The trumpet sounded and the sabbath was over. It was time to go down for our evening meal. Still I lingered, trying to recapture the sense of comfort Josue's words had given me, but already the feeling had faded and I was left alone with the same old restless surge of discontent that sometimes threatened to overwhelm me.

CHAPTER
• TWO •

AND SO THE WEEKS went past. Lazarus finished his last days at the synagogue school and was soon to start the rounds with father, getting to know the clients and the type and amount of textiles they required. But father had gone off for a few days on one of his regular trips around Galilee, which usually combined business with the visiting of friends and relatives, so Lazarus took some temporary employment as a laborer while awaiting his return.

The strip of land he cultivated lay outside the village under the hills, and the "Dove of the Distant Terebinths" wafted to mother and myself when we took out food to him. Without doubt he was far more content digging and hoeing along the furrows than learning the business with father. That shadow hung over him, but with the resilience and optimism of youth, my brother cherished something far beyond father's plans for him in the textile trade. For Lazarus had one of those dreams just impossible enough to come true. He longed to become a teacher, but for this a vast study of religion was required. The best way to achieve such learning was in Jerusalem at one of the Beth ha-Midrash, the schools where the famous Doctors of Law taught.

All this was a dream, a hope in Lazarus's mind told only to Josue and then to me one day in the garden as he clipped the mustard bush into shape. For, although the *hazzan* would recommend him, how ever would father agree? And who was to run the business when father retired if Lazarus was not always there? Many teachers supported themselves while instructing others, but in less arduous trades than buying and selling textiles. Such a competitive business required one's whole attention. If only father were a shoemaker or a charcoal burner, a tent weaver or even a laborer—anything but his present occupation. One could make tents and shoes and still instruct others, but not when one was using all one's time, energy and tongue persuading some lazy Galilean to buy a piece of cloth he did not want.

There seemed no answer to such problems, but Lazarus, undismayed, endured with patience, tended the goats, weeded the onion beds and whistled his songs along the furrows.

Patience was needed, for unknown to us, father's business had been failing for some time. Another man in the same trade had expanded into Caphernaum, a man who was everything father was not when it came to running a successful business, however small. Father's customers were slowly milked away by the new intruder's energetic, flamboyant personality and color-ful selling methods, for not despising the small places, this man made regular monthly trips into the lakeside villages and small towns, giving small gifts along with every piece of cloth he sold. His open rivalry with others in the same field amused the onlookers, but father, who was basically a simple man and detested rivalry, was bewildered by such fierce, unrelenting competition on such a highly organized scale. The man waxed while others waned, and it soon became clear that serious financial troubles loomed unless father adopted not only a better sales technique, but also a more pressing attitude regarding payment from dilatory customers. Father had always enjoyed a modest reputation for giving good value for money, but this was not strictly true. He gave value, but whether he received payment in return was a different matter, for when it came to collecting debts, father was hopeless.

The poorer customers paid as soon as they received their goods, for debt was an evil to them. Not so with the more influential clients. They were only a handful, but the sums they owed were many times the amounts father received from the others. And father, not wishing to offend them, took his payment in trickles or even let the whole debt be paid in kind. On the occasions he was driven to mention an outstanding amount, the house steward, knowing father's weakness for a "bargain," took him out to the barns to unload some of his master's surplus produce plus the promise of a skinful of wine at the New Year. Whereupon father, drowning in the ceaseless flow of the steward's talk (a born salesman), went off with the loaded ass more or less convinced that it was he who had gained the better deal.

But when he arrived home, the story was different. The very word *steward* was anathema to mother, feeling as she did that this breed cheated not only father but their masters as well by putting much of the money their masters owed into their own belts. Father, of course, was never pleased when she informed him that he had been duped yet again.

She could only console herself by crying, "Merciful God, the man will send me to my grave! Levi, it's *money* we need, not two dozen melons and a barrel of salt herring!"

But father, in a mellow mood after a morning's chat over spiced wine, simply laughed. "Ah, woman, what purpose does money serve? I'll tell you," holding up a hand to stem the flow. "You go to the bazaar and buy our food. So," pointing to the fruit and fish, "there is the saving of that task."

"What would I *do* with it!" mother exploded. "I would *save* it! Levi, do you never look to the future? One day there'll be a famine and no food but what we can buy further afield in Egypt. One day when we're old . . ."

"Put your trust in God, woman, and not my purse. We've sufficient for the present and the future is far distant. Besides," chinking the dowry coins on her headdress, "you're still worth a goodly sum should a crisis arise."

"It's all very well to jest," mother grumbled, "but some of these people will be dead before their debts are paid. Suppose they saw us in want—do you imagine they would help us?"

"No," replied father, who, tired of being scolded, was trying for peace, "but rest assured that if any Galileans fall into want, then Herod Antipas, our wise and benevolent ruler"—("That jackal!" cried mother)—"would sell his gold plate and feed us from his own omnipotent bounty. Now there's an end to the subject so rest content."

"It's just not prudent," mother grumbled to herself, beating clouds of dust from the mat. "These people take shameful advantage of you. You're too easy with them by far . . ." And her voice died away into indistinct muttering as she returned to the house.

"Your tongue, good wife," said father meditatively, "is like a dripping roof. It never ceases. It goes on and on and . . ."

He started as mother's head came back round the door. "And don't call that Roman foot-licker omnipotent! Imagine if the *hazzan* heard you! I won't have my own husband accused of blasphemy."

And she vanished within.

But by the time Lazarus left school and joined with father, matters were becoming more serious. There was no longer any need for mother's gloomy sermons, and father no longer jested about his business. When Sarah went lame and had to be destroyed, the realization heavily dawned that money in its own right was a desirable, even an essential commodity.

It was also about this time that a suitable husband was being

30

looked out for Martha. I believe mother would have been happy to have her favorite daughter at home for a while longer, but father thought he had sufficient worries without keeping marriageable offspring for a day more than necessary. However, both women were consoled in that father's choice, after hovering hopefully over one or two of the local bachelors, finally rested on Matthias. This pleased Martha greatly—and mother, too, for her daughter would remain nearby in Magdala and she could go each day to visit her. I felt it in my heart to pity my brother-in-law.

By now Matthias had completely taken over the *naggar's* shop from his father, a widower who, increasingly crippled by rheumatism, was anxious to acquire a daughter-in-law to run their home. So the haggling over the dowry—the *mohar*, as we called it—began. It was a lengthy business, with father making out that he was losing a treasure in Martha (and in one sense he was, for she was as strong and hard-working as a pack mule) and was only parting with her with the greatest reluctance. But Matthias, undaunted, pointed out that he was bringing his health and talents into the family and, having built up a good trade in the neighborhood, a capacity for hard work—which made father look kindly at him.

"Martha's a good girl," he observed lugubriously, "just like my dear wife, God bless her, and I shall miss her in my house . . ." and he gazed soulfully into the distance toward Egypt, as though it were there that Martha was destined to vanish. "However," he roused himself, "the time must come when the chicks must leave the nest."

Matthias looked up, momentarily startled, never having viewed the solid Martha under this appellation before.

"And it is a sacrifice we must all make sooner or later," father continued nobly.

Matthias nodded gravely, totally unimpressed. Father pressed home his advantage. "On reflection, how could anything really compensate for her? After all, what is money compared to a daughter's bright face in your home, her happy smile . . ."

But Matthias was taking all this with a handful of salt and pursuing his own line of attack. He interrupted father's rambling rhapsody over Martha. "Yes, yes, Levi, I fully appreciate your daughter's virtues—that is why I wish to marry her. But remember that she will not be far away—only beyond the spring. You will not have to sacrifice seeing her as often as you wish."

Father looked offended. He considered Matthias to be progressing too fast, and he liked to play this game according to its rules. After all, that was half the enjoyment of being rid of a daughter.

"And is it not time that you had a few grandchildren tumbling about here?" asked Matthias cunningly.

"I suppose so," agreed father dubiously, only partially mollified at the thought. "We . . . ll, let us see now . . ."

So after much arguing under the eucalyptus tree, they at last agreed on a sum mentioned right at the beginning, and Matthias promised to be generous with his gifts—the traditional *mattan*—to his bride. So Martha was betrothed in the early spring, soon after the rains, and they became husband and wife according to our Law. The wedding feast and her entry into her husband's home would take place in the autumn after the Feast of Tabernacles, when the grape and olive harvests were gathered and everyone would be free to come for the week of celebration. Martha was overjoyed at the arrangement and sang round the house all day. Soon she would have a home of her own.

I was glad for my sister's happiness, although I did not envy her Matthias. He was a good-natured, stolid sort of man who, six days a week, had sawdust caught in his long side-locks, of which he was extremely proud and combed often with his fingers. But Martha liked him well enough and, with all the authority of her newly acquired status, sang his praises to me all day. Hearing yet another rhapsody over yet another virtue made me wonder how she knew he possessed such worth, for she had never had a real conversation with Matthias in her life. However, such omissions do not matter in our society.

But while Martha chattered on, my thoughts were running ahead to my own future. In another year or so I, too, would be in my sister's position, and mother, knowing my propensity for daydreaming, would doubtless urge father to select some very orthodox man—the type to insist I go heavily veiled outside the house, a custom the older women still observed, and what little freedom I now had would be even more strictly curtailed. What would happen then to my increasing desire to have a little peace, to be alone sometimes—such simple things yet unobtainable for a woman in my walk of life? Even the tiny boy who crept in and stole our currants had more freedom than I, more rights than mother, who had borne five children and held the strings of the house in her hands. It was unthinkable that any future husband would allow me to go where I pleased; a scandal would erupt at such unknown behavior. But I need not even contemplate such a possibility. Such husbands did not exist. My sister's betrothal filled me with foreboding, and more and more I retreated into my room, wondering fearfully if I must relinquish even this oasis of quiet once I was married with a home and children to care for, and not even the sabbath to call my own anymore. It seemed likely. So much did this prey on my mind that one day, soon after this, I was foolish enough to enlighten my parents as to my feelings. There had been bickering aplenty before, but this time I really exploded.

It was one of those days when for no apparent reason everything went wrong from sunrise onward. Mother was irritable and finding fault with us; father was preoccupied with his own business worries; I had a headache and wanted nothing

33

more than to creep back into my bedroll. Only Martha was oblivious to the tension, lifted above it by her own inner happiness. The noon rest saved us from clashing, for the rains were on again and we could not work outside. With a sigh of relief we all lay down for an hour.

I fell asleep instantly, and in my dream I no longer looked into my room from the terrace or through the half-opened door. Instead it yielded to my touch and swung gently back and, full of happiness, I stepped forward—and mother shook me awake. I had been on the threshold and now, with a start, I was back in reality and nearly weeping with disappointment.

But later that day a better mood returned. The spring air was soft and fresh after the shower and a stillness pervaded the garden. The afternoon wore on, and the last rays of the sun tinged the atmosphere with a mellow, golden light. Figures moved across this landscape from one task to another—figures which I vaguely noticed and even more dimly heard as I stirred the evening meal with an abstracted air. My thoughts were slowly removing from this duty to subjects more absorbing and, unconsciously, my attention was gradually drawn away and then deflected by a cloud of blue butterflies hovering over the garden. Absorbed, I followed their dancing flight, gazing at them so fixedly that they merged into an azure mass against the setting sun and blurred into a vision of blue and gold which drew me down into its center. I hardly dared move for fear of breaking the spell, for blue and gold were all around me. The blue sky was sparkling outside the windows of my room and sunlight was moving in golden motes across the floor. Without an effort I was in the room, hearing the tingling silence all around as I sank down on the warm tiles, waiting in the stillness for I knew not what, turning my face expectantly to the light that poured in through the open window. But the sun was blinding my eyes so that I could not look up to see . . .

"*Mary!*" a voice screamed behind me, and with a violent shock I was back in the garden again.

"*Look* what you've done, you *stupid* girl!" and a resounding slap came stinging down on my arm.

I gasped with pain and then leapt to my feet, trembling with a fury totally alien to me. I believe at that moment I could have thrown the entire meal over my mother, except that it was now a burned mass at the bottom of the pot. Mother was already launching into her usual list of direct questions to the Deity as to why she had been inflicted with so useless a daughter; why it was that this burden was visited upon her and not that feckless woman across the road who deserved nothing better. Reminding Him of her own ancestors' worth, she exonerated her family from producing the undesirable traits so blatantly inherent in me. Finally she beseeched God not to punish her further for the sins committed by her husband and in-laws.

Standing there by the fire, I hardly listened. I had heard it all before many times. But gradually I grew so tired of her wailing (and our mothers *do* wail terribly) that I suddenly rounded on her, screaming hysterically, "Will you be *quiet!* I can't bear the constant noise in this house—and *you* make half of it! If I'm so useless, then send me away! I'd rather be anywhere than herded here all my days. If this is family life, then I hate it! I'd rather be a Roman—*anyone*—than suffer this all the time." Then, unused to such eloquence from myself, I ran out of words, sat down suddenly and burst into tears.

"*Well!*" ejaculated mother after the first shock. "You wicked, ungrateful girl! To think I've lived long enough to hear my own flesh and blood . . . To dare to talk like that! Look what you have—a good home, parents who love you, food to eat and clothes to wear—and you stand there telling me you're tired of it, that you'd rather be a Gentile!" Mother shook her head in an effort to clear her mind of such a blasphemous thought.

"It's a mercy you aren't struck dead at my feet. I've never heard such foolish, dangerous talk. You've some fine notions, daughter, of your station in life—dreaming and idling while the rest of us earn our bread. Well, your aunt was right. You'll come to grief if you don't mend your ways—*and* send your parents to an early grave!"

At last mother ran out of breath and, panting to a halt, looked with satisfaction at her daughter, huddled and weeping, upon the ground. Her words had obviously moved me to repentance, and indeed I was brokenhearted. Once again I had upset everyone; once again mother was ranting at me so that all the neighbors heard, and even father looked uncomfortable. Above all, I knew that I might not get into my room for ages now that all this had happened, and I sobbed afresh at the misery of it.

But mother's bark was worse than her bite, and seeing that I was really upset, she went back into the house without troubling me further. She called to my sister, "Martha, come and help me prepare something if we're to eat at all tonight. Mary can sit out there for a while. She's not fit for anything at the moment but feeling sorry for herself."

Left alone, I brushed away my tears—and then noticed Susan's curious eyes peering at me from across the way. Always there was someone watching! Impatiently I turned back toward the house, but as I did so, I heard father say anxiously, "You know, Miriam, your sister may be right. Mary does seem to be causing problems recently . . ."

Mother wondrously forbore to say anything, and thus encouraged, father continued, "Well, the moment Martha goes to her own home, I'll see about having Mary betrothed. I know she's still very young, but I won't tolerate this all the time. She seems to be getting worse instead of better."

"Oh, I don't think she means it," I heard Martha timidly intervene. "It's been a very humid day for spring, and you know how Mary gets headaches in this weather. People often say things they don't mean when they feel unwell. I'm sure it was just the sun," she persisted anxiously.

"It was not the sun that made her burn my food!" retorted father feelingly. "No, I've decided to have her betrothed in the New Year. She won't find a husband nearly so lenient as her old father!"

Not wanting to hear more, I turned and wandered down to the gap in the hedge, for all the village was indoors now and soon it would be dark. After a while I heard Lazarus coming to fetch me, but I was reluctant to return to the house. So, it seemed, was my brother as he handed me my cloak. But I knew that he had not come to condole with me, for duty, however unpleasant, was always paramount to Lazarus, and although he was sympathetic, I knew he could never really understand how I felt. It was not his fault, for I was a mystery even to myself. For the first time in my life, I found myself wishing I were more like Martha.

"Mary," he began tentatively, "I wish you could realize that we all become tired of our work and even of each other sometimes, but there will always be things in life we don't like and we must learn to endure them. It's the only way if we're to live in peace. But you have been disrupting everything recently. You want to be somewhere else, *doing* something else— at least that is how I understand your constant daydreaming— and it's all foolishness, Mary! Where else could you be but here, helping mother and Martha? And there is no justifying the way you screamed at mother just now . . ."

There was no answer to all this so I waited, mute and miserable, for the next part of my brother's homily. But he, noting my silence, took it as a sign of returning normality and immediately tried to cheer me. "Remember," he continued as we turned back toward the house, "that it won't be for very long. You'll be married in a year or two—which reminds me! Do you recall Barnabas, over at Caphernaum?"

I did indeed and my heart sank, but Lazarus was continuing eagerly. "I usually see him when I go there, and I can tell he is interested in you. He may well come and see father about a dowry this year. I realize you know nothing of him," he added as an afterthought, "but I'm sure you'll come to like him. Anyway, someone will soon come forward if he changes his mind—though I don't think he will. I mean," Lazarus continued awkwardly, for he was unused to paying his sister compliments, "any man would be glad to have you as his wife, Mary. I mean . . . you're not ill-looking . . ."

"Lazarus," I said in one last attempt to make him understand, as we paused outside the house, "I'm not objecting to being at home and doing my work."

"I should think not," he answered flatly. "What else is there for you?"

"It's just that I don't enjoy the same things as mother and Martha—is there enough oil in the lamp every sabbath eve to last over? Has Susan dried her linen before ours? I can bear it for so long and then I must get away for a while, and that's when I usually lose myself in a daydream and upset everyone. I don't mean to but I simply can't help it. I don't think I would so much if only I might have a contrast sometimes—perhaps go out alone for an hour . . ."

"Oh, not this again!" Lazarus interrupted impatiently. "It's just as mother said. You want to run away from your duties . . ."

"No! That's not true!" I cried despairingly. "I just want a little *freedom* . . ."

"Listen, Mary," said my brother forcefully, and he had on his "synagogue" face, which always meant a sermon. "If you do what you are meant to be doing every day, then you are carrying out God's laws. There is therefore no need to go off and think about whether you are enjoying your work or not. It's neither right nor becoming for you to behave like that—especially when we have a code to live by and it's your duty to stay inside its bounds. There is *no* freedom outside the Law."

"Then the Law's wrong," I snapped childishly, disappointed at my brother's lack of support. Then I stopped, fearfully wondering if the Deity had heard this remark. I had already said sufficient to offend Him that evening.

"Mary," said Lazarus sadly, "if you'd only walk in the path allotted you, then you'd reap the blessing of it. Instead you waste your time in useless longings." Then he added in lighter vein, "I must ask father to find you a husband who will send you into the desert one day a week! You will have all the contrast and quiet you want, and I guarantee you'll soon be tired of your own company. However, we'll soon be on our way to Jerusalem—that at least should please you."

Despite myself, I smiled wanly. Perhaps I had exaggerated and been selfish. After all, my brother's path was not an easy one, and yet he never complained. The thought of Passover also cheered me and made me more readily amenable to my lot.

"Perhaps you are right, Lazarus. I'll start again and try to do better."

Lazarus's thin face brightened and he no longer looked like a rabbi. "Let us go and have supper," he said.

And so we went into the house. Going up to my mother, I put my arms around her and said that I would try not to grieve her again. In the way our people have, we all threw ourselves into each other's arms, vowing eternal love within the family. Then father, who was holding the steaming bowl of rice that mother had thrust at him so as to embrace me, roared a reminder that he was not just a statue in our midst but a flesh-and-blood man whose fingers were nearly destroyed holding scalding dishes. Martha immediately ran to take it from him and served me a large portion, while mother beamed approvingly. Lazarus smiled as I handed him the bread, and father sucked his fingers, grumbling at the incredible ways of his womenfolk but pleased that we were all reconciled once again.

Night had fallen outside, but the lamp made a cheerful glow as, squabbling happily, we settled to our meal and, for a while, peace shone out of our doorway.

CHAPTER
· THREE ·

ALMOST IMMEDIATELY AFTER THIS our minds were turned toward the great feast of the Passover, and our domestic life suddenly accelerated with all the preparations necessary for this supreme holiday of the year. Day after day slipped away, with the date of departure creeping nearer and nearer. Then, once more, we were out on the road on the first lap of our pilgrimage south. After the enclosed life of Magdala, I nearly went mad with excitement, anticipating the long, slow journey which, in my view, was the best part of the whole event. Jerusalem was far too crowded to fully enjoy one's stay there, but the wonderful itinerary was an adventure in itself.

The towns and villages were emptying rapidly as we moved down-country, and soon the ground was black with family groups and laden mules meeting and joining up with others along the way, rich and poor alike mingling together. Soon there were thousands and thousands of us passing through the land—Israelites from Tyre, Syria and Egypt; from Greece, Rome, Babylon and Macedonia; from far beyond the empire's boundaries—all converging upon the Holy City to offer sacrifice in the Temple. Day after day the immense caravans wound slowly across the country. From east and west, north and south we came, and as we journeyed along we sang of the miracles God wrought to bring us out from our slavery in Egypt and into this, our Promised Land.

> When the Lord delivered Sion from bondage
> It seemed like a dream.
> Then was our mouth filled with laughter,
> On our lips there were songs.
> What marvels the Lord worked for us,
> Indeed we were glad.

"Indeed we were glad!" I sang loudly as I leaped like a mountain goat along the rocky track, enjoying my freedom to the utmost. Martha was traveling behind with a group of girls all recently betrothed and all chattering away concerning their respective husbands and wedding finery and not listening to each other at all. Lazarus was somewhere in front, only returning to our camp for the evening meal. Mother never queried our scattered ranks, for it meant a budget of gossip at the end of each day. We were almost encouraged to go off and collect as much as possible. I, of course, took full advantage of this indulgence, glad beyond measure to be out on the road again.

Bird song echoed under the blue vault of the sky. Anemones, tulips and hyacinths splashed in vivid streaks along the path and up under the trees. The great forests of oak and terebinth were green oases as we passed in a constant stream. Shepherds were leading their flocks to fresh pasture and, greatly daring, I called and waved to them. If mother had seen, I should almost have been sent home in disgrace. But they could not *all* be vagabonds and thieves. Then I licked my lips at the sight of the great fat-tailed sheep. It was a long time since we had tasted roast meat.

Below me the lambs were leaping beside their mothers while herds of goats and cattle moved slowly across the fields, grazing as they went. The barley harvest was reaped, and now the stooping figures of the gleaners could be seen along the empty furrows. By the time we returned, the wheat would also be gathered. Everything as I gazed around looked fresh and luxuriant after the rains—the blessed rains that quickened our crops, pattered on the roses in Herod's garden and turned Gennesaret into a sheet of pearl; the rains that drew thanksgiving from rich and poor alike.

What a glorious country! As the day progressed, all my cares vanished, as they always did en route for Jerusalem. Turning, I skipped back along the track to join the family group for our evening meal. Father brought Zachary and Matthias to us at the end of each day, and Martha displayed her culinary talents to the latter.

Darkness had fallen by the time we had finished, yet still I lingered up along the track to savor the end of the day. The nights of Nisan were warm and scented with a thousand growing things, and stars glinted over the ancient hills outlined stark against the sky. It was peaceful standing there alone, but mother's voice was calling me. Turning back down the stony path, I returned to the safety of our campfire. Soon we had all retired for the night, huddled together under our cloaks and shawls, trying to identify the formation of stars above us. But my eyelids grew heavy as I drowsily heard the muted swell of voices mingling with the sounds of the night and glimpsed now and again the family fires flickering away in the distance. Somewhere on the road below, the more devout were still singing, and a solo baritone poured richly forth.

> It is good to give thanks to the Lord,
>   To make music to your name, O Most High,
>   To proclaim your love in the morning—

"And your truth in the watches of the night," the tenor voices replied.

On the ten-stringed lyre and the lute

And the kinnor and nebel sounded.

With the murmuring sound of the harp . . .

Their voices drifted up to me, rising and falling with the music, and eventually lulled me to sleep. That is what I always remember going up—the singing. The road to Jerusalem was a highway of song. We sang all day and half the night, and started again each morning.

We awoke at dawn to a rose-washed sky and the ground glistening with dew.

"It's manna come down again!" someone cried, and we all laughed. Each year the same joke was made and each year we all laughed. But we soon set off so as to make the most of traveling at this, the best time of the year, during our brief spring before the blistering heat of summer. In the early morning the air was cool and fresh with the smell of damp earth, and as we climbed the mountain track, the west wind blew in, bringing a reminder of the sea. Now and again we glimpsed the Jordan like a ribbon below us, but usually we did not waste time looking down. We were going up—toward our goal.

Each day we moved slowly closer and closer—and then we were there. Nearing the top of Mount Scopus, we heard the shout that went up from those in front and quickened our step, weary though we were, for we knew what they had seen. Already the joyous song was wafting back to us.

I was glad when they said to me
Let us go to the house of the Lord . . .

Soon our party also reached the summit, and from our vantage point we paused to look down on Jerusalem. It was a lovely sight.

On the holy mountain is his city cherished by the Lord.
The Lord prefers the gates of Sion to all Jacob's dwellings.
Of you are told glorious things, O City of God!

Far below lay our city, tawny as a lion, armored as a fortress and all encamped about with walls and gates, towers and pinnacles, palaces and gardens and, towering like a Colossus over all—the Temple. Bronze and marble gleamed as the sun flashed on its snowy walls, lit on the gilded roof so it sparkled like snow, glinted with the rainbow tints of the hoar frost, lit again in a thousand points of fire and dazzled our eyes. This was our Temple. This was Jerusalem, our Paradise on earth.

As I stood looking down, Zachary pressed forward beside me, his wrinkled face alight with joy and tears of emotion streaming down his cheeks. I heard Elizabeth, Mariam's cousin, speak behind me. She had been staying several weeks in Nazareth since her husband died and had traveled down-country with Mariam for the feast. Joseph was unwell and could not make the journey, so Josue took his place as head of the family. He was staying in Jerusalem, but his mother and aunt preferred the quiet of the latter's mountain-home, Ain Karim, a little south-west of the capital. We ourselves were staying in Bethany with mother's sister and her husband.

"Mariam," Elizabeth said, "I thank God that He has spared me another year to see this sight."

"And, God willing, cousin, you will be with us again next spring."

But Elizabeth shook her head, smiling. She was very old. "Listen," she said, holding up her hand.

Below us the crowds were pushing silently upward, content

to save their breath till they reached the summit, but somewhere back in the throng a woman, anticipating the sight, was
singing softly and reminiscently to herself.

> How lovely is your dwelling-place,
>   Lord God of hosts.
> My soul is longing and yearning,
>   Is yearning for the courts of the Lord . . .

It was the last song of the ascent. Then down, down, down
we came, in leaps and bounds, nearer and nearer, hastening
now. Then those in front were running, nearer and nearer.
Then some were dancing along the way as David did before the
Ark, for very joy. The God of Israel was there in His sanctuary
waiting for us, His people. The end of our pilgrimage was in
sight. Nearer and nearer we came and the singing swelled up
exultantly into the sparkling blue air as we came down past the
great walls encircling our city, past the watchtowers and down
toward the Fish Gate.

> I was glad when they said to me,
>   Let us go to the house of the Lord . . .

The fortified outer door was slowly opening as the mass of
Galileans converged upon it. Now the densely packed crowds
were pushing and jostling through and along the great vaulted
passage. The massive inner gate was opening, yielding to our
rushed onslaught, and already sunlight was streaming into our
gloomy corridor. Swept off my feet by the crowd's impetus, I
was rushed along and through the last barrier. The tamborines
banged, cymbals clashed like bells in my ears, the *shofar*—the
great ram's horn—sounded overhead, and the triumphant shout
went up:

> And now our feet are standing
>   Within your gates, *O Jerusalem!*

And we entered into our city.

Then all was confusion and a bedlam of shouting, singing, dancing, laughing and weeping. Somehow I found myself among a group of Galileans chanting our thanksgiving at the tops of our lungs while, above in the guard room, the soldiers looked down in bored or amused fashion. One was openly contemptuous. But for once we did not care. This was our feast—our city—and they did not belong with either. They were pagans, Gentiles—outside it all.

Then mother tore herself out of the throng and staggered over to me and, with our veils and cloaks pulled asunder, our hair halfway down our backs and three sandals between us, we went off to rescue Martha. "It will be the day," gasped mother, "when I come through the Fish Gate unscathed."

And so the Passover week began, with the city and its suburbs bursting at the seams and overflowing onto the hillsides. Yet still they came pouring in through the Fish Gate in the north and the Sheep Gate, the Fountain Gate from the south and the Golden Gate from the east, through the gate of Ephraim from the west and the Gate of the Gardens—poured in and spilled out again day after day. Trade boomed for the market vendors and the innkeepers, for Passover was the fat which kept them through the lean periods of the year. A multitude of business took place within the gates where the elders presided, sorting and settling a myriad of legal questions and petty disputes amid the tumult of buying and selling. Dozens of lambs among the thousands awaiting sacrifice died on their feet in the crush, and at regular intervals their bodies were flung out beyond the walls to become a festering harbor for maggots and blowflies. Buzzards dropped like stones upon them, and dozens of camels tethered nearby flicked a disdainful glance at this squalid sight, then, chewing thoughtfully, averted their eyes.

But no one else noticed, for it was the Temple which drew

and fixed our attention. It was a magnificent sight, and no true Israelite failed to experience awe and pride each time he entered its walls.

Passing through into the immense outer Court of the Gentiles, we looked about with renewed delight. There was the great portico built all around, roofed with cedar and paved with colored stones. On the eastern side lay Solomon's Porch, with its triple colonnade of pillars overlooking the Mount of Olives and the Kidron Valley. Facing south, the central aisle of the Royal Porch soared ninety-two feet above us. From this vast outer court a flight of steps led up to the outer wall of the sanctuary. Thirteen gates led into the Temple proper, the most splendid being the Beautiful Gate. The first court was relegated to the women, then another fifteen steps led up to the Court of the Israelites for the men. This latter was entered through the Nicanor Gate, an immense bronze structure requiring twenty men to open it each day. On a slightly higher level and sealed off with a balustrade was the Court of the Priests. Here the high priest blessed the people. Here the beasts offered as a holocaust were sacrificed on the great altar. Finally twelve more steps led up to the Temple itself.

Standing below in the outer court, we looked up at its pavement fifty feet above us and then craned our necks to see its pillars soaring yet another ninety-eight feet above that. I understood why we always spoke of "going up" to Jerusalem as my eye followed the majestic ascent of courts, steps, balustrades and galleries rising tier upon tier to the summit, to the Temple porch itself. There the eye must halt before the great cedar door sumptuously adorned with gold. This door stood open from dawn until sunset, with only a richly embroidered veil concealing what lay beyond—the *qadosh haqedoshim*—the Holy of Holies where, each year on the Day of Atonement, the high priest placed the incense upon the rock.

Far below in the outer court, the business of the Temple was being transacted amid the crushing throng—a business that happily blended religion and cold finance, pious devotions and the manners of the marketplace. Rabbis and their disciples debated soberly while prayers were droned to a background of agitated squabbling as the money changers haggled over their rates, for foreign currency was unclean for Temple usage and countless Israelites were cheated each time they visited Jerusalem for the feasts. Children ran about screaming excitedly or crying from sheer weariness, while their mothers rested under the porticos chatting to friends not seen for many months. Baskets crammed with doves and pigeons were kicked aside as the porters strove to contain the sacrificial beasts, which further increased the uproar. The ground was slimy with their droppings, and I could tell from Martha's look of distaste that she was longing for several thousand gourds of water to sweep it all away.

"Well, Herod must be given praise for this at least," father remarked, gazing at the pinnacles glinting high above. "It was worth all those years of building to see an edifice like this in Jerusalem."

"And after all those years it's still not completed!" mother snapped. "And what do you mean by *praise*? Do you think the tetrarch designed it himself? Have you not heard of Solomon— and I don't mean Zachary's ass? Give Herod praise indeed! For what reason and for whose glory do you think this was built?"

"Hush, woman, or you'll have us all arrested!" father whispered urgently, looking hastily about. "To speak like that with spies listening everywhere!"

But mother, totally unrepentant, was already waving enthusiastically to a group of women under Solomon's Porch and bustled over to them directly. Father breathed a sigh of relief.

"Come, Lazarus, we'll go and get our beast and see how much they try to rob us because we're Galileans." A happy thought suddenly struck him. "By heaven, I hope we encounter that thieving rogue we had last year! I never finished that dispute with him."

And, grimly optimistic, he strode off to the gate, with Lazarus following resignedly. The long afternoon wore on and still we lingered until our lamb was slain. Then we set out at last to Bethany, where we were to have our Passover meal on this the fourteenth day of the month of Nisan, the first day of the festive week. Uncle gave us a warm welcome, while aunt was regaled with all our histories since she and mother last met. Then, with our preparations over, we settled to our Passover meal of roast lamb and bitter herbs and plenty of the red sauce, *hasereth*, in which to soak the unleavened bread—our banquet of the year! The Cup of Benediction was passed around the table and we heartily joined the rest of Bethany in singing the Grand Hallel. Then, replete with food and wine, and with our long journey over, we finally settled to sleep.

So Passover week began. Each morning we set out for Jerusalem, pausing briefly on the Mount of Olives for our favorite view of the city before descending. Once through the gates, its cosmopolitan atmosphere embraced us. Lazarus, his task of escort over, vanished into the synagogues, while mother and aunt went straight to the bazaar, firmly quashing my plan of visiting the upper town with its open squares and gardens of the rich.

"We'll go one evening when it's quieter, Mary," said my aunt. "And *no*, you can't go alone!" she added firmly, reading my thoughts. "You'll come with us to the bazaar—and look ahead! That water carrier almost soaked you. Miriam, I declare your daughter has her eyes shut half the day!"

So we struggled along between the mud-brick and limestone houses, under lines of dripping clothes and down through narrow alleys, cobbled and stepped and effectively blocked now and again by a loaded ass.

"A man was killed here the other day," aunt remarked

conversationally. "The beast slipped and plunged down on him. It's miraculous that it doesn't happen more often."

"These streets are a positive scandal," grumbled mother, holding up her skirts. "Take care where you tread, Martha, or your good sandals will be ruined."

"Too late," my sister replied resignedly as she squelched after us. "I should have taken your advice and worn my old ones."

"Mercy on us, they cost me a good drachma! Be sure you clean them the moment we return—and do I see your best tunic?" pulling aside Martha's cloak. "I know it's Passover, but why dress thus for the bazaar?"

"Perhaps Martha thought we might see Matthias today," aunt guessed shrewdly, "and she wanted to look her best."

My sister blushed guiltily, but at that moment mother trod in something undesirable and the subject was forgotten.

The streets of Jerusalem were appalling indeed. Mud filled them in winter, choking dust in summer, and filth and refuse all the year round. The main thoroughfares were swept clear once a day to observe the Law, but the results were simply pushed down the side alleys to fester there. In the hottest months it was unbearable. The place was black with flies and mosquitoes, and disease spread unchecked.

The noise too was indescribable—a constant babel as the shopkeepers and stall-holders argued, haggled, cajoled and cursed from dawn to dusk. The itinerant smith bellowed for trade as he set up his charcoal furnace and anvil and was soon soldering, brazing and banging away with the sparks flying about his enormous frame. A soldier with a damaged shield at his feet stood leaning on his javelin and watching intently as he awaited his turn. An old crone pushed past hawking her dates and fig cakes—the finest in Jericho! Then screams of abuse as a stall overturned and oranges rolled in all directions. Grinning urchins appeared from nowhere, grabbed their bounty and vanished again. Suddenly a quarrel among a group of traders

51

erupted into violence, and the jostling crowds quickly gathered to savor this entertainment. Then just as rapidly it dispersed as a group of cloaked and crested cavalry nudged through to investigate this latest fracas. Their mounts moved cautiously, instinctively nervous of slipping on these stepped streets, unlike their humbler but surer-footed relatives, the donkeys. Across the way a potter sat crouched over his wheel, hands smothered in wet clay and oblivious to everything. The barber flashed his razor in the sunlight. Sawdust flew about the carpenter. A scribe wandered past with pen and ink horn at his belt, watching for likely customers. Only the laborers stood mute and unoccupied, waiting to be hired.

Suddenly we heard the crush and din of a foreign caravan loaded with jewelry and linens, oils and perfumes. The caravan was escorted by swarthy merchants colorfully clad in embroidered tunics and silken turbans. Rings glittered on every finger. The penetrating odors of balm and nard hung heavy and expensive in the air while the gorgeous bale of emerald silk they flung contemptuously before them, unrolling it like a carpet, drew covetous looks from the society women passing in their litters. The old men gossiping in their dim shops among the flickering oil lamps nudged each other joyfully. This would rob the upper town of its trade. Visiting Israelites from Persia and Babylon had already gathered, the former richly clad and with fat purses, the latter sable-cloaked and sober but with a cautious eye for a bargain. Passover pilgrims were always in a spending mood, and the merchants' arrival invariably coincided with the big feasts. But the chapmen moved away, scowling at these intruders on their pitch. Not so the beggars and cripples, who fawned on them for alms. Martha and I watched, entranced, for the *rokels* were beings both foreign and fascinating in our closed society. They were pagan, too, of course, but by our provincial standards their caravan was as exotic as a retinue from Solomon's court and to be accorded the same respect.

Only the Pharisees could command a similar following, albeit for different reasons. Passing through the crowd, they were saluted on all sides with lengthy ritual greetings while others came forward to kiss the hands of these upholders of the Law. Many were worthy of the respect shown them, but there were many also who placed such absurd emphasis on outward ritual and the minutest observance of the Law, that soon they were like fettered and blinded men. Days might be spent devoutly ruminating whether it was lawful to kill a flea on the sabbath or simply pull off its legs to prevent it hopping further! Such an outlook effectively stultified any spiritual progress.

"I'd prefer ten gossiping old women to one Pharisee," declared father whose famed imitation of a Pharisee and his foibles was the delight of his cronies.

So the days slipped past. All through the week the mingled odors of incense and burning flesh hung over the city, sickening us at first, but after a while we ceased to notice it. Four times during the day at the sacrificial hours, the seven silver trumpets sounded from the gate of the Court of the Israelites, and immediately we prostrated ourselves in the dust, acknowledging the solemnity of the moment.

Much of our holiday was spent visiting old friends and entertaining new ones at our uncle's house, who thoroughly enjoyed these invasions, being the most hospitable of men. Sometimes he and father took me with them to the Pool of Siloam, and while they bathed, I sat under the portico and watched the children splashing about. It was said that from time to time an angel came to stir the water, and whoever entered the pool immediately afterward was healed of his infirmities. But father said it was the desert wind and we were not to believe such nonsense. Still, it was a favorite place of mine.

Later in the day mother, Martha and I went up into the Court of Women to attend the service and receive the traditional blessing from the high priest.

> The Lord bless you and keep you. The Lord smile on you and
> be merciful to you. The Lord turn his gaze toward you and
> give you peace.

It was comforting to hear the familiar words again—words given by God to Moses as a blessing for the children of Israel. Somehow it confirmed our belief that, no matter what happened, Yahweh would never forsake us, that the Holy City and the Temple would stand forever as a sign of the fidelity of His people who alone accorded Him the worship he desired. As if confirming this, the haunting melody of "The Lily of the Law" surged up in unison as the service ended. We remained in the city for the evening offering, and then, with hundreds of others, retraced our steps to the surrounding villages for the night as the sun set and the *shofar* sounded the end of another day in Jerusalem.

On the last evening we left our uncle's home to camp outside the city so as to be on the road north at first light. From where we lay I could see the watch fire flickering on the Phasael tower of Herod's palace and hear the distant howl of the wild dogs as they roamed the Plain of Shephalah. At regular intervals came the cry of the guards high up on the Antonia, and the answering hail faintly repeated from the watchtowers around the fortress.

"All's well, indeed!" grumbled father. "It would be well if they returned to their barracks and I could enjoy a night of unbroken sleep."

"The Antonia *is* their barracks," mother stated heavily. "They're simply keeping watch over their own property—and I well know you can sleep through any amount of noise!"

Father opened his mouth to protest, thought better of it and closed it again. Martha and I giggled. We usually spent a great deal of the holiday giggling.

We awoke to hear the Nicanor Gate rumbling open like a distant growl of thunder. The sun was rising over the Moab mountains, and father and Lazarus were already gone to the Temple to recite the morning Shema facing the sanctuary and to bring back, father threatened, a string of camels to cope with mother's purchases. It was always sad leaving Jerusalem, and I wished I might linger awhile, but mother was already gathering our belongings and Martha was openly eager to be home again. Before long we were out on the road heading north, and as we passed each town and village, my spirits sank lower and lower. By next spring I, too, would be betrothed, and I wondered if father had anyone in mind yet. Even life at home would soon be a new trial with Martha away and I no substitute to mother for her—and with one pair of hands less in the house, more work would inevitably fall on me.

That spring as we trudged back into Galilee with our holiday over, my future seemed bleak indeed.

CHAPTER
• FOUR •

BUT LIFE IS EVER unpredictable and changing like the dust of the desert, which is gathered up and dispersed by the winds. Within a few weeks of our return, our life in Magdala was suddenly and irrevocably altered.

During the blistering summer that ensued there was a drought, of short duration but fierce, and it caused great suffering among us. As the heat grew worse, the flies and mosquitoes, always prolific in our climate, covered everything, bringing disease in their wake. Water was strictly rationed, so to assuage their thirst, the children stole soft fruits from the bazaar and, brushing off the fat blowflies, pushed the rotting flesh into the mouths of other infants. It only required a few to sicken before the infection spread rapidly around the lake. Dysentery was rife, bringing, in its turn, dehydration, wasting and great weakness. Wine and fruit juices only aggravated the illness. With our poor facilities, strict hygiene was not possible to lessen the spread of the epidemic. This kind of sickness is common in our country, but I had never seen it so virulent as during that summer drought. The very young and the old had no resistance and went down before it. Mothers gave their share of water to their children, but to no avail if they had already sickened. The sun burned down, the flies swarmed, the ground cracked open with the heat and people sat listlessly in their doorway, away from the dreadful white glare outside.

Before long there was news of several deaths around Gennesaret. As the villagers attended the burials, they wondered fearfully where this illness would strike next. We wondered also, and within days we were enlightened.

Early one morning, just after daybreak, I was lying on the roof thinking idly that I must bestir myself when I heard footsteps shuffling through the garden and into our house. A moment later a piercing wail arose and, rushing below, I saw Zachary in the doorway. His old frame was bent over his stick and tears were flowing down his beard. Father was trying to comfort him while mother held Martha, but my sister sank to her knees and rocked to and fro in an agony of grief. Matthias was dead. No one noticed me standing there, and I did not know what to do, so I turned and ran to the garden hut until I was needed. Later that day I learned that Matthias had fallen ill through drinking polluted water in a house at Caphernaum. He had also taken food that may have been tainted, for the people were very poor and ignorant and knew nothing of infection. His body was still lying in the house, so father went with the other men to bring it back for burial.

Hardly had a week passed since this event when, to our intense anxiety, mother also sickened soon after visiting Susan, who had two or three children lying ill. Susan was always a bad manager and sickness baffled her even more, so mother had recently spent much of her time helping her neighbor. Now she too was ill. Martha put aside her own loss and stayed beside her night and day. She refused my help, saying there was no reason for others to be infected, and besides, it eased her own sorrow to be busy. Martha was a better nurse anyway.

I had never known mother to be ill before, so to me it was

inconceivable that with her strong constitution she could not overcome this local epidemic. But mother, who had drained her energy nursing in the neighboring houses, had no reserves of strength to draw on and grew rapidly weaker. On the sabbath eve she lay half-conscious and wandering in her mind. Martha sat like a statue beside her, while father, Lazarus and I huddled in a corner of the room, waiting. No children played outside. It seemed as though the whole world had come to a standstill, and I, who loved a quiet life, now dreaded the awful silence in our home.

Toward evening mother awoke and knew us. "What day is it?" she whispered.

"The day of preparation, mother," Martha replied, giving her a few sips of water.

"Ah," mother said.

She lay unmoving for a while, then, turning her head to my sister, "The psalm we sang in Nisan—going up . . ."

"Which one is that, mother?"

"Our song—when we came home again—from exile."

So Martha sang, softly and falteringly, the familiar words mother loved.

> Deliver us, O Lord, from our bondage
>   As streams in a dry land.
> Those who are sowing in tears,
>   Will sing when they reap.
> They go out, they go out, full of tears,
>   Carrying seed for the sowing.
> They come back, they come back, full of song,
>   Carrying their sheaves.

When she had finished, mother feebly patted her hand and drifted into sleep. We watched in turn throughout the sabbath, but she did not know us again and died in the early hours of the first day. There was no time for tears. Anna and Deborah came in when they heard the news and moved mechanically about their tasks. Martha told me to get food for Lazarus and father, who was already in deep mourning and unrecognizable with his beard shaved off. By the time the sun rose, the body had been washed and anointed and wrapped in a shroud, and the hands and feet tied with linen strips, for burials follow fast on a death in our climate. As many relatives and friends as could come at such short notice now arrived at the house, which was soon full of their wailing and keening. Then for the last time we looked at our mother, and immediately the veil was lowered over her face. I could still hardly believe she was dead. Then, an hour before noon, Martha, myself and the other women led the way out to the burial ground in the hills, with father and Lazarus carrying our mother on an open litter and the flute players following behind.

My loss came home to me as we halted outside the great cave. It suddenly seemed a place of horror, with its network of tunnels and chambers, each belonging to a family and con-taining generations of our villagers—a veritable charnel house of bones. The thought of mother lying there on the rock shelf in the airless dark filled me with terror, and I sobbed wildly as her body was carried past me down the slope and into the vast limestone cavern.

Mariam, who had heard the news while visiting friends nearby, came up and led me away down the hill as behind us the great wheel stone crunched along its groove and came to rest over the mouth of the cave. Anna was preparing the burial meats as we entered the house, and father was weeping quietly in the hut as he searched aimlessly for our best wine. Lazarus went to help and sent him indoors to our relatives—and so the customary visits to the bereaved began. They helped fill the void and pass the days for us. But I missed mother more than I thought possible, and at night I dreamed of her wandering in the darkness of the cavern and beating her hands on the great stone, and I awoke screaming. I was a sad trial to Martha and had almost forgotten Matthias.

But the tomb was not long closed. Although the sickness was lessening around the lake, father had been unwell even before mother died, with the seeds of our local fever in him. His ill health was increased by constant anxiety over his failing business. He was troubled too that Martha was officially a widow so soon after her betrothal, and then came the shock of mother's death a few days later. After the burial he lost all interest and energy and instead sat wrapped in his own thoughts, though we tried to rally him gently from this inertia.

Then to our great grief news came up from Nazareth that Joseph, his oldest and dearest friend, was gone. No more would he stay with us and we hear his hammer tapping cheerfully on our roof, or his answering hail from the garden hut when we called him in at dawn. This second blow broke father in his weakened state, and his grieving frightened us. Neighbors came to sympathize, for they all knew Joseph, and to all of them father replied with the tears trickling down his face, "We grew up together, he and I . . . we were always friends . . . he was like a brother to me . . . Did you know that?"

"Yes—yes, Levi, we know," they soothed, but father did not hear and continued murmuring brokenly, "Impossible to measure all he did for me . . . we were like brothers . . ."

"Was there ever such a friend?" they said to each other to comfort him.

"He was here by my side when I married Miriam, God rest her dear soul. Joseph my friend . . ."

And his tears flowed afresh. If you realize all that the word *friend* embraces in our language, then you will know also how much my father loved Joseph. He could not forgive himself for not going to Nazareth when Joseph was first unwell, and now he was too weak to attend the burial. Lazarus was sent, therefore, with many kind messages to Mariam and Josue, whom we would visit as soon as father could travel.

But father had lost the will to fight and sank rapidly. He seemed strangely lost without mother to scold and chivvy him; he had relied on her more than he had realized. Now he wandered weeping around the garden in the cold night air, and we wept also to see him in such a pitiable state. Before he died, I sat beside him, willing him to live. The sickness was gone from the village; the drought had lessened; there was no need for him to leave us, but I felt tangibly that he was drifting away and cried out in fear for Martha. The thirty days' mourning for mother were scarcely ended before we were weeping afresh at our orphaned state.

Father was buried as the harvest was gathered in—a scanty one after the drought. Once more the house was filled to overflowing as it had been only recently. All father's old cronies were there, easygoing Galileans, shaken now and silent, for father had always been well-liked in the district. Josue was there, of course, to take Joseph's place as head of his own little household. He forbade his mother to come, for she was exhausted. Amid the ritual sighing and noisy rehearsal of our parents' virtues he sat, compassionating us in our loss, for the mere mention of his own father brought tears to his eyes. In the evening he said farewell, for he planned to leave at dawn and we should not see him before he went. Martha gave him food for his return journey to Nazareth. When Lazarus thanked him, "Are you not our friends?" he asked.

When everyone had left and the house was empty once again, I did what I had never done alone before—I went down to the lakeshore and wandered along it in the fading light. Martha and Lazarus were too preoccupied to think of me, but there was little pleasure in this late-won freedom. A fresh breeze had sprung up, ruffling the plumy heads of the reeds; overhead the gulls wheeled and screamed their harsh cries; it was a lonely sound. Little waves slapped against the boats as they rode their moorings. On the far side of the lake, a light gleamed and was gone. The shore was deserted as far as the eye could strain. I wandered back and stood in the shelter of the thorn trees. It was only now that I was fully realizing that mother and father were dead—that their bodies were lying in the hills behind me. But I did not know if they were happy. "The souls of the just are in the hands of God"—but would I see them in some other life? Would there be a resurrection of the dead one day? No one seemed to know. Even the great Doctors could not decide.

Leaning against the cool bark of the trees, I felt the scalding tears run down my face. I wished that I had been able to tell mother that I loved her more than she thought. I wished that father had given me his blessing before he died. I looked out over the lake feeling sad and hopeless. The wind whispered in the branches above me and rustled the dry leaves at my feet. One thing I did know, and it brought anguish in its wake— "Their place will know them no more." Already they had voyaged far. I shivered and turned abruptly toward the comfort of the lamps flickering in the houses above. The birds had stopped singing. Soon it would be dark.

A few days later a swollen-eyed Martha set out to visit Mariam at Nazareth, leaving me to look after Lazarus and run the house. In the past few days I had scarcely noticed my brother's presence, but now I looked around and saw that all his usual jobs had been done as if there had been no break in the routine of our lives. But even as I thought this I heard Martha returning. She had only just left Magdala before she met Mariam on the road coming to see us. The two bereaved women ran to greet each other, and then my sister brought Mariam back to the house.

After greeting and condoling with her, I sat down in the

doorway while the two women talked quietly in the room behind me. Later we took a meal together, which Martha cooked.

"Mary, is the bread ready yet?" Martha asked as the vegetables simmered over the fire.

Startled out of my lethargy, I was ashamed to confess that I had not even thought of baking bread. Since our parents' death I had scarcely done anything in the house, living in a kind of listless limbo and relying on neighbors to help us. But already Martha was lecturing me. "For years, Mary, you have baked the bread each morning, and it is more than time you began again. I will grind some barley this evening so there will be no excuse not to have any tomorrow. But now we have nothing fresh to offer Mariam. That is no way to serve a guest."

I felt mortified, but my sister's homily roused me. While Mariam was in the garden playing with Susan's baby, I hurried out to ask Anna if she had a surplus loaf. Fortunately she had, but Martha was not pleased. She detested borrowing; it was the mark of a bad housewife.

The following day Mariam returned to Nazareth. She intended to travel back with a family as far as Cana, where her son would meet her. Lazarus had made his farewells earlier and was gone out to milk the *hazzan*'s goats. I was already at my hated task of mixing the dough and wondering if I had salted it too much. Then it occurred to me that mother would not be scolding me anymore or father asking if my salty bread grew on trees around the Dead Sea, and tears began to trickle down into the bowl, making the mixture more saline than ever. Then Mariam's heavily veiled figure bent over me to bid me farewell.

I went down with her to the gap in the hedge, and we stood on the road waiting for the group she was to travel back with to arrive. Eventually it came straggling along, and she went forward to join them, only turning back for an instant to say, "Mary, you have all three lost your parents, but Martha has lost

64

a husband as well, and Lazarus is not strong. Be a good sister to them; help them all you can."

That night I awoke to hear Martha weeping quietly beside me. I bent over her, thinking she was grieving for mother who had loved her best, and touching her shoulder, I whispered, "Martha, you mustn't fret like that. Mother wouldn't want—"

But my sister, turning toward me, did not hear and, clutching at my hands, sobbed wildly, "Oh, Mary, he's dead! He's dead!"

And I realized with a sudden shock that I had forgotten that in a few days' time, now that the harvest was in, Martha's wedding feast was to have taken place.

Then I remembered Mariam's words and felt ashamed of my selfishness. Martha had carried the burden of everything lately, hiding her own grief without a word of reproach to me. I was so absorbed in my own sorrows that I had noticed nothing and no one. Overcome with remorse, I put my arms around her and tried to comfort her. It was the first time I had felt close to my sister.

When the days of mourning were over and the house empty once again, we began to return to some kind of routine. The first problem Lazarus had to solve was how we were to live, for father's death had left us with little money. We knew that payments were due from several clients, but as father had trusted his memory rather than any written record, Lazarus was unable to trace them. My brother was not long enough employed to have learned much, so we were greatly relieved when some customers came forward and readily paid their debts—people whom we were unaware owed money. Various sums were paid in reluctant trickles, but the bulk was never retrieved, and this, as we expected, was owed by the wealthier clients. Their stewards came to Lazarus feigning ignorance of any recent goods and demanding records of such deliveries. Lazarus, armed only with a handful of father's ill-jotted notes, was no match for the glib-tongued servants who, with shoulders shrugging and hands spread out in bewilderment, called on heaven to witness their innocence in the matter. So Lazarus, unaccustomed to such flagrant dishonesty, was forced to turn away, angry and baffled and sickened with the humiliating business of begging around the country. Indeed he often looked so tired and ill when he returned that we pleaded with him to cease such a thankless task, and after several more failures he eventually agreed.

But nothing could persuade him to continue father's trade, particularly one that had long been failing. Besides, he possessed neither the inclination nor the enterprise for such an undertaking. So the remainder of the cloth was sold and Lazarus looked for new employment. Obviously he had to have some less arduous job than traveling around Galilee in all weathers, as father had done quite happily for years—but what? For a day or two he and Martha discussed moving down to Bethany in Judea, for our uncle had indicated after father's death that he could find Lazarus employment there should we decide to leave Magdala. But although we were grateful for this offer, we all three felt reluctant to accept unless circumstances forced us. Galilee was our home and we loved it, and I certainly had no wish to be living in my aunt's house and beholden to her, for she was very fond of ordering peoples' lives.

Fortunately Zachary intervened soon after this. A month after Matthias's death the old man sent to Bethsaida for his nephew to come and manage the business, intimating that he could find him a wife in Magdala if he wished. So Jude, who was a skilled man, arrived in the village and settled in the *naggar*'s shop beyond the spring. Then Zachary, who had a good opinion of our family, offered Lazarus a job as apprentice to Jude, and my brother was thankful to accept. At first he earned little, for he was totally unskilled, but it was a way of learning a secure trade. The nephew too was a pleasant man and a patient instructor.

Setting aside his dream of studying and becoming a teacher, Lazarus now had to work to support us. Even marriage was impossible for him until Martha and I were settled into our husbands' homes. Most of his contemporaries were looking around for prospective wives, but no father-in-law would welcome Lazarus into his family while he lacked even the sum for his bride's dowry.

But Lazarus, although he seemed to have grown older and more serious than ever with his added responsibilities, did not complain. He worked all day at the *naggar*'s, still milked the *hazzan*'s goats, helped me in the garden and learned to do household repairs. Josue came occasionally, and it was almost like the old days to see them talking under the eucalyptus tree and Josue sketching patterns on the ground as he demonstrated the replacing of a roof beam. It greatly pleased Martha and me to see them together, but Josue could seldom stay long.

However, we women had our own domestic troubles in trying to run the house on a drastically reduced budget. Martha had the few pieces of jewelry mother had left, including her own dower gifts, which she was determined to keep. Being a frugal housekeeper, she managed our family purse as best she could. By forgoing all but necessities and relying on the produce of our tiny garden, we managed for food, never realizing till then how much we had previously relied on father's payments in barter. What would we not give now for a barrel of salt herring and two dozen melons! Even new sandals or the replacement of household utensils provoked a small crisis if the need occurred at the wrong moment.

But our heaviest burden was the dual system of taxation. What we owed to the religious authority was heavy enough— twenty-four dues in all, not including the didrachma for the Temple tax—but the imperial levy we thought scandalous in our straitened circumstances—a direct poll tax that went straight into Roman coffers or, in the case of the Galileans, to the tetrarch to finance yet another of his extravagant schemes. Lazarus went white with anger each time it was paid.

Martha suffered, too, in her own way. She greatly missed mother's company in the house, and I was a most unsatisfactory substitute. Not surprisingly, my sister felt lonely, and although she worked harder than ever, the joy was gone from it for her. She often sighed, where previously she had sung. All her friends were now married, and although she was a widow according to our Law, most Magdalene women of like status seemed three times her age, with children and grandchildren to occupy them. So poor Martha did not really belong to either group. She never spoke of Matthias, but I knew she missed all he represented—a husband, children, a home of her own and, with it, her fixed place in our village society. Needless to say, she found it the hardest trial to attend the wedding feast of Josue's cousin, James, who was marrying a local girl soon after the date arranged for my sister's own celebrations had Matthias lived.

It was nearing sunset as the procession wound up the road toward the house of Cleophas. James's father stood in the doorway awaiting his new daughter while his wife, Mary, assisted the clustered attendants in lighting their lamps. Everyone loves a *mistitha,* and the villagers of Nazareth were no exception. Leaving their domestic tasks, they ran from their homes singing the ancient bridal songs in greeting.

> Who is this that makes her way up by the desert road
> All myrrh and incense—all gaily clad,
> Leaning on her true love's arm?

Carried on a litter, the bride drew near. With one accord, the guests surged down the road to meet the procession. Esther's face was veiled and the gold coins of her dower gifts glittered like stars on the band around the black hair lying loose on her shoulders. James walked beside her, turning now and again to smile at her. She smiled back with her eyes, the only part of her that was visible. All the men, led by James and Josue, had set out an hour previously to walk to the house of the bride's parents and escort her into her new home. Josue was at his cousin's side as the indispensable friend of the bridegroom who rejoiced in their happiness, supervised the festal arrangements and saw that all ran smoothly. Tears streamed down Martha's face as she watched the happy, laughing group. It might have been her. And so the first day ended.

On the second day of the festivities, after the evening meal, came the presentation of the wedding gifts to the bride. Seated under the *huppah*—the traditional canopy—and surrounded by her ten bridesmaids all arrayed in white and holding ornate little lamps, trimmed once more and burning brightly, Esther looked for the first and last time in her life as regal and happy as a princess.

"Tell us, fairest of women," the bridesmaids sang, "how shall we know this sweetheart of thine?"

"Know? Among ten thousand you shall know him," answered the bride as James stepped forward, singing,

See how fair is the maid I love.
Soft eyes thou hast like a dove's eyes half-seen beneath thy veil.
Fair thou art and graceful, my heart's love.
For beauty Jerusalem itself is not thy match.

"And see how fair is the man I love, how stately . . ." Esther echoed, drawing aside her veil as the bridegroom sang,

69

Rise up quickly, dear heart, so gentle, so beautiful,
Rise up and come with me.
Still hiding thyself as a dove hides in cleft rock or crannied wall.
Show me but thy face, let me but hear thy voice—
That voice as sweet as thy face is fair.

Later that evening, as the women sat with the bride and her attendants, James came over to speak to his wife. He had obviously been told of Martha's loss, for Esther immediately rose and went to my sister and, taking her hand, spoke long and kindly to her, and wished her such happiness again in the future as she now had herself. She was a pretty girl, with red cheeks and black eyes that shone with her own overflowing happiness, and Martha's tears nearly burst out afresh.

"It's God's will, Mary," she said, blowing her nose resoundingly. Nevertheless, she could not bear to stay the whole week and we left early.

CHAPTER
• FIVE •

TEBET AND SEBAT SLIPPED past, Passover came and went, and it was summer again. The worst of our grief was over and we were accustomed to there being only we three when the lamp was lit in the evenings. My brother was gradually becoming more skilled in his work, and it was a pleasant sight to see him planing or polishing a piece of wood, totally absorbed in his work. Once he had really proved himself, then Zachary guaranteed him a partnership with Jude and would, of course, pay him a better wage.

The reason behind this merging of our two families was simple. We knew by now that Zachary was persuading his nephew to take Martha as his wife, but Jude refused to be hurried into marriage, although he promised his uncle to give the matter some thought. Martha, I knew, was agreeable to these potential arrangements, but she was also anxious that my betrothal should be quickly settled so that Lazarus might be freed from the task of supporting us and could thus realize his dream of studying in Jerusalem. So, despite our financial troubles, Martha and Lazarus looked forward to brighter days.

But as their spirits lifted, mine depressed. Since our parents' deaths the pace of our life had slowed considerably, and I now

71

frankly enjoyed the more lenient atmosphere in our house. I moved about with greater freedom and was in no haste to lose it again. I unconsciously hoped that this way of life might continue indefinitely.

The thorny question of my betrothal had been postponed for the past year, but now my brother and sister were anxious to have all our futures settled and the plan for mine was surfacing again. But since father's death most girls of my age had become betrothed, and there was a temporary dearth of bachelors in and around Magdala. Barnabas over at Caphernaum had once seemed interested but so far had said nothing definite to Lazarus. The remaining suitor was a local widower whom the *hazzan* recommended highly, but my brother refused even to consider this grandfather who was old enough to be going up the hill to join his ancestors. All this was going on in the early summer, at the time of the shearing festival.

Then suddenly, to Zachary's great annoyance, it seemed that Jude had transferred his fluctuating attention from Martha to me. For Matthias's sake, Zachary wanted his nephew to marry Martha, but, shrugging his arthritic shoulders, he conceded there was little he could do if Jude decided to the contrary. But for the present the nephew kept his own counsel and said not a word to his uncle or to Lazarus. Discretion kept him silent until he became fully clear in his own mind as to whom he favored. He did not wish, after all, to offend the old man who had given him a far better livelihood than he had made from his previous job over at Bethsaida.

But when I heard of this sudden change of plan, I was horrified, feeling that events were rushing ahead and sweeping me along with them whether I would or not. With our parents dead, surely I should at least be consulted as to whom I marry? Seeking out Martha, I spoke vehemently against the fickleness of Jude, expecting wholehearted support, but my sister seemed surprised at my outburst and not slighted at all.

"But, Mary, you must be sensible. It is for Jude to decide whom he'll marry, and Zachary is only turning him toward me because of Matthias. Besides," she added generously, "you're the pretty one, not me. I don't wonder at his changing his mind."

"But, Martha," I cried desperately as I saw my placid life slipping from me, "you must be married before me. You're the eldest. It wouldn't be right . . ."

"Of course I'll be married before you," my sister replied comfortably. "As a widow I can remarry almost immediately. Indeed I'll be in my new home before the harvest is gathered! If Jude decides in your favor, then I know Simeon will take me. He's been a widower for a year now and he's a good man. I was fond of Judith, God rest her—and it's shameful for those two children to be living with his sister. I should love to have them as my own, and I know Simeon misses them and wants them back with him."

So Martha chattered on, totally unworried as to her future. She would settle quite happily with either man and looked forward to the day when she and I would be living within a short distance of each other in Magdala. She made me feel incredibly selective with the practical way she organized both our futures.

"But, Martha," I began tentatively, "I don't wish to marry Jude—that is, supposing Zachary's not mistaken in the first instance—or Barnabas. Could I not wait until there was someone else, someone more suited to me . . .?"

"More *suited* to you!" Martha was astonished. "Whatever has that to do with it? When will you wake up, Mary, and start being a little more realistic? Your husband will want you to care for his home and children, and provided you do that—and most women can if they have any sense at all—even you, Mary!— then you will be well enough suited, unless," she continued with some warmth, "you are hoping he'll let you go wandering off as you've been doing recently when you're meant to be collecting the water or buying the fish."

I looked up guiltily. However did she know that?

"I suppose you imagine that Magdalene women don't have eyes! I *trust* you to come back from your errands directly, but you do nothing of the sort. Susan was telling me only yesterday that she saw you climbing the hill path until you suddenly noticed her. I felt so shamed that I couldn't think how to excuse you. What ails you that you must go roaming about all the time? It's not becoming when you're soon to be betrothed. In fact I'm surprised you have any offers at all! I'd no intention of mentioning this, as I'd hoped that Jude would decide and everything be settled at last—including your wandering! It's very wrong of you to deceive me, Mary, and selfish, too, when Lazarus is doing his best for both of us and you not caring about your reputation at all! I don't know what I'll tell our aunt when I go down to Bethany next week. She'll be expecting good news of us all, but I'll not have much to say about *your* prospects if you continue like this! But rest assured that once you're married, there'll be no roaming up in the hills when you're meant to be down in the house. The idea! You know, Mary, there are times when you're completely beyond my comprehension."

I felt utterly miserable. I knew it was wrong to go off like that, but I sometimes felt I had to when all the doors started closing in my face. If only I could open the right one and get back into my room. I had not seen it for over a year now. Would it still be the same? I could not reenter however hard I tried, so I had thought of going up into the hills where it was quiet and no one could disturb me. I thought I might be more successful there. But Susan had suddenly appeared and spoiled everything.

"Mary, are you listening to me? God bless the girl, she's off in a daydream again!"

I blinked and tried to fix my attention on what Martha was saying.

"Now I know you're not very pleased about Barnabas, but you can't stay at home forever. I certainly wish for your own sake that there was someone whom you'd really like, but you're in no position to wait until—Merciful heavens!"

I looked up at her sudden exclamation as she turned eagerly to me. "Why did I never think of him before?"

And while I gazed at her expectantly, she clapped her hands in triumph. "Josue, of course! No, it's not so singular," she insisted as my mouth dropped open in astonishment. "We've known him all our lives and you couldn't hope for a better husband—and Mariam would make you so welcome," my sister chattered on encouragingly.

"Martha!" I almost shouted to drown her voice. "Will you cease marrying me to every man you know! What *would* Josue think if he heard of this? That you and I have been urging Lazarus to start matchmaking. Oh, I should die of shame!"

"But he's still unmarried," Martha persisted.

"And able to approach anyone he wishes to marry without being assisted by you!" I cried.

"Perhaps you're right," Martha conceded doubtfully. "It is certainly not our place to say anything."

"I should think not," I muttered thankfully.

"Even so," she persisted, unwilling to abandon her idea, "you would think that he would be married by now. All his friends are, and half the mothers around Nazareth must have him in their minds as a suitable son-in-law."

"Oh, really, Martha," I cried angrily, "you're just like the rest of the women here! You think of nothing else but who should be married to whom and if not, why not? I don't like Barnabas because he's as dull as soaked flax, and from what I heard down at the spring the other day, Jude might not be so interested in us as you think. There is a cousin over at Bethsaida whom he visited recently, and even Zachary can't object to a blood relative! As for why Josue is waiting before he marries, well, that is his concern, not ours—and I wish you wouldn't make it ours. Let him wait but 'though he tarry,'" I quoted sarcastically, "'I will not wait for him.' So there's an end to the matter."

Having disposed of my two suitors and demolished Martha's fond hope of seeing me as Mariam's daughter-in-law, I now hoped for peace. But my sister was shocked at my irreverent misquoting of Israel's declaration of faith in its coming Messiah coupled with my intransigent attitude.

"You shouldn't speak like that, Mary. It's a wicked thing to parody those words. And I don't believe a word of that gossip about Jude. I'm sure I'll be telling aunt next week that you'll soon be betrothed to him."

I was angered at Martha reiterating this after what I had said. "Betrothed to Jude!" I cried. "Forced to live out my days with that constant hammering and noise! I'd go mad within a week!" My voice rose to a shout. "Once and for all, Martha, I will *not* marry a carpenter!"

A sudden sound made me turn. I had not noticed Lazarus in the doorway. Now he came into the room and put down his bag of tools, and immediately I felt stung with remorse. I wanted so much to please him and Martha and not be a burden to them, and yet I felt miserable at the prospect of Barnabas or Jude as a husband. Martha was right. There would be no more wandering once I married. But perhaps Lazarus would let me wait a few more months? He was kindhearted. Let Martha be married, and I would stay at home awhile longer.

"Forgive me, Lazarus," I said going over to him. "I didn't mean to say that. I was angry and—"

"Martha is right," he interrupted abruptly. "You shouldn't parody sacred words like that—and you must be married soon."

He turned to face me. "I've been talking to Zachary today, and his nephew has promised to give him an answer by the end of the month. Martha will be home from Bethany by then. Once I know if Jude is interested in either of you, then I shall know what to say to Simeon and Barnabas should they approach me. I know we've waited long enough, but for Zachary's sake, I want Jude to have first choice. And there is nothing amiss with Barnabas, Mary," he said, seeing my expression. "I should hardly allow my sister to marry a man I did not approve of myself. So everything is settled."

I had never before heard my brother speak like that, and for a few moments I was speechless. Then I saw that he really meant what he said and there was to be no respite for me, and tears of self-pity welled up.

"You're both against me," I wept. "You don't try to understand . . ."

"Don't be foolish, Mary," Lazarus intervened. "We only want your happiness, but you don't seem to realize how selfish you're being. How can Martha be married when she is troubled about you? And you've condemned Barnabas and Jude for no reason I can comprehend. Well, one of them will be your husband by the end of the month—and there will be no more argument! I'm head of the house now."

This was a new Lazarus, and at that moment I did not like him at all. Turning abruptly, I ran out of the doorway and down toward the gap in the hedge. My sister made to follow me but I heard Lazarus say, "Leave her, Martha. She'll not stay out long in this heat. She'll soon be back."

I ran through the garden and out into the road. Then, without thinking, I turned down toward the spring and came to a panting halt under the pepper tree. Screwing up my eyes against the blazing sun, I looked around. No one was abroad, and the village slept in the noonday heat. The little road winding out into the fields was deserted, and clouds of dust hung in the scorching air where a handful of sparrows squabbled in the ditch below. Through the gaps between the houses, I could see the lake shimmering in the heat; a stork sailed lazily over the empty boats and assumed a motionless stance in the shallows.

To my surprise I found I was shaking all over and tears were running down my face, for Lazarus's sudden ultimatum had surprised and frightened me. All through the past year I had lived pleasantly enough in a kind of dreamy limbo, and so long as I was left in peace for some part of the day, then I did not greatly notice events around me. But standing under the pepper tree, I realized sadly that I had been so immersed in my own private world that I had not even noticed my selfishness. Of course Martha wanted to be married again and have some status in the village, and Lazarus could never think of his own plans while he was still supporting us. Of course my future must be settled quickly. I must cooperate so as to free him, and then no one need worry about me anymore.

Filled with these new resolves, I wandered down to the shore and sank under the laurel bushes out of the dreadful heat. But as I lay looking out across the lake, my good intentions faltered. How wretched to have Barnabas or Jude as a husband! Barnabas was so orthodox—and so fat! I would always be cooking for him. And Jude, though kind, was a perfectionist in all things, no matter how small. There was not a nail but in its proper place in the workshop, Lazarus said. Even the sawdust was swept up three times a day. However would he tolerate my careless ways? I groaned aloud with the misery of it all. And with either man my scrap of peace would vanish for ever.

Then, remembering my recent resolve, I tried to look at the problem from another angle. Perhaps Martha was right. Once I was married, I should be too busy to think or even to want to climb up into the hills to see the sun rise. Going against one's obvious duty only brought unhappiness and hurt others. Martha had told me that. I would reap the blessing of it eventually. Lazarus had said so.

So I argued and rallied myself under the laurel bushes. Closing my eyes, I tried to imagine myself in my own home, but all I could see behind my heavy lids was Susan's house full of noisy, fretful children. Then suddenly I thought of my room. During all the recent disturbance it had eluded me, but now my eyes blinked open and I sat up.

The sun was burning down through the leaves and I knew I must quickly remove myself from the shore. One could fall ill staying out in such heat. I must seek shelter, and I knew where I should find it. It was well known in Magdala that the house above the lake was closed for the summer and only a few servants left in charge, and they would not be about at this time of day. I would steal up now and see if my room was unchanged. Then—and only then—could I return home and leave my room with a quiet mind. If I might see my room once again before I was betrothed, then I could force myself to relinquish it forever.

Sick and dizzy with the sun, I did not try to differentiate between the room I saw years ago as a child and the place of retreat in my mind. Besides, I argued to justify my action, had not Josue once said that I should visit it as often as possible? And it would be cool up there in the orchard.

My head reeled again as I scrambled to my feet and, staying in the cover of the laurels, hurried along the shore and up the white, dusty road curving above the village.

The great gates were closed at the entrance, but, squeezing in through a gap between pillar and hedge, I found myself in the little orchard. Trees were everywhere, and beds of herbs in the clearings. Insects hummed in the vines on the wall, making a soporific summer sound. Silence. Far away a gull cried over the lake and a boy shouted in the distance. It seemed to come from another world. It was shady in the small plantation, and down the grassy aisles motes of sunlight danced in the air. I stole through the trees, holding my sandals and savoring the coolness beneath my feet. A bird hidden deep in the massing foliage of the olives chuckled suddenly, sang a brief cascade of song in the stillness, then sank into silence again. I heard everything with a peculiar clarity. The wicker gate clicked open. A twig snapped underfoot and petals showered down from the espaliered rose as I came out into the blazing heat again.

Once more I found myself on the graveled path beside the house. Looking down over the terraced gardens, I saw the fountain, my childhood's delight, still flinging its spray in the air and heard the cool tinkle as it splashed into the mossy basin below. There was no sign of a servant anywhere, so, greatly daring, I ran barefoot down the steps and, enchanted, bent over to touch the upturned faces of the water lilies. Pushing back my veil, I bathed my face and hands. Then, swinging my sandals, I looked up again at the house. It seemed certain that the servants were in their own quarter at the back, so I did not hesitate a moment longer. Running up the steps and through the garden, I stole onto the terrace.

The shutters on the windows were only half-closed, and I wondered if the cage of singing birds were still inside, but not a sound came forth from the room. Tiptoeing forward, I pushed open one shutter, and a shaft of light filtered into the gloom. The room, as I had thought, was empty, and the birds were nowhere to be seen. Sitting on the wide ledge, I peered into the dimness and dared myself to enter. The next moment I had slipped over the sill and down onto the wood-tiled floor. I was in there at last. My heart was thudding with excitement as I stood in the gloom, looking about and wondering if I might push back the shutters and let in the sunlight again as I first remembered it scattered in pools of gold across the floor.

Suddenly a muffled sound made me spin around, my heart jumping with fright. The sofa, formerly in the center of the room, was now pushed back into the alcove at right angles to the window and, to my horror, someone was lying on it.

"Who's there?" said an old man's voice querulously. "Is that you, Simon, waking me like that?"

And as I stood there, transfixed with fear, he peered at me, muttering irritably, "Who are you, girl? What do you want?"

And as I stayed mute: "Are you dumb, girl?"

Rising shakily to his feet, he slowly tottered toward me and pushed open the shutter with his stick. Daylight streamed in as his shortsighted eyes looked down and focused on my terrified face. For a few moments we gazed at each other in silence.

"Humph!" he said at last. "For a while there I thought you were my granddaughter. But you're not, thank God!" And he peered closely at me again to make certain.

He was a very old man indeed, with white hair poking out in wisps from his elaborately rolled turban. His striped *chalouk* was crumpled, his bony feet were bare, and I noticed he had crumbs in his beard. His pale, watery eyes had a childlike stare.

"I was asleep and you woke me," he stated simply, and looked vaguely around the room.

Struggling to speak, I gasped out the first words that came to my lips. "I hoped to see the birds."

He did not seem surprised but simply turned, nodding and muttering, and tottering to the sofa, sat down with a grunt. "They've gone!" he suddenly announced, staring down at his hands. "His father died, so they've both gone to Rome to claim the estate. My grandson's gone with them—a nice boy but too fond of wine."

He shook his head and, cracking his finger-joints, murmured sadly, "It was a mistake giving up my home and coming here to live with them. I should have known it wasn't the right thing to do. I was happy in Rome—independent. However," and he brightened visibly, "we might go back now all this has happened. It would be far better for us to live in the Roman villa than stay here in this backwater."

I had no idea what he meant, but I was no longer afraid. I moved across to him. "But who cares for you here?"

He looked up. "Oh, she left a few servants, but they don't trouble me. Her absence gives them a holiday, too. There's little peace when *she's* back. She has a sharp tongue, my daughter."

I recalled the thin-lipped woman seated outside on the marble bench and thought he might be right. But the old man had fallen into a reverie and seemed to have forgotten me.

"I—I must go now," I murmured awkwardly as I moved away. "Forgive me for having wakened you."

For a few moments he looked at me absently. Then, taking in my words, he became suddenly alert. "No—don't go yet! Stay here and bear me company. Let me think . . . Ah, yes!" And rising again, he shuffled from the room.

Clearly he was anxious to detain me there for a while, and I was loath to disappoint him. He was so very old and seemed lonely. But even as I thought this, he returned carrying two painted boxes. I went over as he opened them and saw they were full of crystallized fruits. I had never tasted such sweetmeats before and gazed at them with delight.

"They're mine," he announced proudly. "Imported. I thought you would like them."

I put one in my mouth. It was delicious. The old man crowed

with laughter at my ecstatic expression, and together we sat on the sofa and ate the contents of the first box. It was almost unbelievable that I was there in my room eating exotic fruits! Beside me the old man sucked greedily and rambled on about his old house in Rome where he had lived before his wife died and all the good things he missed now he was living with his daughter in Galilee. After a while I hardly listened.

What good fortune to encounter someone so old that he lacked all curiosity and accepted entire strangers without a hint of surprise. His advanced years had made him a child again—a lonely child. So, as I had no wish to return home yet, we bore each other company. While he ate and talked, I looked around, savoring the coolness and stillness of the dim room. It was virtually unchanged. To think that I was sitting here un-challenged—nay, invited! I pondered my position with awe. How I should love to be here alone. Then perhaps it would happen again—the silence flooding in and . . .

I looked around sharply, suddenly aware of another silence. Why, the old man was sleeping again! Taking the box, which threatened to slide to the ground, I gazed at him dispassionately and wondered what mother would think if she could see me now. How hotly she would disapprove of the entire family in this house—Israelites living in Rome and absorbing most of its ways, and only half-observing the Law when they returned home. It was rumored in Magdala that the old man's son had bought his title as a Roman citizen, and I had already heard of the grandson called Alex—a Greek name. What a comedy if it were not such a scandal! I wished I could have told Martha so as to witness her reaction.

But thinking of my sister jolted my memory. I must return quickly before anyone noticed me slipping down the road, for most of the villagers would still be indoors. The next moment I started again as, somewhere beyond the room, I heard dishes clattering and then footsteps. I hastily thrust on my sandals as the old man blinked sleepily at me.

"I must go now," I said urgently and sped over to the window.

He held out his hand as if to detain me. "But you'll come back?" he pleaded.

"Yes, indeed!" I cried, climbing onto the sill, for I wanted very much to return to my room. Besides, it seemed ungrateful to disappoint him after his kindness. "I'll come as soon as I can—but when will your daughter return?"

"Not for another three weeks—and time passes slowly when you're alone." Then, anxiously, "Did you like the fruits?"

"Yes, yes," I cried, impatient to be off, but as I jumped down onto the terrace, he called suddenly:

"Your name, child, your name?"

"Mary," I answered timidly and slipped off along the colonnade.

I sped back through the silence of the orchard, out through the gap and, keeping under the trees, ran swiftly down the road to the lakeside. To my relief, half the village was out collecting water and I was able to hurry back without being accosted. I entered the house quietly, but Lazarus was not there, and when Martha returned from the well she found me busily preparing the evening meal as if nothing had happened. Obviously relieved at my change of mood, she did not upbraid me for my absence, guilelessly assuming that I had crept back during the afternoon and taken refuge in the garden hut, as I sometimes did during the worst heat of the day. Judging by my quiet preoccupation with the cooking, I had been visited there with calmer thoughts, so Martha said nothing but went off to prepare for her visit to Bethany.

I was secretly elated at her pending departure, for all my earlier resolutions of relegating my own wishes and dreams to oblivion and concentrating on becoming a good wife instead—all these had vanished—at least until Martha returned. Then I would renew them. But in the meantime, with my sister away and Lazarus out at the *naggar* all day, I would have a golden opportunity to visit my room again.

CHAPTER
• SIX •

MARTHA HAD BEEN AWAY nearly a week. During that time, to my vexation, one or two unexpected visitors arrived to spoil my plans and delay my visit to the house above the lake. Now the end of the second week was nearing and I was determined to slip away. But tomorrow was the day of preparation, and I should be too occupied to contemplate going further than the well. I resolved that I must go that afternoon or not at all. It would not be difficult, for Lazarus always took his food to the workshop and would not return until the evening. So once more, as the sun reached its zenith and the women retired indoors, I slipped out down the deserted road, hoping as I ran that Susan would not visit the house and discover my absence.

The sun glared down unrelentingly as I entered the orchard and was immediately enclosed in its shade. Once again a bird hidden deep in the olives sang a sudden mosaic of scattered notes as I approached his hiding place, then fluttered off among the mulberry bushes. Hardly glancing now at the fountain, I climbed onto the terrace—and paused. On the marble seat along the colonnade sat the old man. His hand beat time in the air as he sang some old song in his quavering voice. Oblivious to everything, he looked out over the garden, absorbed in memories of the past. It seemed wrong to disturb him, and besides, it gave me a wonderful opportunity to enter my room alone. I would go and talk to him later.

Creeping to the door, I pushed it open, entered and closed it behind me. I was alone in my room at last. I had no desire to walk around, looking and touching—it was enough that I was there savoring the stillness and almost hearing the tingling silence. I stood motionless, my eyes shut, absorbing it all. This was *my* room, *my* place, where I belonged. Perhaps it would happen again, as it had in the old days before our parents died and everything went wrong and I was shut out. It could not happen anymore down in Magdala—it was too noisy. But here, as nowhere else, the door could swing back in my mind. Already the air was hushed and expectant as when I first came, as if it breathed a welcome, recognizing its rightful owner. Even now behind my closed lids the light was filtering through. Soon it would flood in and then . . .

My eyes jerked open. I spun around, then froze. A man loomed above me in the doorway, his silhouette black against the light which now poured into the room. Behind him stood the old man, his eyes fixed fearfully upon me. There was a moment's pause and then they both came into the room and the old man sat down suddenly on the sofa. The younger man's eyes traveled slowly around, glancing over me as if I did not exist, to rest finally on the old man, who gazed back dumbly.

The younger man remarked in a bantering tone, "Well, grandfather, I've been home two days now and you never mentioned we had guests. It was well that I returned early. My mother was anxious that you were alone so long, but I see that you've been conscientiously attending to your duties."

Walking across to the table, he poured a cup of wine from the flagon and drank it in one swift movement. Then he wiped his mouth with the back of his hand and refilled the cup—all in total silence. Fascinated and terrified, I watched him, still shocked by his sudden appearance in the room. The silence grew until, turning around and jerking his head in my direction, he asked briefly and without interest, "Who's this?"

The old man fluttered his hands distractedly as if struggling for speech, and even I could see that he was obviously terrified of his grandson, who suddenly barked savagely, "Are you dumb as well as deaf? Who is she?"

"Just—just a child. She came with a message," he lied. "But she's going now—aren't you?" he appealed to me. "Run away now—quickly."

With my eyes fixed on the younger man's face, I backed away a little. I did not know the penalty for trespassing, and I had no reason to be in the house and the old man was too frightened to give me one. All I wanted now was to go home. But the grandfather's attempt at effecting my escape had deceived no one.

"Wait!" the grandson's voice rapped, and I froze again. "You—come here."

And sitting down on a carved chair, he motioned me toward him. I went slowly over and stood before him. There was a brooding silence as he gazed down into his wine, and I glanced at him covertly, as I had at his mother years ago. He looked more like a Roman than an Israelite with his closely cropped hair and clean-shaven face that was already fleshy. In a few years' time he would run to fat. I could not see his eyes, but judging from the sullen set of his mouth, I thought him bad-tempered and unreasonable.

At last he spoke, still swirling the dregs in his cup. "Why is she here?"

"I don't know," the old man whispered. "She came in one day when I was asleep."

"She simply entered the house and was standing here when you wakened," his grandson murmured.

"Yes—and I knew nothing of her being here today until you saw her through the window and called me." Then a thought struck him. "It was the birds! She came to see the birds! I expect it was simply a jest," he faltered as the younger man's eyes traveled around the room in search of these creatures and finally came to rest on me.

"So," he said softly, "you simply walked in here one day—from curiosity, I must presume?"

I nodded eagerly.

"And where are the birds?" he asked benevolently.

He looked so agreeable now that I no longer felt so afraid.

"Oh, they're gone," I told him coming forward a little. "They're not here anymore. I saw them the first time I came but—"

Then I cried out in pain as, catching my arm, he twisted it viciously, his face suddenly contorted with anger.

"The *first* time!" he snarled. "How long have you been a guest here?" Jerking me forward, he thrust his puffy face into mine. "Have you taken aught from that old fool? Any jewelry? Any money? *Have* you?" And he twisted my arm again.

"No! No!" I screamed, terrified, as the old man tottered across, wringing his hands.

"Alex, don't hurt her, I beg you! She's but a child. Let her go now. I've given her nothing of your mother's, nothing at all," he cried frantically.

At that moment I was released so abruptly that I staggered and fell away from him.

He thrust forward his bullet-shaped head to hiss savagely, "Imagine if I took you down to the village and told the good orthodox folk there that you like to visit the homes of your betters and take expensive gifts from doting old men. What price your reputation then? You'd bring disgrace on yourself and your family—and no man would marry you. You'd be publically expelled from the synagogue, for the *hazzan* would

90

draw his own conclusions." Leaning back, he smiled silkily at me. "You'd be better dead," he announced quietly. "The villagers might think so, too. I wonder what penalties the Law has for one so young yet so corrupt?" he mused.

Terrified, I gazed at him only half-understanding his words and not knowing if he were serious or not. The whole episode was a nightmare beyond my experience. I knew that I had trespassed, but could not imagine why he was treating me thus.

Suddenly he turned away and, pouring out more wine, assumed a bantering tone again. The speed with which his moods changed was frightening.

"Well, old man," he remarked, looking up at his grandfather, who stood silently beside me, "I must concede that after Rome this is indeed a dull place—but in truth . . . !" And he gestured with contempt toward me.

Plucking up courage at his grandson's altered tone, the old man ventured timidly, "She is just from the village and means no harm. I was glad of her company with you all away."

The younger man chuckled, distressing his grandfather anew by deliberately misconstruing his words. Sipping his wine, he took no further notice of us. The old man and I looked at each other, and with a slight indication of his head, he intimated that I should go.

Trembling still, I rose from the floor and wrapped my veil around myself again. "I will go now," I whispered. He looked in such good humor that I did not think he would refuse. He must know that I had not taken anything, and the way he spoke of me to his grandfather made me think he would be glad to see me gone.

Instead, he took a peach from the bowl and began idly to peel it with his teeth.

"Why?" he queried at last, still not looking at me. "I was told you like to visit here. But perhaps you don't like me?"

I did not know how to answer. Suddenly he leaned forward,

the spiced wine heavy on his breath. "Surely you like me better than this old fool?" he said, jerking his head to the figure behind me, and as I remained silent, "You're hard to please," he remarked pleasantly and, lifting his cup, he yawned suddenly. His eyelids drooped.

Twisting my veil, I pondered my position. He might eventually fall asleep after drinking so much, but I could not risk waiting that long. I must return before Lazarus discovered my absence. If only he would say I might leave! What ailed him to behave thus? I had never encountered such a man. I felt I was moving in a maze of unknown standards and conduct. But bewildered and frightened though I was, I realized from the old man's reticence and my own recent experience that this was a man to be placated at all costs, lest another terrifying eruption occur. I felt I must say something—something that would please him and also deflect attention from the old man. It was monstrous that he spoke to his relative in that fashion.

"I do like you," I whispered. "You are very kind—but I must go home now. Forgive me for having trespassed, but the room was so beautiful. It was wrong and I ask your pardon."

A pause, and then his eyes opened. "Oh, you *do* speak—and with a pure Galilean accent! Harken, old man—praise from the *am-har-arez* instead of curses!"

Sipping his wine, he smiled as the tears began trickling down my face. "Now what ails you?"

I began to sob with fright. Why did he ignore everything I said? The old man stood beside me, not daring to utter a word, but it seemed that his very timidity only helped prolong my ordeal. I must do something or this situation might continue indefinitely until he fell asleep or released me from sheer weariness. Fighting back my tears, I resolved on my escape. The door was behind me and I was fleet-footed. Once I was out, I did not think him capable of pursuing me—and I simply must leave now if I were to be back before Lazarus.

As he turned again to the wine flask, I gasped, "I must go now!" And whirling around, I ran toward the door. It was my undoing. I should have stayed until he drank himself into a stupor. I heard the cup shatter as he threw it down on the table.

"*You!* Come here!" came the snarl behind me, and I could no more move another step than if I had been nailed to the ground. In two strides he covered the distance between us and savagely wrenched me back. His face was livid with rage.

The old man tottered toward us, a look of dread on his face. "Don't hurt her, Alex, I beg you. She's but a child . . ."

But his voice was drowned as his grandson rounded on him, shouting furiously, "*Silence!* Unless you want it known how ill you guard my father's property! My mother would not be pleased at the tale I'd tell her—and you'd not have a home by the time it was ended!"

His face was scarlet, and the old man quailed as he spat viciously, "Don't cross me, old fool! She's borne you company long enough. Now it is my turn."

And seizing his unresisting grandparent, he dragged him across the room and out onto the terrace. I saw the old man stumble and clutch the pillar, then stagger off down the colonnade. Dumbly I watched his grandson come down into the room and slam the door with a force that shook the house. If the servants heard they were too well trained to answer. Lurching toward me, he grabbed my shoulder. Gasping with pain, I tried to wrench away, but a swinging slap across the face knocked the breath from me and sent me reeling back against the table. Feeling half-dead with terror, I tried to stagger to my feet, but before I could recover, he brutally felled me again, blotting out the sunlight, and my room—*my room!*—was dark with his shadow.

*   *   *

The door slammed behind me, and somehow I was on the terrace again. My breath came in hysterical gasps and my legs hardly supported me, but still at the back of my mind the thought drummed persistently—Lazarus will be home soon. I must hasten.

Suddenly I became aware of the old man looking out from behind a pillar. His face wore a piteous expression as he tottered toward me, wringing his hands. Drawing a deep breath, I smiled tremulously at him, for I did not wish him to be unhappy. The old man had been kind to me.

"I must go now," I whispered, not for the first time that day.

"Wait!" he said urgently, and reaching into his belt, he thrust a small purse into my hands and at the same time darted a furtive look at the house.

"Take this—and remember you must not tell anyone you've been here. Do you understand?"

I nodded mutely to reassure him.

"The fault was yours for trespassing," he persisted. "It would go ill for you if this was made public knowledge. You would not wish that?"

I shook my head mechanically and he looked relieved.

"Go now before you are missed," he mumbled and, turning, shuffled off down the colonnade. I never saw him or his grandson again, for his daughter and her husband decided to remain in Rome and the two men left to join them there. Within a month the house was untenanted.

I went slowly down through the orchard and out onto the road, uncaring if I was seen and feeling icy cold. The birds had started to sing again as the day grew cooler, and the massing foliage of the olives blew silver in the wind that had sprung up over the lake. For a few moments I stared dully at the scene, then turned and went up through the village and into the house. Fortunately the women were busy preparing the evening meal so, acknowledging their calls with a lifted hand, I passed on with quickened step, pretending to be in haste.

Once I was safely home I pushed the little purse into my bedding and sank down, trembling violently. The rancid smell of the oil lamp suddenly sickened me. I had never noticed it previously, but now I wondered how I had endured it all these years. However, it was essential that I be myself again when Lazarus returned, so, still trembling, I rekindled the fire and put rice and vegetables on to cook.

Then I bathed my face and rearranged my hair and veil. My reflection in mother's little mirror was pale and strained, but thank God there were no bruises where his hand had struck me—only a dull red mark which in the dim light would not be noticed. Sitting down, I tried to compose myself, but my hands still shook and, despite the fire, I felt cold.

My brother found me huddled over the embers, but mercifully he was too tired to talk much or notice my silence, and I was thankful when he went out immediately afterward to his friends. Even then I dared not think of what had happened. At any moment a neighbor might enter and I should betray myself if I allowed my thoughts to dwell upon my terrible experience. There was so little privacy anywhere that I could not indulge myself in tears—and no time for it, either, with all the preparations for the sabbath and the visitors who usually came that day.

I was forced to contain my feelings and remain outwardly calm during the next few days so as to assure Martha on her return that all had gone smoothly during her absence. But lying on the roof at night, my whirling thoughts crystallized and the full impact of what I had done in going alone to that house—and the consequences of my unlawful visit—struck me with such stunning force that I could hardly bear it. I felt sick with rage and misery and guilt. Anger at myself for the crass stupidity that took me to a room I had once glimpsed years ago as a child! Unfair anger, too, against my brother for giving me such an ultimatum regarding my future that I had fled to the consolation of my room. Ah, but it was useless and wrong to blame Lazarus. I was the guilty one, preferring daydreams to reality.

But *he* was real—that man—for whom the feelings of the *am-har-arez* were there to be trampled upon. They would both go their ways—the old man anxious to forget, and the grandson vicious, bullying, corrupt and caring nothing for such a casual encounter as ours, which he had doubtless already forgotten. Thank God Martha was away that day, for I could not have returned home and faced her. Thank God, also, that I was not seen going to and from the house. My reputation would have been ruined forever.

Before I realized it Martha was home again, arriving one evening with such a large budget of news and gossip from Judea that she scarcely enquired of home events in her absence. But Lazarus told her how well I had worked, staying in the house and attending to everything, and this made Martha beam with approval and kiss me delightedly before flying out to relay her news around Magdala. Now that my sister was back, I knew that the question of our betrothals would soon be settled, but I no longer cared. Indeed I wished to be married as swiftly as possible, for suddenly I had no wish to be alone anymore. Even my views on Barnabas and Jude had changed, and I was willing to accept either. But this goal was not to be so easily achieved.

Zachary's nephew came one evening and told Lazarus he had finally decided for his cousin at Bethsaida. My brother was vexed that he had delayed so long in telling us, but at least it meant that Simeon would have Martha, and Lazarus planned to see him when he returned to Galilee from his business trip into Egypt, and settle the matter then. But for the present my position remained unchanged. Barnabas might come forward, but he too traveled widely and no one knew when he would return to Caphernaum. So my hopes in that direction seemed tenuous, but Lazarus told me to be patient. Some bachelor would begin contemplating marriage, and one always started an epidemic. I should not have more than a few weeks to wait. But a few weeks and then a betrothal period of several months before I could go to my new home seemed interminable. Now I felt I should go mad alone in the house, for Martha would be married as soon as Simeon returned. I felt thwarted and utterly miserable, and berated Jude and Barnabas for their fickleness— to my sister's surprise, for I had had little good to say of them previously. I do not know what might have happened following this impasse in our family affairs had not another matter arisen to divert our attention.

One morning in the month of Sivan Martha suddenly resolved to clean the whole room—a thorough scouring—and with my assistance she cleared the entire place of chests and household utensils.

"Mary," she called going back into the empty room, "take these up to the roof until we've finished."

And gathering up the bedrolls, she tossed them over to me. They fell in a tumbled heap across my arms and I heard a loud chink as a small purse dropped to the floor and, from its mouth where the strings had loosened, there spilled a handful of coins, a small bracelet and a pair of earrings. We both gaped down at them, Martha in amazement and I in horror. All this time the purse had lain inside my bedding, for I had not had the heart to open it, caring nothing for the old man's gift given to assuage his conscience in the hope that it would keep me silent. But until now I had not thought it contained aught but a few coins. The jewelry was an unpleasant shock. Now as it all lay on the floor between us, I felt my face go crimson as I frantically sought a reason for their being in my possession.

"Mary!" gasped my sister in astonishment. "How is it that you have such things?"

Useless to say that I did not know. I decided to take the only course open to me, although heaven alone knew where it might

97

lead. "I suppose they were . . . gifts. They were given to me."

"*Gifts? Given* to you!" Martha echoed in bewilderment as she lifted the purse and its contents. The stones of the bracelet changed color in the sunlight, and the tiny earrings seemed lost in her red hands. She seemed lost also, groping for speech.

"But . . . *who* gave them to you?" she managed at last. "Mary, answer me. How could anyone *give* you . . . Oh, merciful heaven!" she said as a thought struck her. "You must have stolen them! Oh, Mary!" And she begun to wail hysterically, which brought Lazarus in from milking Sheba.

"Martha, be silent!" he cried above the noise. "The whole of Magdala can hear you! What in heaven's name is amiss?"

"This!" wept my sister, holding out the purse. "Mary had it hidden in her bedroll. Oh, the disgrace! What would mother say if she were alive now? Mary, what possessed you?"

"Martha, will you be silent!" Lazarus interrupted impatiently. I could tell from his look of sheer incredulity that he knew Martha's supposition to be wrong, but nevertheless he was determined to solve the mystery. Taking the jewelry and coins from my sister, he turned to me. "Mary, are these yours?"

"Yes."

"Did you steal them?"

"No."

"How is it that you have them?"

"They were given to me."

"Who gave them to you, Mary?"

There was no escape, and my voice faltered as I answered, "The old man who lived in the house above the lake. He is gone now, back to Rome."

Behind me Martha gave a gasp either of horror or incredulity, but my brother's voice was expressionless as he asked, "Sister, why did you take gifts from him?"

It pained me so much that Lazarus should ask such a question that I knew I must tell him the truth—but only part of it. No one would ever know of my encounter with the grandson, only how I had rushed from our home that day and, to escape the heat, had gone up into the private orchard that I had remembered from the past. Then I lied. I said that I had encountered the old man there and not in the house. I did not dare admit that I had entered it, either of my own accord or by his invitation. Instead I said that he had spoken to me and was not angry at my trespassing. Indeed, he wished me to stay and talk to him, for he was lonely with his family away. Then he had pressed the purse on me—an old man's unthinking, extravagant gesture—and I had felt unable to refuse for fear of hurting or offending him.

"He gave you all *this*—for a few moments of your company?" my brother asked incredulously.

It seemed foolish to say that he had, so I was forced on the spur of the moment to admit that they were given to me on a second visit. Lazarus was astounded. "You went *again!* When?"

"When Martha was away and you were at the *naggar*. I pitied him," I added desperately so as to make the whole episode sound as innocuous as possible, but in my country, where women lead such enclosed lives, it was a heinous enough crime. My guilt, too, increased tenfold, for I had never lied to my brother and sister, and I now felt my sins mount up around me like another Babel.

Lazarus never doubted my word for an instant. At last, convinced that he had all the facts, he stood pondering them in silence. But Martha, listening aghast throughout, now gave vent to her feelings.

"Merciful heavens, I don't think the girl realizes what she has done! It's a miracle no one saw you! Praise be the whole family is gone and no one the wiser! I'd never lift my head again if this went around the village. What would Simeon think to have you as a sister-in-law? And how would *you* get a husband if this was noised abroad? And it only happened because you won't listen to reason or take advice! You simply run away and do the first foolish thing that occurs to you! And to think that when I came in and found you preparing the meal, I imagined—God preserve me!—that you had had a change of heart! And you were planning even then to see that man a second time—because you pitied him!—and waiting till Lazarus and I were away before you went!" Grasping my shoulders and giving me a vigorous shake at each word, Martha continued energetically, "You *wicked—foolish— deceitful*—girl! I thought your roaming about shameful enough, but I never dreamed this would happen!" And she turned to Lazarus. "I think we must accept uncle's offer and have Mary married now, even though it's out of Galilee. It may be weeks before someone here comes forward, and I won't leave her as your responsibility all that time."

I did not fully hear the end of Martha's outburst, for I was totally unnerved by the sudden discovery of the purse, and my brother's questions also found me unprepared. I was further distracted by Martha's ranting reaction and the awful silence from Lazarus. Too worn down to combat it, all the accumulated misery of the past weeks surged up unchecked. Bursting into tears, I sobbed, "I know it was wrong, but he was *kind* to me!"

And venting all my grief on them, I rounded on my brother and sister. "And you were *un*kind! *You* drove me from the house! You are *both* to blame!" I wept furiously.

Lazarus waited until I had finished before saying quietly, "Mary, I don't believe you realize that what you did was incredibly stupid and wrong, and it is a miracle, as Martha said, that you emerged with your reputation unblemished. Only think if you were seen there! Many of the local men are employed in the gardens, and especially during this sabbatical year, when there is little work in the fields."

I shivered. I had not thought of that.

"Imagine," Lazarus continued, "if they had seen you in the

orchard taking gifts from that man—what conclusions they would draw—and rightly! Indeed, it is only because you *are* my sister that I can credit you with such stupidity. But there are some things that you *must* understand and observe, and to act as you did . . ." and his voice died away.

I knew I had hurt and bewildered them, but suddenly I felt angry. Angry with Lazarus for being kind and understanding. Angry with myself for being forced to lie—and such clumsy lies! And this same anger I directed against the only people on whom I could vent it—Martha and Lazarus. They knew nothing of my misery as they stood there judging and condemning and telling me of my duties.

I rounded furiously on my brother. "That is all you ever speak of—observing the Law and acting in the right way to others! Did father think of his responsibilities—did he act justly—when he left us so poor that we must be married to anyone who will take us? None of this would have happened if you weren't so intent on hastening me into marriage."

"But it was only yesterday," Lazarus said pointedly, "that I heard you bewailing the dearth of bachelors in Magdala."

"Yes . . . yes," I agreed in flustered tones, "but I had different views earlier . . ."

"And how can you say that we have been left in poverty?" asked Martha, hurt at my wild accusations against father. "We've had hard times, Mary, but we live the same as others . . ."

But, frightened and confused, all I could hear was the door of my room crashing shut behind me. And *he* was left there to desecrate it with his presence—his shadow falling darkly across the sun-dappled floor—and I was left outside. He had usurped my claim. He had taken it from me. My room! My room! I could never enter it again. My grief broke over me like a wave.

"Live!" I screamed almost beside myself. "This is not living—herded here with no peace day or night! My God!" I ejaculated,

"If you had been in such a room where you could move and breathe and almost hear the silence—"

I stopped abruptly. I had said too much. The faces of my brother and sister were expressionless as they stood together and looked at me.

"I entered the house but once," I said desperately, "when he gave me the purse. That is the truth," I lied again.

My eyes met my brother's and he looked away. Tears were spilling down Martha's cheeks, and her roughened hands plucked unconsciously at the fringes of her shawl. I knew they were grieved because they loved me and could not understand my deception. I was unable to enlighten them further, and their love pained me, so I turned and left them.

A week of silence passed, and then Lazarus told me what he had decided to do. As there was no likelihood of a husband coming forward in the near future and no question of my remaining alone in the house after Martha was married, my brother had resolved that our uncle's offer, made to Martha on her recent visit, should be accepted. Our relatives knew that Martha would easily obtain a husband—if not Jude then definitely Simeon—but I posed a problem if neither Jude nor Barnabas offered. Since our parents' death, aunt had continued to take an interest in our family affairs. Her opinion of me had not altered over the years, so she had recently urged our uncle to find me a husband in Judea, where I could then live under her eye.

Martha was told of this proposal when she arrived in Bethany. My sister had thanked our aunt, and indeed was grateful for the offer. She was quite convinced, however, that Jude would choose me, so nothing of this was mentioned to me on her return home.

But now Lazarus had sent a message to our relatives, telling them all that had happened and accepting their offer of a temporary home for me until uncle had found a husband for his erring niece. Indeed, it had already been intimated to Martha that there would be no difficulty about this. I could be betrothed after the rains and in my new home by the summer of next year. Once I was safely settled I could visit Magdala with my husband, but it was essential that I be watched in the interim. Our friends and relatives would simply be told that I was gone on a visit to Bethany; then later it would be announced that I had fortuitously found a husband down in Judea and no one except uncle and aunt would ever know that I had been sent away in disgrace. Lazarus would have said nothing but simply accepted their offer, but I had deceived Martha and told lies and might do so again. It saddened him to send me away, but I had proved untrustworthy and must be protected from myself. Everything was arranged, and he and I would leave immediately after Yom Kippur and join the caravan going down for the Feast of Tabernacles.

To the stranger these may seem elaborate precautions for my brother to have taken, but in our country a woman's reputation is a priceless asset—indeed her only one—and without it she is nothing, a social leper. That I had twice entered a stranger's house and accepted gifts was an appalling crime. Only my emerging from it unscathed robbed this incident of its full horror. Nevertheless, my behavior was still impossible to understand and hard to forgive. Something drastic must be done, therefore, to ensure that it would never happen again.

I wept bitterly that Lazarus was so disappointed in me and that our relatives knew of my disgrace. Aside from this, however, I was almost relieved at the plan for my future. I would be married soon instead of waiting endless weeks, and although I loved Galilee, I simply wanted, in my present state of mind, to be as far away from it as possible. Perhaps down in Bethany I would not be haunted by recent memories. I would become a different person—a happier one. I was fond of my uncle, too, and knew that aunt, though strict, was basically good-hearted. Once the initial scolding was over, nothing more would be said of my transgressions. So I made no resistance to my brother's plan.

Martha was kind in a brisk fashion, reminding me that she and Lazarus would be in Jerusalem next spring for the Passover and that Simeon would join them for my wedding feast in the summer. She made it sound so pleasant that I tried to enter into a like mood, for I had caused her great anxiety and yet she was always so quick to forgive.

"I am sure it sounds splendid, Martha, and with us settled, Lazarus can also be married once he has finished his apprenticeship and earning so much more. Then one day he can come to Jerusalem and enter the Beth ha-Midrash at last."

"Yes, indeed!" my sister enthused, "and it will be wonderful to have you so near each other. Why, Mary, it's almost a blessing, your going to Bethany—and I shall come down to visit you whenever Simeon is away on business."

"You must indeed," I answered. "I am only sad that everything prior to this has grieved you so much, but I'll recompense you for it. I shall be a different person in the future."

Martha, generous as always, swept me delightedly into her arms. "That is the right attitude, Mary. Don't look back and repine but think how happy we'll all be in a few months' time."

It seemed then as we went out amicably to the garden that the twist in my tangled life was at last unraveled, and the future took on a brighter glow.

CHAPTER
• SEVEN •

BUT MY TROUBLES WERE not ended. Indeed, they had scarcely begun. It was not until the month of Tamuz that I began to suspect that all was not well with me, but I ascribed it to the excessive heat, which always oppressed me and hoped that it would pass. But lying on the rooftop one night, relieved that the faintness and nausea that had dogged me during the day had now faded, there drifted into my mind the casual conversation I recently heard down at the spring. Now its full impact struck me with stunning force, and for a moment my heart stood still.

We had gone to collect the water, and I was walking behind Martha and Susan when I heard my sister call to me to hasten. She remarking afterward, "This summer heat never pleases Mary."

"It doesn't please *me*," Susan replied brusquely, shifting her pitcher to a more comfortable position, "but for different reasons. She has little to complain about."

Trudging listlessly behind, I had taken small notice of the conversation. Susan was with child again, as she was most years, but she always came to the well each day for a gossip, having left the latest baby in charge of the oldest girl. Susan took her sickness and dragging fatigue as a way of life.

Now, lying on the roof with my thick cloak clutched tightly around me, I stared up at the star-lit sky, my heart thudding with fear. "Oh, merciful God, not that!" I whispered again and again. Despite my wrappings I shivered, trying desperately to find a glimmer of hope that I might be wrong. For the present I could only wait and pray.

But I had no faith in prayer. In my increasing despair I felt the ways of God moving slowly and inexorably against me. Had not aunt and mother prophesied that I should disgrace our family? When Lazarus told me there was no freedom outside the Law, had I not said that the Law was wrong—the Law given to Moses, our greatest prophet? Had I not said before my own family that I envied the Gentiles and would prefer to be numbered among them? He had not forgotten. Now His hand was reaching to deal out retribution. If my worst fears came true, then I would be cast out from all that symbolized family life and security within a God-given code.

The days passed by, and during this time a further blow fell. My uncle, a man of few words but swift action, had found me a husband, a young widower with two children and a baby. I could be betrothed immediately I arrived in Bethany. Indeed, our relatives would prepare a special meal, and my husband and step-children would be there, the latter anxious to meet their new mother.

Uncle sent the kind message, "I know Mary will approve him and she will not long be a guest in our house." Aunt was providing my wedding garments as a gift, for, childless herself, she was eagerly anticipating all the preparations necessary for a *mistitha*. In normal circumstances I would have found it easy to sympathize with her feelings and be grateful that everything was progressing smoothly, but it was not to be. Martha

106

chattered on with all the information she had been able to glean from uncle's message, but I was deaf to it all. I felt no curiosity about the man, for I knew by then that I would never be his or, indeed, any man's wife. My thin thread of hope snapped and despair closed around me. On the day the news came up from Judea, I went into the garden hut, sat down and tried to face my future.

There was no question of redress; I could not trace the man responsible. There were no witnesses; I could not prove that I was not a willing partner. Of my own volition I had gone twice to a stranger's house and accepted money and jewelry. Who would believe that it was from the old man and not his grandson? People would draw their own conclusions. Furthermore, I had deliberately omitted any mention of the younger man to Lazarus—he was not even aware of his existence! How could I confess now—weeks later—that I had lied, that I had suppressed the truth out of fear, never dreaming in my ignorance of any consequences?

And would Lazarus believe me, knowing that I had lied before? He would be entitled to think that the old man did not exist at all—that it was the younger man I was protecting when my visits to the house were discovered. As these thoughts passed through my mind, my courage failed me and I groaned aloud. Soon everyone would know. The scandal would run like lightning around the lake. The *hazzan* would publicly condemn me. He had already spoken harshly against those who did not fully observe the Law and fraternize with their occupiers; they were not true sons and daughters of Israel. What would he *not* say of me?

We would have to leave Galilee and settle elsewhere. Lazarus must seek new work—and would Simeon want me as a sister-in-law? I had ruined *their* lives as well as my own. Now I understood what Martha meant when she accused me of being selfish. Such actions always reached out and touched others. Now at last I must face the reality that loomed unrelentingly wherever I turned, almost paralyzing me with fear.

For although I was ignorant of much of the Law, I knew, nevertheless, that our moral code was rigid, clear-cut and strictly defined to the last detail. It held justice in full but the penalties were harsh for transgressors—especially for women who hid their actions and then professed ignorance when time eventually betrayed them.

In a few weeks' time I would be betrothed. The penalty for a woman who was unfaithful during her betrothal was death by stoning. How much more heinous to come to a betrothal bearing another man's child! I must confess *now*, therefore, before I was committed in any way—but how? Despite the heat I shivered. Sunlight slanted across the sanded floor and shadows flickered on the slatted walls and over the wine skins. Children were playing outside in the road, and I could hear Martha singing to herself as she pulled vegetables in the garden. It seemed unbelievable that all this was happening. How could I go out *now* and tell her? But I must. Then I heard Susan call to Martha and felt reprieved.

During the following week I tried to steel myself to make my appalling statement to my sister, but I found it difficult to find a suitable opportunity. Whenever I missed a chance to speak to her, I promised myself—next time I'll tell her; I really will—*next* time.

But she and Lazarus were so happy, with everything running smoothly in their lives and the future so much brighter for us, that my courage constantly failed me. I wished desperately that Martha would notice my fatigue, my lack of appetite and the nausea that overtook me in the early hours of the day. When she did notice, she ascribed it to the heat, so buoyant was she with the coming fruition of all our plans—that Simeon was on his way home and that I was happily reconciled to my new life in Bethany. In such a mood all else passed her by. But I knew that she must notice something by the first of Tisri, the day we celebrated the feast of the New Year. I knew that Lazarus and I would not be making our journey or stopping at Nazareth for Josue to join us.

In a way I was right. We did not make that particular journey, for as Elul waned, news came up from uncle that an unexpected caravan was already coming down from the north, or so he had heard. Why not send Mary down-country now instead of waiting for the feast? I would be perfectly safe with the other families, and he would watch for its arrival in Jerusalem and meet me there.

Hours after this message reached us, the caravan in question came straggling around the lake to Caphernaum. I had no time to think, for Lazarus was instantly amenable to uncle's suggestion. Immediately half the neighborhood came in to say their farewells, knowing I should be staying several weeks in Judea. I could scarcely comprehend my situation. Friends and excited children came flocking in, bringing little gifts and messages for relatives in the south. Normally I loved these heartwarming farewells when a villager left Galilee for a while, but now, shocked beyond belief at this sudden quickening of events, I wanted frantically to talk to Martha. If only I could approach her! But the scourge of our life—lack of privacy—prevented my planned confession during those last hours, and suddenly the caravan had arrived at Magdala.

Panic-stricken, I ran into the house, where Martha was rolling up some tunics she and the other women had hastily made for me in the past two days.

"Martha," I gasped, "I must speak to you . . ."

"But everyone is waiting to bid you godspeed," she laughed. "See, there's Anna and Deborah coming, and even old Zachary tottering up the road!" At that moment Susan also looked around the doorway. "Come now, Mary," chivvied my sister, "it's time you left."

I could not speak. Drained, helpless and hopeless, I went out into the road. I was too late in confessing and now felt gripped in the hand of my inevitable fate, for whether I was discovered in Galilee or Judea, the disgrace would still be the same. The sun was fully risen as I clung to Martha, knowing somehow that this was the last time I should be so close to her.

She, misunderstanding, kissed me and tried to cheer me. "I know it's hard leaving Galilee, Mary, but," she said, lowering her voice, "remember what we were speaking of—all our plans—and how happy we'll be very soon."

I turned to my brother. "I will go now," I whispered.

My brother looked pale and strained now that I was actually leaving, for he disliked sending me away. His thin hands nervously clenched and unclenched as he looked at me anxiously. "You are not angry with me, Mary? You've been very silent recently."

I shook my head.

"I know uncle's chosen a good man for you, and as there are children to consider, it is as well that events have moved more swiftly than we planned. I don't wish you to travel alone, but it's a large caravan and you'll be perfectly safe if you stay with the women and don't wander beyond its confines. And be sure to help our aunt, Mary. She has been very good to us. Now you must go, for they are waiting for you. Farewell, sister; God bless you."

He turned back to the house and I gazed sadly after him. I felt as I had with Martha, that we should never be on the same terms again.

"Lazarus," I said, going after him, "whatever happens, you'll always remember me as your sister and love me, won't you?"

"Why, Mary, what a strange girl you are!" and Lazarus,

laughing, took my shoulders and shook me gently. "What an extraordinary question! You're only going to be married. But if it sets your mind at rest," seeing the tears in my eyes, "then even when you're old and have grandchildren playing about your feet, you'll still be my little sister, and Martha and I will always love you. Now," reverting to more practical matters, "if you stop at Nazareth be sure to visit our friends and tell Josue to *wait* and not set out next month until I arrive."

Then Lazarus lifted me on my donkey and secured my water skin and other bundles. Immediately our neighbors crowded around. Clutching a handful of keepsakes and to the cry of "Don't stay away too long, Mary!" and "Bring me some Jericho dates!" I went forward to join the moving stream of travelers. Soon the villagers had faded to black specks in the road behind me and finally vanished in the cloud of dust raised by the caravan. I had left Magdala, my home and family, forever.

I do not remember much of the journey now. There were many families traveling down-country, and although I did not join any one, I was, nevertheless, easily assimilated among them. I was also relieved to discover that there was no one I recognized in the throng, for I was in no mood to fraternize with my fellow countrymen. We passed Cana and Nazareth, and at the latter, having no intention of visiting our friends, I watered my animal hastily lest Mariam arrive at the well and see me and then waited outside the village until we set off again. The caravan was the slowest I had ever experienced, and I could not decide if this was an agony or a relief.

Three or four days passed, and then came a surprise. After Nain, instead of bearing eastward toward Scythopolis, we turned down toward Engannin and were soon straggling deep into Samaritan country. I knew that if Lazarus had realized we should not be taking the Jericho route, he would have insisted on my waiting until he could accompany me. But I was now traveling with a tolerant group, none of whom objected to reaching Jerusalem via Samaria and Shechem, although my brother would have protested strongly to the contamination of crossing Gentile territory. For a while I felt utter misery, knowing that I need not have left home so early if only this fact had been known, but now it was too late. I should mention here that we regarded the Samaritans as no more than heathens whom we had long ago cast out from the Israelite community as being worse than Gentiles, for they had deliberately turned away from the true faith. I once recall father, tolerant though he was, quoting from the Talmud that "More unclean than the flesh of swine is bread proffered by a Samaritan."

But I was in no state to care about anything. I felt too ill. I had gone down to the well at Engannin to fill my skin and, stumbling on a jagged stone, had slipped and fallen on the wet slope. Since then a dull pain had crept around me which the rough journey and uneven motion only aggravated. I almost wept with relief when we stopped at nightfall outside the city of Samaria. By now the pain gripped me in an iron band and I could do nothing but wander about whimpering behind my veil. The cold air seemed to worsen it, and yet the perspiration poured down the sides of my face. I went over to one of the fires and made a pretense of joining in the conversation with the women, but the pain soon drove me to my feet again. Somehow I struggled through the communal meal and then, pretending I would retire to sleep, I went to the outskirts of the encampment, and sat huddled in my cloak in the shadows.

Oh, what was to become of me? There were another thirty miles stretching ahead to Bethany, and I could not travel another step! Weeping silently, I rocked back and forth trying to ease the pain. Why had I not told Martha? I could not have been in a worse position than now. If only events had not suddenly accelerated, then I might still be at home and not alone with a group of strangers in hostile country—and so frightened! But gradually, to my relief, the pain eased a little and I fell into a fitful sleep through sheer exhaustion.

I awoke in the early hours while it was still dark and found the pain still nagging at me. Once we began traveling it might well become worse, and I could not endure another day of it. But I was not going any further. I had evolved a plan and at last made a decision. I would go into Samaria now, while the rest of the caravan was sleeping, and find help there. Even in this country it was still a religious duty to provide shelter for one in need. I would wait in the city until dawn, and then find some woman to aid me. I would ask her to send an urgent message to Lazarus and Martha that I was lying ill in Samaria.

They would come swiftly, knowing I was waiting unprotected in Gentile country, and then I would tell them my story. Although I dreaded the shock and grief it would cause, at least in this neutral ground between Galilee and Judea, where no one knew us, we might decide what was to be done—for I knew they would not disown me. Aunt and uncle must know, but perhaps the whole episode could be a secret between us five for my brother's and sister's sake, so that their futures would not be ruined by my scandal. Perhaps uncle could end the betrothal plans by telling my future husband that I was very ill and he would be wise to choose someone else. Perhaps I could stay in Samaria until after the birth, and then leave the baby with someone before returning to Galilee.

These confused, half-formed plans whirled in my head as I climbed slowly to my feet. A dull ache dragged at me but I did not dare stay with the caravan, for they would put me on a litter and carry me to Bethany, and that simply must not happen. As we had camped on the fringe of the city, it did not take me long to stumble through the lifting darkness toward the first house I saw. I took my donkey with me in the hope that I would not be missed in the caravan until it was too late—if they noticed my

113

absence at all. An unclaimed donkey would be remarked upon instantly. Now I crept behind the solidly built dwelling, which stood, screened by trees, in its own garden and made my way into the stable built alongside. It was still dark and I huddled down in the straw to wait, with my cloak drawn tightly about me. Two plump donkeys were tethered at the far end of the stable, which was cozy and warm compared to the raw air outside. By hiding here I could also ensure that anyone from the caravan passing to water his animal would not see me.

Time passed. A gray light stole in through the doorway, and the first cockerel greeted the dawn. Just as I gathered my courage to leave this haven and seek help, footsteps sounded outside and, to my relief, two women entered and immediately saw me in the straw. I struggled to my feet, striving to be calm and praying that they would give me shelter and not send me back to the caravan. They continued gazing at me in surprised silence. One was a middle-aged woman, plain and capable-looking, while the other was much younger—not more than twenty—dark and attractive. I thought vaguely that she might have Egyptian blood in her. Neither offered to address me, so I opened my mouth to speak. To my horror I found that tears were running down my face, and I could hear myself sobbing weakly. My pain and all the accumulated tension of the past few weeks had broken me completely.

"What ails you, girl?" the first woman asked, not unkindly but as one who expects an answer. "What are you doing in my stable? Are you lost? Are you sick?"

I grasped this last question gratefully. "Yes, I am sick. I was with the caravan but I'm too unwell to travel down to Judea. If you would only send a message to my brother in Galilee and give me shelter until he comes to fetch me, I should be so grateful. I cannot go any further, and I know my brother will repay you for your kindness."

The woman looked long and hard at me in silence and then

asked, "Do you have no friends on the caravan who would help you, who would accompany you home?"

"No," I wept. "No one. I'm traveling alone to my relatives in Judea."

The woman shrugged. "Then it would be just as simple for you to go on than return. It is almost the same distance to travel."

"No! No!" I cried wildly, "I can't go on! I am far too sick!" I was now terrified that she might force me to return to the caravan.

She weighed me up in silence again. "What *does* ail you?" she asked eventually.

My heart sank at her persistence, and I knew I must seek help elsewhere in Samaria, from one less inquisitive. Unwilling to reply, I lifted my cloak and moved heavily toward the door. I felt her shrewd eyes on my back. As I stepped over the threshold, her voice behind me stated calmly, "You're with child, aren't you?"

If a thunderbolt had fallen at my feet, I could not have been more aghast. Clutching the doorpost, I turned and gazed at her with terrified eyes. I was lost. Now she would not help me. Indeed, she might take me back to the caravan and tell them of me. My plan to protect Martha and Lazarus crumbled into dust.

"Judith," said the woman, still gazing at me, "have those animals fed and watered and then return to the house. You, girl, come back in here or my donkeys will trample you. They are not very courteous when they're hungry."

Judith took the beasts to the stone water trough in the yard, and I was alone with the woman. Too shocked and fatigued to do aught else, I sank down into the straw again.

"You're not married, of course?" her voice came from above me.

I shook my head mutely.

"I thought not. But perhaps you are betrothed and have been

115

a little indiscreet? So," and she shrugged her plump shoulders, "it is not unknown and easily forgiven."

"I am not betrothed," I answered heavily. "I am traveling from Galilee to Judea to be betrothed at my uncle's house. My parents are dead. My future husband is not the father of my child, and my brother and sister do not yet know of my condition."

There was a silence then, "I see," she said. Another pause. "Why don't they know?" she asked at last. "And tell me again why you came in here?"

I looked up hopefully. She did not seem unduly shocked or censorious. Perhaps she *would* let me stay after all. Scrambling to my feet again, I went over to her. "They don't know because I was not able to tell them before I left. It was all so hastened and unexpected. And now I don't want them to suffer for me and so I thought . . ."

And, relieved beyond measure to find a sympathetic listener, I poured out the whole miserable tale. Then, with my eyes fixed imploringly on her face, I waited in silence while she digested this information.

"Will anyone notice if you don't rejoin the caravan?" she asked at last.

"Oh, no," I cried eagerly. "No one knows me and I didn't associate with any of the families. If I *am* missed, then it will be thought I'm further up or down the line until it's too late—and even then they will not know whom to tell of my absence, for I informed no one that I was going to Bethany. I don't wish my relatives to know of me until I've seen my brother."

"How do you feel now?" she asked abruptly.

"Very well," I said in surprise, and indeed I had almost forgotten my pain.

"If you rest, then you should recover," she remarked.

I looked at her expectantly.

"You may stay here," she pronounced, "until your brother

fetches you. Come into the house before you are seen. Your donkey can remain here. Come quickly now."

As I thanked her effusively, I felt as if a great burden had been lifted from me. Salvation, however temporary, was being offered. I followed her gratefully through a side entrance into the house, where I was immediately taken up to a small room at the end of a passage. Here I was given food and told I should remain there until my brother came. With my mind flooded with relief, I ate and drank with a better appetite than I had experienced for weeks and soon after fell into a deep sleep.

Several days passed, and then one morning the woman entered the room and signed Judith to leave. I had not seen her all this time and now looked at her expectantly as she sat down beside me. I guessed that she had a message for me from Magdala.

To my dismay, she took my hand and, looking gravely at me, said, "Mary, you must take courage for I have bad tidings to give you."

My heart missed a beat. I could not imagine what she meant. Lazarus would surely come, knowing I was sick?

"I sent the message to your brother and sister in Galilee, saying that you wished to see them—that you were with child and—"

"Oh, why did you say that?" I wailed in disbelief. "I was to tell him myself! I simply wished him to know I was sick!"

"Indeed?" she murmured. "Well, I must have mistaken what you meant. But I'm grieved that, despite all the trouble I've taken on your behalf, your brother will still not be coming here."

"Not coming?" I whispered. "But why?"

"He says that you are no longer his sister. You are full of lies and deceit, and now, by associating with a Gentile and bearing his child, you have brought shame on your family and they have lost their good name. He refused to look at the token you sent, and when he was told you were lying in Samaritan country, said, 'Let her stay there among strangers for she is no sister of mine.' Then he cursed you."

There was a silence in the room. I lay back on the bed and stared at her, shocked beyond words, for I had no reason to disbelieve her. However could I have dreamed of escaping the retribution I so richly deserved, or of protecting Martha and Lazarus from the results of my folly? My brother's words were just. I had lied and lied, deliberately deceiving them. It was only right I should suffer—but to know that my own brother had cursed me! In our country it is a solemn and dreadful thing to curse a member of one's family, and this meant that Lazarus, generous and forgiving though he was, had reached a limit where he could no longer excuse my behavior. He had always lived for the Law, studying it intently, and had small patience for those who tried to reach out beyond it—and in his sister lay no exception.

There was no hope for me. I had once longed to be free like the Gentiles and not shackled by the Law. Now I lived among people considered worse than Gentiles. Now I was free to go anywhere I wished—except home to my brother and sister. Soon the whole of Galilee would know about me. Already I was an outcast, condemned by Lazarus (I could not believe he had Martha's support) to stay in this Samaritan wilderness like the scapegoat driven out from Jerusalem into the desert at Yom Kippur. But the sins that weighed me down were my own.

At last, through my agony of mind, I became dimly aware of the woman asking me what I planned to do.

Bewildered at such a question, I gazed dully at her. "Do?" I repeated slowly. "I have no home now, no family. What *can* I do?"

"Well, you can't remain here indefinitely," she replied briskly. "This is not an inn, and even if it was, you would need money to pay for your board. However," she continued, "I'm

118

not completely devoid of feeling, so I'll tell you what I propose to do. You may stay here until the child is born, and once you're fully recovered you can repay me by working in the house. We'll decide later what can be done with you."

But already I was weeping with relief and thanking her incoherently for her goodness, her kindness—no mother could do more. I felt bitterly ashamed that I had once nourished such a contempt for the Samaritans, for they were more merciful than many a one professing the true faith. But for days after this I was ill with shock at the news from Magdala, the knowledge that everyone knew of me. Despite the proffered aid, I feared for my uncertain future. Never had I felt so desolate.

Now, looking back, I know that I was an innocent, gullible fool. But at the time I was ill and in the depths of despair. I was also very young and had no reason, not knowing the ways of the world, to disbelieve the woman (my rescuer!), convinced as I was that I had erred beyond redemption. The truth, however, was that she and her husband kept a small brothel on the outskirts of the city and, at the time, needed a replacement for a girl who had fallen ill and died. I had unwittingly presented myself in an ideal condition for her to exploit. Knowing that I was alone and would not be traced for weeks once my disappearance was noted, she gave me shelter. I was given my brother's "message" so that I might feel totally alienated and dependent on her charity. In fact no message had been sent at all. They knew that by the time I was found, my reputation would be lost, for I had freely chosen to stay here in a Samaritan brothel, and they would ensure that my long-hid condition would also be known. Nothing more was required of them but to pose as saviors in my distress until I, full of gratitude, promised to repay them for their goodness. This too would be told to my relatives, and I should have no opportunity to relate a different tale.

While I was lying in that house, the caravan continued its

journey and eventually arrived in Jerusalem. Our uncle went from Bethany to meet it. By the time he came most of the travelers had already dispersed, but he remained by the Sheep Gate thinking I had wandered off to one of the bazaars while awaiting him. Time passed and he grew annoyed, then anxious as he paced up to the Fountain Gate and back again. The last remnant of the caravan had long since vanished into the city and there was no one he could question about me. For the remainder of the day, he scoured the streets but was finally obliged to return home and tell our aunt that the celebration must wait, for I had completely vanished. Another day passed and still there was no trace of me, although my future husband and several friends joined the search, never dreaming that I had not arrived in Jerusalem at all. An urgent message was sent to Lazarus, who came down immediately, accompanied by Martha, who refused to be left at home.

By this time three weeks had passed since I had left Magdala. My disappearance caused a sensation around Gennesaret and became the main topic for weeks. After conferring at our uncle's house, the little search party was finally forced to conclude that I had vanished somewhere along the route and, consequently, they went nearly mad with anxiety. Had I wandered off alone and fallen in a ravine and perished? Had some wild animal attacked me and dragged me off? Had I been captured by brigands or any of the other countless hordes of bandits and mercenaries which haunted the slopes above the trade routes— the very reason for traveling in a large group? My brother and sister were almost convinced by this time that I must be dead, but a tiny spark of uncertainty drove them to scour the countryside—still with no success. The Feast of Tabernacles came, and Lazarus and my uncle waited in Jerusalem to question the countless pilgrims, looking for one who might have been on the caravan traveling south the previous month.

Eventually they encountered one or two women who did indeed vaguely remember me—and that was all.

Six weeks had passed since my departure from Magdala before my disappearance was traced to Samaria. Lazarus had not realized until then that the caravan had not taken the Jericho route, and now he cursed himself for not checking such a basic fact. His fears increased at the thought of my vanishing into such hostile territory. Leaving Martha with our aunt, he and uncle set out again from Bethany to go up through Ramah, Michmash and Bethel into Gentile country and comb every place for me—if indeed I was there at all.

Time passed, and as they moved northward toward the city of Samaria, I lay desolate and helpless in my room, believing myself forsaken by God and man. Ill with shock, I lived in a kind of stupor, my mind devoid of everything but misery. Then during Kislev, as the early winter set in, my child—a leaden weight which never quickened—was born before its time. A girl. During all the weeks of waiting, I had somehow felt sure that it would be a boy and was already prepared to hate it as I did its father. But when Judith left the room to fetch me a caudle, I felt compelled to reach across to the bundle lying beside me on the chest. Almost unfeelingly, I pulled aside the coarse wrapping to see once and for all the result of my sufferings. With the knowledge that I must suffer still more in the future, I tugged roughly at the covering swaddled around the body until it fell open—and then my heart stood still.

I looked down at the perfectly formed limbs, the minute features, pinched and bloodless. Every detail was there—the dark crescent of lashes, the tiny cleft in the chin, even fingernails on the hands like pale starfish laid against her cheek. It was no replica, no reminder of anyone I hated—it was just a babe. I longed to reach out and touch the dark, fluffy down on her head, but I dared not. I was too moved to weep, and I felt I

121

should die of grief if I actually put my hand on her. It was strange that in all my emptiness and misery I yearned, nevertheless, that this stillborn child should have been a living warmth in my arms. Not everything in life would be lost to me if my daughter had survived. The old adage was true: The sins of the parents are visited upon the children. I did not deserve to have her. I had been allowed to look on her just once, so I might know what I had lost. She had been taken from me so I might be totally alone. There was no other answer to my fearful desolation. This was the crushing weight of divine justice, and it would require an equal measure of mercy to lift it—but I knew I would never feel that now. Grieving quietly, I drew across the cover again.

Then someone came and took my baby away.

For two weeks I was ill with child-bed fever. A physician came at one stage, but I was too sick to know either friend or stranger. However, fate decreed that I should survive, and I slowly regained my strength. It was during this period of convalescence that the woman (I never knew her name) came to my room and enlightened me at last regarding the business of her establishment, and ended by reminding me of my promise to repay her for the charity shown me in my outcast state.

I cannot describe my feelings on learning this. In my weakened condition I could neither speak nor think coherently. I felt numb, frozen with horror. Now indeed I was in a living hell. Looking back, I marvel that I did not sink under such a blow considering my age, my whole upbringing and background, and the mental and physical shocks to my system. But the human spirit is stronger than the flesh which longs to surrender and die.

"You've had a child, that's all," the woman's voice continued, "but you're fully recovered now, thanks to all the care and attention we've given you. Now I want you downstairs again as

122

soon as possible, and you can start earning your keep."

I drew in my breath sharply, but she went on, "Tell me you won't and you can go out *now* on the street, and with winter coming on I wouldn't advise it. Pity about the child—she would have been a good investment for the future—but you'll soon forget her. The physician said you're unlikely to bear another, which is all the better . . ."

At this point, for some reason, I started to sob weakly and at last said feebly, "I *can't* stay here."

"Very well, you can go—but where? And to whom? You've not forgotten what your brother said, I hope, or the fact that half the country knows all about you. No one wants you now. You don't belong anywhere. The penalties are always harsh for people like you—but you should have thought of that months ago. Now," she continued more pleasantly, "if you stay here you'll find I'm not a hard person to please. You'll be living in a warm house with plenty of good food—I feed my girls well— and the best in clothes. There's a garden for you to walk in, and the servants will bring you all you require from the city, within reason, of course. I'll tell you now that this is an establishment of quality, and I pride myself on its reputation. You may consider yourself very fortunate to be here, for I'm very selective regarding our clients. Discretion is our motto. Now, instead of staying here all day, I suggest you sit in the garden and get some color into your cheeks. And think about what I've said."

And she rose and bustled out.

I lay motionless, knowing there was no need to think at all. I knew that she meant what she said about casting me into the street, where I would surely die—and I could not seek shelter elsewhere. Even the most charitable Samaritan could only offer me a temporary home. Ultimately I had nowhere to go. Every face was turned from me. Every hand lifted against me. It was

123

to be—the sickening realization of what I must become, with loneliness my lot for the rest of my life—however long it might last.

That night I stared sleepless into the dark, with my future laid open before me. I felt that, if only I knew how, I might take my own life and be finished with everything. But, as a gray dawn crept into the room, I realized that my fear of death and the hell that awaited me was greater than the misery I now endured. Realizing that there was no solution yet unable to be reconciled to such a life, I finally ceased to wrestle with the problem, and numbness settled upon me.

The other women in the house often came in and tried to cheer me, but most of them were foreigners and I found it difficult to understand their accents. Judith was the most frequent visitor and often brought her little girl with her—a lovely, dark-eyed child of three years. I could hardly bear to look at her. Did not Judith care about the future of her child?

It was about this time that Lazarus and my uncle returned to Bethany, resigned to the fact that I must indeed be dead and dreading breaking the news to the women. But on their arrival at the house, Martha and my aunt were waiting with appalling news. A Caphernaum man and his nephew passing through the outskirts of Samaria while following the road down to Shechem had seen me walking in the garden—the screening trees were leafless now—and recognized me as the Magdalene woman the whole of Galilee was talking about. The nephew, wishing to confirm his uncle's opinion, had immediately entered the garden, where I was taking my exercise as the woman had ordered. I did not know the man or what he wanted, gazing at me so intently and, terrified, I turned and ran back to the house. But before I could enter, the proprietress came out and, approaching, addressed him in honeyed tones of welcome and apologized at the same time for my behavior.

"You must forgive her. She is only recently arrived here from the north and is unwell. She has lost a baby, too, poor dear girl—but I am sure that you are most welcome—"

But the man interrupted her. "What is that girl's name?"

"Why," she crooned enthusiastically, "I can see you're quite taken with her. Her name is Mary. A pretty name for a pretty girl, do you not think?"

But she was talking to herself, for the nephew was already out in the road again. She returned to where I stood in the doorway. "Well, you're quite a success already, pale though you are!"

Sickened, I turned away and, going up to my room, tried to dismiss the episode from my mind. But this same incident was related to my family when the two travelers reached Judea. On their return north a few days later, it was also repeated there— the scandal of my long-hid condition—and now many people recalled my wandering habits after our parents died. Lazarus, however, instantly pinpointed my visits to the house above the lake, and my lies and reticence when discovered. Now it seemed I had deliberately taken flight into a house of ill fame, leaving them for weeks in ignorance of my whereabouts, thus confirming uncle's opinion that any good in me had long since died. How could I have inflicted such suffering upon them all this time, sending, even now, no word of regret, no plea for forgiveness? Obviously no one was forcing me to stay at that house, yet I was there—sitting in the garden where anyone might see me! Such brazen behavior was beyond belief and past forgiveness.

Martha and Lazarus were at first stupified with shock and disbelief, which, as confirmation of the story grew, turned to grief. My brother fell ill at Bethany so brokenhearted was he. Martha bore up, with the help of our relatives, who did not forsake their niece and nephew because of me. My poor sister was forced to accept the facts retailed about me, yet still remained incredulous that I had pretended to be so happy when last talking to her of my proposed journey to Bethany. But uncle said I must have been born full of deceit and depravity.

When Lazarus asked, as he lay recovering, "Could we not send a message—to be really sure . . .?"

"No," uncle answered firmly. "No one is keeping her prisoner there. It is for her to come to us. She could have sent a message to you all those weeks, knowing the anguish you were feeling when she vanished . . . giving her up for dead. Well, she's dead to me now."

Lazarus sighed and turned away. He was too ill to argue and knew too well, anyway, the customs of our country to hope that I could ever be reinstated. Besides, uncle had urged him and Martha to leave Galilee, for they would find it difficult to stay in Magdala now. This offer, which they accepted gratefully, made it impossible that I should ever return to live with them even if Lazarus should try and seek me out.

So at the end of that winter, my brother and sister journeyed home to gather their belongings. It was a brief visit. I shall never know the full extent of all the grief I caused them. Although they never referred to me in public so as not to antagonize our uncle, I knew later that, despite everything, including, not least, my seeming lack of love, I was still a sister to them—a sister who had a foremost place in their hearts and prayers.

Back in Magdala they found things sadly changed and felt glad that they had a new home waiting for them in the south. Jude now owned the *naggar*'s shop, and Zachary hobbled over to tell Lazarus that he could no longer work there, for his nephew, recently married to his Bethsaidan cousin, was horrified that people, including her, might recall that he had once considered me as a possible wife. The news that I had borne a child also appalled him, lest an accusing finger be pointed in his direction. Understandably, he wanted no dealings with our family at all. Simeon, too, withdrew his suit for Martha, who was so stricken at the time that she hardly noticed it. But the women were kind to them and bitterly upbraided me for bringing such sorrow on my brother and sister, who deserved only happiness after all their work since our parents died.

"We will come and visit you at Passover no matter what our husbands say," promised Anna and Deborah and a weeping Susan, who was wondering how she would manage without Martha to borrow from and help with the children. The *hazzan*, too, although he thundered denunciation in the synagogue, quietly told Lazarus that he would always recommend him should he ever study in Jerusalem.

So when the first days of spring arrived, Martha and Lazarus left Magdala, their empty home with the little garden now neglected and overgrown, where the tethered Sheba (sold for a tiny sum to the *hazzan*, for they had spent their small savings in searching for me) was already turning her attention to the abundant feast awaiting her, including mother's flowers just nodding into bud against the wall. They left quietly at dawn when no one was abroad—down the hill, past the *naggar*'s shop and onto the road winding down to Cana, to meet up with a group there.

"Soon it will be Passover again, and Mary was to have been married a week or so after. I told her that Simeon and I would stay after the feast and help her, and she said that it would be wonderful—and she was lying, Lazarus!" Martha burst out. "All the time she was lying." And she began to weep again.

"Hush, Martha," said my brother, who was trudging beside the donkey (they had been forced to pay also for the hired one I took with me into Samaria). "We must forgive her and try not to speak of her again. It will only anger our uncle and we are beholden to him now for a home."

"I can forgive her," said Martha, "but I can't *understand* . . .

127

Perhaps it's my fault. I should have been stricter with her after mother died. But I trusted her—and you don't expect your own sister to lie to you!"

"I shouldn't have let her go down alone—and I should have checked the route! If she'd gone with me, at least she'd not have ended in a Samaritan brothel—God help her!"

"Why didn't she tell me about the child?" said Martha, pursuing her own thoughts. "Something could have been arranged. Poor Mary; I'm sure the fault wasn't hers. Always wandering about daydreaming, and I always scolding her for it. Perhaps she was too frightened to tell me . . . Perhaps if I'd been kinder, more ready to listen, she would still be with us."

And so they journeyed on, blaming themselves.

During that early spring, as my brother and sister traveled down to Judea, I too was forced to leave the only home I had and to start my own form of journeying.

During the winter I recovered my health, for I was without doubt well fed and cared for, and regular exercise in the garden helped hasten the process. Then the day arrived when Judith entered my room with the woman's instructions to make me ready so that I might repay my benefactor for her kindness.

Dressed in the softest linen and with my hair curled and interplaited with jeweled ornaments, I sat listlessly staring at the array of bangles, gorgets and anklets lying in my lap. Meanwhile Judith mixed black antimony with a few drops of olive oil and darkened my brows and lashes. Sikra reddened my lips and the ashes of the al-khanna dyed the palms of my hands. The other women crowded admiringly in the doorway.

Giving me a brisk shake, the woman pointed to the sparkling heap and told me to choose any jewelry I wished.

"That will cheer you," she said.

And so my life in that house began. From now on I must not

think of the past at all. My family had cursed and disowned me, so I must also forget them if I was to stay sane. My heart ached for other reasons now, yet the other women seemed happy enough—although I spoke but little to them.

Judith, however, became my friend and one day told me her story. She had been stolen from her mother at three years of age and now no longer remembered her home. I knew little of the others. They were soft, indolent, tolerant creatures, content with their clothes and jewelry and comfort. But I had never desired such things—only peace of mind—and my life was now an unplumbed well of misery. It was obvious that I would never fit into their establishment.

It was early spring, over six months since I had vanished into Samaria, when Judith told me that she would soon be leaving the house. A merchant, a regular visitor, had announced his intention of taking her back with him to Egypt to make her his wife, for he had been a widower for several years. The woman was highly flattered and for a large sum in compensation she readily gave permission. This was magnificent proof of the quality of her establishment. Judith was very happy, too, when she told me this one sabbath evening as we sat in the garden together. But I listened with a heavy heart, for I had become fond of her. She was quiet and gentle and defended me from the woman's criticism. I should greatly miss her.

"But you've known so many men, Judith," I said. "What can he be to you?"

"That is true, Mary, but until now I have never known what it is to be loved. Furthermore, he is taking me away with him— something I never dreamed could happen. I thought I would finish as one of the servants here, cooking and cleaning and seeing my daughter take my place. But to belong in society again, in a country where no one knows me; to be a wife with a husband, and my daughter still young enough to forget all this . . . Oh, Mary, it's like a dream! I can't think of anything at the moment except that he loves me, and one day I will love him as much in return."

After she had returned to the house, I sat on in the fading light. To imagine being taken from this house—to be reinstated and given back everything with increase like Job of old. Her gods were kinder to her and more merciful in their dealings— but then she was not an Israelite and had no code to obey. I suddenly recalled standing between mother and Martha in the Temple and receiving the old blessing from the high priest: ". . . The Lord turn his face toward you and give you peace." But God had turned away from me and I would never know peace again.

A bird was singing beyond the wall in the Adar evening, filling the still, cool garden with its song. The young trees were misted with green and raindrops still trembled in pearls along the branches from a recent shower. Time passed, yet still the bird sang on as if joy and hope were its constant companions. I rose and paced restlessly along the path. Oh, what *was* that yearning at hearing an unseen bird singing through the evening air in a deserted garden? It brought only anguish in its wake and filled me with longing for—I knew not what! Perhaps it reminded me of better days—a nostalgia for sabbath days in the garden at home—better things—and to know that I had lost them forever! Turning abruptly, I ran back into the house and up to my room.

A spark of feeling had at last arisen in me, despite my numbing misery. My hard-won control snapped and was replaced by a simmering anger. A year ago I was Mary of Magdala; now I was nothing, utterly nothing. "You'd be better dead." *He* had said that to me. I had promised myself that I would not think of him again, but my rage was such that now I deliberately dragged him to the front of my mind, cursing my fate and the man who had caused it. How many others had suffered because of him, and he neither knowing nor caring!

How many other lives had he made a living hell! Hatred followed fast on the heels of my anger, a bitter hatred that rose like bile and nearly choked me. Raging, I cursed him with all the venom I possessed.

"You devil!" I whispered. "You *devil!* If you knew how I hated you, you'd die of it. You'd *die* of it," I gloated with malignant satisfaction. "I'd give my right hand to see you fed to the jackals. I'd sell my very soul to see you rotting in hell. As long as I live, I shall hate you. I shall die hating you. You devil!"

Suddenly a door banged below and I started. Then, recovering myself, I shivered. What an evil house this was! The softness and luxury smothered it, but it was there in the very atmosphere, prevalent and insidious, watching and listening and ready to creep out from every corner. Darkness had fallen while I crouched there, and now it pressed around me like a thick, stifling blanket. The anger and hatred, so foreign to my nature, vanished as, amazed at myself, I jumped up with all the old misery flooding back. I must go down and sit with the others or the woman would come looking for me.

As I turned, the darkness seemed physically to engulf me again, muffling and dragging at my footsteps as I groped toward the door. I seemed to hear inside my head and all around me my own whispered maledictions. Dear God, what had happened that I should talk like that!

I shook my head vehemently to rid myself of the sound, but to my bewilderment, the whispering grew louder, a buzzing and murmuring that rose in a discordant babel till a crescendo of noise dinned in my ears and reechoed through my mind. I was deafened by it, drowning in it. The suffocating darkness terrified me and, fumbling to the door, I wrenched it open and nearly fell into the passage—and immediately the noise ceased. Closing the door behind me, I drew a shuddering breath of relief, which caught in my throat as I suddenly became aware of a faintly menacing atmosphere around me.

131

The passage stretched ahead, dimly lit by one small lamp. Not a shadow flickered along the walls, and apart from its tiny pool of light, there was nothing but impenetrable darkness between my room and the stairs. A dozen steps would take me to them, and even now I could hear the other women as they chattered and laughed, whiling away the sabbath evening—and yet I could not move. Along that passage lay nothing but horror.

Feeling icy cold, I clutched my veil around me, urging myself to go forward and not to be foolish. But ingrained in every fiber of my being and surfacing rapidly now was the native superstition that caused us Jews to observe minutely each particle of the Law lest we incur God's displeasure and ill luck befall us. I was already convinced that divine wrath had marked me out, but the episode in my room that had left me shivering in the passage now made me wonder fearfully if malevolent forces had been sent abroad to persecute me. Like all my countrymen, I believed in evil spirits. They were a commonplace like flies that swarmed everywhere. Not for nothing was their master called Beelzebub, lord of flies. Had I fallen so far that this was permitted to happen to me? Then the justice of God was more terrible than his wrath. But it could not be. Surely not. It was my imagination, my recent illness, the strain of my terrible life. I stood there in the tingling silence, berating my cowardice, but still I could not move toward the stairs. Then suddenly the door opened below and Judith came up with a lamp, looking for me. I almost wept with relief.

But three days later Judith left for Egypt. She went off with her husband and daughter in the early dawn, and I watched them for as long as I could from my window. Then she was gone. With my head aching, I returned to my bed. With all my heart I wished her happiness—but how I would miss her! I was glad for her child; it distressed me to think of her in this house. But my only real friend had vanished into another country.

Worse was to follow. Within a week of Judith's departure the woman told me I was free to leave the house, for they had somehow acquired an Abyssinian girl to replace me. She was the same age as myself but with a lively temperament, good health and attractive into the bargain. It had become increasingly obvious that I had been a bad investment and she should not have troubled me in the first place.

Though I had gained strength during my convalescence, my health began to fail again beneath the strain of trying to look and sound cheerful to avoid complaints. I had long known that my position was in jeopardy, but I lacked the energy or inclination to care. For me, life was not worth living either in or outside the house. I suffered increasingly from excruciating headaches, which racked me for hours. Insomnia followed in their wake, leaving me a hollow-eyed wraith. My appetite decreased, and I became thinner and more faded. I was no use to anyone.

Thus, without a moment's warning, I was sent into the street one morning with a wallet containing a few of my belongings and a handful of coins. The woman, who was not totally bereft of feeling, told me that she had waited for the warmer weather before dismissing me. Her last words as she escorted me from the garden were, "If I were you, I would go and see if your brother will take you back."

I turned and stared, wondering how she could mock me with such a vain hope, but already the door had closed behind her. Still I felt nothing but shock and bewilderment at the sudden change in my life. At least the house had been some form of shelter. Then the realization struck me that I was homeless, and for a while I felt overwhelmed. All that morning I stood by the stone wall bordering the garden, watching the passersby and wondering where I should go. If only I had a friend. Then the woman's husband appeared and ordered me away from the house, shouting and gesticulating as though his establishment were so respectable that it could not bear the contamination of my presence near it.

As I walked slowly beyond the outskirts of town, I suddenly became aware of streams of people wending their way along the roads, and I realized with a shock that soon it would be Passover. Hundreds were passing through Samaritan country, and I stood watching them for a while, not enjoying the painful memories such a sight evoked. I, too, must go south to Jerusalem. I dared not return to the familiar country of the north and bring even more shame on Martha and Lazarus and all our relatives there. But even as I thought this, there came a shout from a caravan of swarthy Babylonian merchants. Two women were calling and waving to me.

Like seeks like, I thought bitterly—but who was I to judge? It would be companionship of a sort. Lifting my wallet, I went forward to join them, and so one phase in my life closed and another opened.

CHAPTER
• EIGHT •

GYPT. ONCE THE ZENITH of civilization and now a
granary for Rome. Once the crook and flail, the emblem
of "My Majesty" the Pharaoh, was everywhere revered,
but now the people had grown lazy, tainted by foreign settlers
with their customs and their gods.

The caravan had eventually brought me to Alexandria, one of
the greatest cities in the Roman Empire, and now three years
had passed since I had left Israel. My new home, founded by
the Grecian conqueror, lay spread along the flat coastline, its
white buildings reflecting the sunlight. Gardens lay to the east,
behind stretched the western desert, and dominating the whole
port was the great lighthouse towering above us. Avoiding the
large community of Greek-speaking Jews, I blended instead
into the cosmopolitan background of this friendly country. My
health improved, I learned to speak their language and even
made some friends. I had rooms in the center of the city.
Siamon the Egyptian kept me, and I was as content as a woman
in my circumstances can be who has no family or relatives to
claim and who wanders as an outcast in her own country. The
women were tolerant and the children around me unquestion-

ing, and I found much in Egypt that I liked. But after two years Siamon died and I was alone again. For a while I felt forlorn and unprotected, but my neighbors were so kind that I could not feel dispirited for long.

Then, unexpectedly, I had the good fortune to be taken as a concubine into the house of a provincial landowner. It happened at the time of the rising of the Nile waters, when Sopdet the Dog Star rose over the flooded land. I had gone out early one morning to paddle ankle-deep in the shallows, searching for clams, when I heard a whimpering on the dyke behind me. Turning, I saw a small monkey gazing wistfully down, one paw reaching to pluck my hair while the other held a thin gold chain attached to his collar. I had early learned that the Egyptians loved all animals and birds and kept a great variety of pets in both house and garden, unlike the Israelites, who regarded them as either unclean or beneath contempt—and certainly not sacred! The Egyptians had many gods in animal form, and such species were not to be hunted and killed. This monkey had obviously strayed and disliked his new, watery environment. Speaking softly, I raised my arm, and immediately the eyes in the wizened face brightened and he ran, chattering, down onto my shoulder and sat joyfully hugging my neck. At the same moment I heard singing in the distance. Wending its way between the canals came a group of slaves carrying their master in his chair.

For many days now the rising Nile had flooded the land, as it did each year. But now *akhit*, the inundation, was receding and crops were being planted in the rich silt deposit left behind. The land was irrigated through an ancient system of canals, and the earthen dykes served as roads between the fields. Along one of these paths came the slaves, singing of the coming season as they took their master to inspect his estate.

Akhit is come,
Sebek the crocodile god is glad,
His sacred lake is filled—
Now the season of perit is nigh,
The cereals sprout green,
We go out to the fields rejoicing. . . .

The chair stopped before me as I stood on the dyke holding the monkey. Then, "Kheti! Kheti!" called the man. He held out his *naboot* and immediately the monkey swarmed up the long knobbed stick and into the chair to play with the thick, beaded collar round his master's neck.

"My heart was grieved at losing him," he said, and as I haltingly replied in his own tongue, he interrupted, "You are a wanderer in my land. Follow my chair if you wish."

The eyes were kind beneath the fringe of the heavy wig, so forgetting Siamon, I crossed over the dykes and was taken into the household of Ani the landowner.

At first I was enchanted with the whole estate. The wood-built house with its latticed windows was large and airy, and the sunny courtyards around it were laid out with flower beds and fish ponds. All was enclosed behind high brick walls. Crops grew in abundance on the estate, flax was cultivated and fields of wheat and barley—*iot* and *boti*—ripened in the sun. Vines were trained along the walls while palm trees and the *rehet*, or sycamore, favored by the Egyptians shaded the paths and terrace where the mistress of the house ordered the blue and white lotus to be grown for her eyes to rest on while she dined. The birds of the air and the spoiled wildfowl of the Nile ran tamely before my feet hoping for largesse. Monkeys screamed and chattered through the windows, and as the sun reached for its zenith, a pet gazelle came shyly to the open door to ask for water. Ani kept three greyhounds in the house, and Nofret had a favorite saluki constantly at her feet.

As his wife, she shared in all his business and social life, including the management of the estate—totally unlike the Israelite woman—and was respected by the entire household. There were two other concubines living with me in a separate wing of the house but I was the only foreigner. Nevertheless, Ani grew fond of me, calling me *sonit* or "sister," meaning "loved one."

For a few months I was happy. My quarters were pleasant, with the traditional blue ceilings and colorful mats adorning the walls. A round table stood in the window, surrounded by chairs with latticed-work seats. Three carved chests completed the furniture of the room, with, of course, the indispensable fly whisks!

Tui and Napalta, the other two women—or girls, they were so young—adored jewelry, and Ani gave them boxes inlaid with ivory for their necklaces and bracelets—copper ones studded with turquoise from the mines in Sinai. The silly creatures thought they should have gold ornaments like the ones Nofret wore. To me he gave a figurine of the cat goddess, Bast. It was as well, for I had no desire for jewelry and even less for an image of one of their hard-faced gods, but it was made of pure alabaster, which I liked—"from Hat-Nub in Middle Egypt," I was told. Another time it was a gift of balm—balm from Jericho! For one fleeting moment I saw the oasis and the fragrant bushes bending in the breeze.

Time passed pleasantly. There were servants for everything—for the kitchen, the laundry, the brew and bakehouses, the fields and gardens. There was a pedicurist and manicurist for the master and mistress, a sandal bearer who also stood by their chairs to whisk away the flies and, of course, musicians. The Egyptians loved music, and while they were dressed, while they were shaved or bathed, while they ate and entertained the *darabukkeh* drummed softly in the background. The bow was drawn sweetly across the strings of the *rab-es-sha'ir*, mingling

138

with the jingling *tar* and the soft clash of the *sagat*. Nofret sat beside Ani, looking very beautiful in her plain linen sheath, her hair elaborately oiled and dressed and her eyes heavily rimmed with kohl. Colored beads hung around her neck, and the *kholkhal*, the silver anklet of married women, gleamed beneath her dress. The table was covered with fish and quail, wheat bread and sweet cakes. There were dishes of stewed fruit, *botarikh*, the caviar from the bouri fish and a plenteous supply of strong beer, the national drink of Egypt.

It was the last happy day I spent in that household. The following morning Nofret's mother came with Seneb, her dwarf-servant. From the first she disliked me. She saw that Ani favored me, a foreigner, and resented that he called me *sonit* as though I were Nofret. Her black eyes bore into me, she whispered poison into her daughter's ears and set the dwarf to spy on me.

Nofret had always been distantly kind to her husband's concubines, but now she was frightened. Like all Egyptians, she believed in magic and was morbidly preoccupied with death, and her mother, jealous of my place in Ani's household and affections, warned Nofret of the undesirability of my presence, how ill luck could befall her husband, who had gone the way of many of his countrymen by taking a stranger under his roof. How would his Ka, his spirit, fare in the afterlife as he stood before Thoth to render an account of his deeds while the jackal, Anubis, stood beside him holding the scales of justice? To Ani she was more subtle, only quoting in his presence the words of the sage: "Beware of her who comes from a far country and who is unknown in her city. Turn away as she draws nigh and rest not your eyes upon her."

But it was Seneb who sealed my departure from that house. Dwarfs were a familiar sight in Egypt, often working in the laundry or tending the household pets. Seneb came and was put to work with the animals, a task he enjoyed. He particularly adored his mistress's saluki, which romped with Nofret's on the terraces. He was loyal to his mistress to the extent of sharing her likes and dislikes, and so he hated me. His eyes followed me everywhere, and I would often glimpse his stunted form sidling in the shadows behind me, for what reason I could not tell; but hatred in itself is a wearing weapon.

One day I went to my room and found on my chair a twisted circlet of gold wire intertwined with lapis lazuli and carnelian. It was a lovely object and one I did not expect from Ani, who had looked at me with troubled eyes since his mother-in-law had arrived. But now it seemed that, despite her malice, he had set the seal of his approval on my presence by this gift—a gift worthy of his wife and not me. I was pleased and resolved to wear it that evening, sure that he would visit me when he returned from inspecting his harvest, for it was the season of *shemu*. As I dressed my hair and arranged the circlet, I thought I heard a footfall below the open window, but though I called, no answer came. So the noon wore on. Suddenly I heard Ani's voice and, rising, turned toward the doorway. The next instant Nofret and her mother stood before me, with Ani following reluctantly behind. I looked at him, but he would not meet my eyes.

"See, daughter. Seneb was speaking the truth. She now wears your jewelry and flaunts herself before you in your own house."

For a few moments I was speechless; then the horrible truth dawned on me, I turned to Nofret to protest. But her dark eyes were full of pain, which so hurt me that for a while I gabbled meaninglessly to her in Aramaic. I stopped and tried to explain in her own language, but I was so shocked that my memory failed me and I could only utter odd words and phrases.

"It is not true . . . I found it here . . . I thought it was a token . . ."

"Ani!" Nofret gasped and turned to him.

140

"This is all foolishness," Ani rasped. "It was my gift to you. How then could I take it and give it to my concubine?"

"Is he speaking the truth, Nofret?" her mother shrilled. "You know how he dotes on her. But perhaps she stole it instead?"

I felt sickened at her wickedness. I loved both Ani and Nofret and would not be the cause of strife between them. Better to leave than cause them pain.

"Of course Ani speaks the truth," I said boldly above her noise. "Seneb the dwarf brought it here to make mischief between us. Only Nofret and her mother have the keys to Nofret's jewel chest. And you know," I added to the latter, "that Ani gives gold only to his wife. Nothing else is precious enough."

And removing the circlet, I gave it to her.

Her mother saw that her plot to disgrace me had failed. In her impulsive stupidity, she had not imagined I would or even could defend myself. Now, in order to clear herself of any suspicion, she hurriedly accused Seneb of stealing the second key from her. "He will be whipped and dismissed instantly."

"And I will go also," I declared, aware that my life would be naught but misery with this woman. "I will not be the cause of any sadness between the master and mistress of this house."

Ani looked at Nofret, who made a fainthearted gesture as if to detain me, but I walked past them into the garden. I will leave tomorrow, I thought as I paced up and down the terrace, trying to form some plan for my future. Then I froze as malicious eyes looked through the bushes at me and the next instant Seneb sprang out, blocking my path. Although he barely reached my waist, I instinctively recoiled from the enmity within him.

"Foreign woman!" he spat, "I was happy here. My animals loved me. Now I have nothing. My mistress has beaten and dismissed me even though I obeyed her orders. Why could you not leave when you saw we hated you—foreign woman?"

I could only gasp at such reasoning. He seemed to harbor no

grudge against his mistress but only saw me as the root cause of all his woe.

"Now I am homeless. My mistress will not recommend me to another household and I must travel to the city to seek employment. I hate the city. I wished only to stay here with my animals."

But I could feel no pity for his plight. What cause had he to blame me for his misfortune, willing as he was to carry out the corrupt wishes of his former employer?

"Go back to Alexandria and join the *ut*—they will take you without recommendation," I advised him contemptuously, referring to the guild of workers which dealt with the mummification of the dead, an essential but socially unacceptable position. "But beware lest you fall in the natron baths and be pickled before your time."

And I walked away—but suddenly a small rock hit me as the dwarf vented his malice. Ignoring this childish gesture, I ran along the terrace, past the acacia tree toward the steps leading down to the courtyard. A saluki was sleeping on the broad wall, and as I hurried past my ankle twisted on the rough shale and I lurched against the animal. There was a frightened yelp, a scrabbling of paws, then the poor beast fell with a sickening thud to the courtyard below. With a hoarse cry the dwarf rushed past me and down the steps to his mistress's pet. By the time I also reached the bottom, he was cradling the dying beast in his arms, rage and grief distorting his face. I knew he thought I had deliberately pushed the saluki to its death.

"Now I will kill you. I swear by Set I will kill you for what you have done."

His anger frightened me, for I knew what the beast had meant to him. I left the house at dawn the next day. As I walked along the dirt track to the town, the harvest was being brought in from the flat fields that stretched in all directions to the desert. The peasant farmers were busy with sickles and winnowing forks. Young boys with their tunics, or *galabiyyas*, tucked up beneath their belts carried trawl nets down to the river. I heard them splashing through the reeds and papyrus and calling to each other. The storehouses and granaries were filling rapidly. Outside each one sat a cross-legged scribe with his papyrus scrolls and ink cakes, laboriously recording each product as it arrived.

It was nearly noon when I finally wandered into the outskirts of Alexandria, to be greeted with delighted cries from my friends. I was surprised and touched that they were so glad to see me again, and did my best to slake their curiosity regarding my life on a landowner's estate. But somehow I could not settle into the old ways again. After Ani's spacious house and gardens, I found my two rooms in the city cramped and the lack of privacy intolerable. I had become accustomed, also, to a softer style of living and a gentler manner. But I had to forget Ani. So, of necessity, my life went on as before. But sometimes in the evenings, so as to gain some peace, I went a little way into the desert and wandered about on the plateau among the ruins of old temples and former glories of Egypt.

One evening I stayed longer than usual. I was not unhappy but pensive, wondering how I would fare in the future and if the good health I now enjoyed would stay with me, and it was nightfall when I turned back toward the city. Emerging from the ruins, I walked down through a man-made corridor of masonry, seeing ahead and below me the flaring lights of the town. Then something made me glance back over my shoulder—and I suddenly froze in my tracks.

Two lines of broken columns and statues formed the long, ghostly avenue in which I stood. Stars glinted high above, and below on the sand stood the squat figure of Seneb the dwarf. In the clear moonlight his whole attitude exuded menace, and fear caught in my throat as I instinctively backed away. I had almost forgotten him, but now it terrified me to think that he had remembered me—had followed me to Alexandria—had spied on me—had followed me here. For what purpose?

Suddenly his voice came hissing down the avenue toward me. In the stillness and emptiness around, it seemed more menacing than a shout. "You advised me well, foreign woman. So now I work for the *ut*. It was all they would give me. Look!" He pointed suddenly to one of the statues. "Do you see him? I swore by him. I swore by Set . . ."

Weathered and crumbling though it was, I could still discern in the granite above me the doglike head of the god Set and heard again the yelp of the saluki. Horrified, I looked back at the dwarf, who was still watching me intently. Then his hand, as small as a child's, moved slowly inside the short coat, or *suderi*, he wore over his long tunic. Suddenly a knife gleamed in the moonlight—probably one of the instruments of his terrible trade. Seneb meant to kill me indeed. Was he evil or mad—or both? As he moved slowly down the wide avenue toward me, I turned and ran across into the shadowy maze of pillars and boulders, stumbling across the rubble and ploughing through the soft sand, my feet weighted by it as though in a dream. Flap, flap came the sound of the *balgha*—the heelless leather slippers he wore—as he pursued me. Looking back, I saw his grotesque figure darting among the pillars, the knife glinting in his hand—and I knew I could not outrun him. My breath came in painful gasps as I fled among the ruins, emerged into the desert again—and suddenly the ground gave way beneath me as, amid a cascade of sand and rubble, I slid down a sloping shaft until a large boulder stopped my further descent.

For a short time I lay bruised and breathless, and too terrified at the sound of the dwarf's feet above me to feel anything but thankfulness at this odd deliverance. Then, fearful that Seneb might also fall into the shaft, I rose and stumbled down and down into the darkness, the realization dawning as I progressed that I had unwittingly entered a tomb; but the

144

menace of the living outside overcame any fear of the dead within.

Arriving at the bottom of the shaft, I found myself facing a long corridor with various chambers and passages leading off in all directions. In the dim light statues of the Egyptian gods gazed down as I passed swiftly along. The jackal, Anubis, god of the necropolis and of the western horizon—Anubis, who watched over the burial rites of all men and, placing their hearts on his scales, balanced them against the feather of Truth until the ibis-headed Thoth pronounced them *maa-kheru*—true of speech—or mendacious. Osiris, ruler of the underworld, and his wife, Isis. Horus the hawk, god of light, and in one side chamber, the inscrutable cat, Mut. How I loathed these stony faced gods. I fled onward, ignoring the smaller shafts leading no doubt to smaller vaults, till I finally came to an extremely ornate door with Nut, the goddess of the sky, carved upon it, her arms spread protectively against any intruder. I had found the main burial chamber—and to my dismay the seal on the door was already broken. I listened, but no sound came forth. No member of the dead person's family would have done such a thing and thus incur the anger of Thoth, so I could only assume that brigands or grave robbers had already discovered the tomb entrance and plundered the main burial chamber. Despite the keen watch kept by the authorities and the heavy punishments meted out, such crimes were still committed.

Cautiously I peeped around the door—and gasped in amazement. The chamber was small and lined all around with turquoise blue tiles, and in the center on a large slab stood the painted coffin of the deceased. This had been broken open with some force and the lid thrown hastily on again, but, judging from the bandages hanging from the sides of the inner coffin, all the jewelry that had adorned the body had been ripped off. Averting my eyes, I gazed around the room, the contents of which had obviously been disturbed as if someone had been rummaging for small, precious objects to take away quickly. The entire chamber was piled high with beds and chairs, chests and stools. A chariot stood in the corner and a small boat leaned against the further wall. Scattered all around and in some disarray were vases and ornaments, gilded drinking vessels and plates, mirrors and tools, clothing and linen and even a meal set out at the foot of the coffin. In the dry atmosphere it was still intact. If one or more persons had recently stumbled upon the tomb as I had and stolen the smaller valuables, then there was every reason to suppose that they might return any night—this night!—to complete the task.

Suddenly I stiffened. A scuttering sound in the passages outside. Could it be rats? Then as I listened intently there came the sound I dreaded—the soft flapping of heelless slippers. Seneb had been too close behind me *not* to find my hiding place. Full of dread, I tiptoed behind the chariot as the steps grew nearer and halted outside. A pause, then just as he made some movement toward the door, I panicked and, moving further back into the alcove, accidently kicked a vase lying there and sent it rolling across the floor. I thought my last living moments had come as I waited, terrified, for the dwarf to rush in, but instead the heavy door began slowly to close and, too late, I realized what Seneb was about. The door had no handle on the inner side, as in the manner of burial chambers. I was entombed below the desert—a far worse fate than the one originally planned.

With a cry I darted across the floor, but already I could hear the retreating flap of his slippers along the passage to the shaft.

After ensuring that the door was certainly proof against any efforts of mine to open it, I sank despairingly on one of the chairs. So this was to be my end—buried alive in someone else's grave. I must suppose there were worse ways of dying. As yet I felt no real, overwhelming fear, so inevitable seemed my fate and so great my relief at escaping the dwarf's knife—in fact I felt only a great thirst after my lengthy pursuit. Rising, I wandered to the foot of the coffin, and there among the food was a tightly sealed jar of wine. Well, I thought with a wry smile, let me at least enjoy my last hours. Breaking the seal, I retrieved a dusty cup from the floor and sat down to my lonely vigil. Time passed and drowsiness crept over me. I calculated that it must be nearing dawn, and with this last thought I fell into a light doze.

I do not know how long I slept, but it seemed no time at all before I suddenly jerked awake and found the empty cup still lying in my lap. There it was again—the sound of muted voices further along the passage, coming nearer, and then I heard the door of the anteroom next to the burial chamber open and people enter.

Cautiously I rose and, tiptoeing to a slit in the wall, peered through. I guessed immediately and with mixed feelings who they were, judging from their somber looks and laden baskets. It was the custom each year on the feast day of the dead person for his heirs to visit the tomb and burn incense before the wall slit so that the terebinth resin, or *sonté,* could reach the nostrils of the dead and inform him of their caring presence. Fresh food and wine were also laid on the offerings table before the slit for the dead man's Ka, or the spirit which had left the corpse but remained in the tomb—the hut-Ka. Prayers were then said by the father or eldest son reminding the gods of the deceased virtues and begging clemency for him.

Here now was an opportunity to make my presence known— but with what results? The penalty for breaking into a tomb was heavy indeed, and especially so for a foreigner like myself. Would they believe my story? Seneb would hardly affirm it, and they would simply think that I had imprisoned myself accidentally while investigating the chamber—and such desecration! A clawlike yellow hand hung over the coffin edge and I could not bring myself to replace that pickled limb. And the vanished jewelry! Perhaps I would be accused of stealing it on a first visit and, returning to gather more, of having sealed my own fate. Nevertheless, it was better than dying of starvation or being killed by the brigands who were bound to return and finish their task of plundering the chamber.

"You are beloved of all your family," the man's voice began, "beloved of your father and your mother and your sisters—you, our son; you, our brother." (So it was the *khet* or dead body of their son the parents were mourning.) "Food you have given to the hungry and water to those that thirst. The naked you have clothed and those who had no boat you have ferried across the river."

The pungent odor of the resin wafted through, and I moved to the further side of the chamber as it caught in my throat. The cloud of *sonté* grew thicker and I stifled a cough. I had no desire to interrupt them till I had thought out my story. They were obviously deeply attached to their son, and my presence in his rifled chamber would require a very convincing explanation. Coming as they did through the anteroom, they had no reason even to check the seal on the main door.

"Spirit that was in him, heart of his several forms, witness not against him before the Guardian of the Scales. Ka of his body, defend him. Khnum, strength of his limbs, weigh the balance with truth."

As the father's voice addressed the Ka of his son, I suddenly realized another superstitious belief of the Egyptians—the Ba, or human-headed bird that flew around the passages of the tomb to frighten off intruders. If they heard the flapping of its wings in the actual burial chamber, they would have to open one of the lesser doors and release it into its proper environment. As none of them had ever seen or, I suspected, wished to encounter, a Ba, they would doubtless hastily retire before it flew out angrily among them. I had nothing to lose. If I was discovered then I must confess and hope for clemency of some sort, but now there seemed a chance to escape by playing on their naïve beliefs, to which they would be particularly liable in such a setting! Already I could hear the father ending his address and the sighs of the family gathered with him.

"Depart with peaceful step toward the other world. Trust not in length of days for the gods dwell not in time. Man carries into eternity all his deeds—good and bad, they are there beside him. What madness then to practice evil! But he who comes blameless to the other world shall live there like a god."

There was a pause and then a stirring as they rose to their feet and prepared to leave, murmuring among themselves. Stealthily I lifted a fan and fly whisk from the assorted domestic objects scattered on the floor. Moving around the chamber in my bare feet, I began to imitate the sound of beating wings. I could almost hear the mourners freezing into stillness in the anteroom. There was a whispering and, as I beat more loudly against chairs and walls like a bird trying frantically to escape, a frightened whimper broke from the mother and I distinctly heard the word *Ba*. Judging from the noise I heard, the younger children were already crowding around the door leading to the passage, and soon the sound of their feet faded up the passage and away into the shaft. But the parents remained, overcome by the thought of this terrifying bird actually in the burial chamber of their son, where, according to their beliefs, it should not be. It was unthinkable to allow it to remain there, but they were obviously terrified of the consequences of opening one of the doors and releasing it. Fortunately for me, however, conscience and duty to their dead prevailed and, to my intense relief, I heard one of the smaller doors being unsealed. Furiously I beat the fan as it opened the merest crack, and I heard the woman gasp, "Flee now, husband, lest it emerge while we are here."

Not a moment too soon, I thought, as they sped after their offspring, for the resin was almost choking me and I doubted if they would believe that the Ba of the tomb would also cough!

149

A short while later I also cautiously emerged from that twilight place and looked thankfully around. What a blessed relief to be out in the world of living people again! Everywhere was deserted, and the morning sunlight heartened me as I hastened back to the city, pausing only on the outskirts to buy bread and fruit to eat as I went along.

But my mind, after the terror of such a night, was far from easy. Seneb would soon discover that I was still alive, and my presence in the city might only urge him to try and kill me again. I could not spend my days looking fearfully back to see whether he followed me. I must leave Alexandria. It had held no happiness for me anyway, since I had quit Ani's household. I determined to gather my few belongings and board one of the boats journeying up and down the Nile until I found a place that attracted me and where I felt I could settle. Having resolved this, I wandered on through the outskirts of the city. The place was barely astir and I paused curiously outside the ut, the huge building where the dead were brought for preparation. Seneb and his co-workers were still slumbering, and only a servant or two were there preparing the saltpeter baths and the resin for anointing. Cautiously I pushed open the door, a morbid curiosity compelling me to peep in.

I found myself in a gallery and immediately before me a flight of steps led down to a great tiled chamber with rooms leading off on all sides. A servant was washing down a marble slab in one of them. A bath of saltpeter lay directly below me, and I noticed with a shock that a woman was lying in it. Her face was only just below the surface of the water, but even at that distance it seemed vaguely familiar. Surely it was not . . . I could not rest until I had confirmed it for myself.

Swiftly I descended the steps and ran across to the bath. I bent over her, then, still doubtful, plunged my arm into the water and, grasping a handful of the black, floating hair, I pulled the woman's head above the surface. It was Nofret, wife of Ani.

Good God, when had she died—and of what? Judging from her features, she had not been lying in the natron for long. Seventy days was the usual span for the literal pickling of a body after removing the brain and internal organs. Poor, gentle Nofret. I laid her head back in the water and, oblivious of my surroundings, stood quietly grieving. Then I thought of Ani and for one moment wondered if he might take me back, for I knew how much he had loved me. It seemed an unworthy thought with his dead wife here before me—and what of his mother-in-law? Her shadow was still there. No. That happy episode in my life was past and gone. I thought too of dying here in the city and falling into the hands of Seneb the dwarf, and shuddered. Turning, I retraced my steps and came out again into the street. I left Alexandria that same day and never returned.

After several days of haphazard journeying, I finally found my way into the village of Matariyeh under the shadow of the great pyramid of Gizeh. It had a flourishing Jewish community, but, as I always did in Egypt, I avoided them and took lodgings with a peasant woman who took pity on me when she saw that I was unwell. I had been in low spirits when I left Alexandria, and this, coupled with my rough voyaging on the boat, had given me some kind of fever. I had, of course, been used to a more ordered life, both in the house of Ani and in Alexandria, and if I had known then that this was to be the beginning of several years of wandering, I believe I should have lain down in that village and never risen again. But my only thought was that, with my health restored, good fortune might yet favor me again. So for several days I lay in that house recovering my strength, giving the old woman sufficient money for my keep and a little surplus to buy some wine to cheer her, for she was a widow with two sons dead and a daughter living several miles away. A guest of any sort gladdened her, and the wine loosened her tongue as she related to me the entire history of her life.

"And where is your home?" she finally asked.

I saw no harm in telling her, knowing that she could never have heard of a tiny village in the northern part of Israel. But, "Magdala—in Galilee?" she said immediately. "Yes, I've heard of Galilee before. There was a young family here once—it must have been over twenty years ago, for I was only recently married myself and nursing my first baby—poor Huni, he's been dead these five years now. She was a young mother too and grateful for the help I gave them. Poor things—strangers in a strange country, and they mixed but little even with their own people here. Often when the Jews journeyed back into Israel they were asked if there was any news to be given to relatives there, but they seemed reluctant that anyone should know of their whereabouts. I even suspected them of running away from some wrongdoing, but that was before I knew them properly."

The old woman poured out more wine, then suddenly slapped the table. "Nazareth! That was the lady's birthplace, though they were living somewhere in the south, near Jerusalem, before they came into Egypt. Mariam—I remember now. She was exhausted when they arrived. What a journey— and in winter—with a child only a few weeks old! I never knew why they came at all. Joseph and Mariam and their little son, Josue. I think I came to love that child as much as my own."

It was as though my fever had left me, and I felt like ice from head to foot. During the past few years I had tried to forget everything of my past life. I had nearly succeeded, so long as I was kindly treated and enjoyed good health and a comfortable life in some man's household. But now, sick and in low spirits, I felt as though a deep wound was slowly tearing open again as I heard, like a body blow, those old familiar names. And such names! I did not doubt for an instant whom she meant. Egypt was suddenly a foreign land, and I a stranger wandering through it. A wave of homesickness engulfed me as the woman

152

settled back and prepared to continue her reminiscences.

Interrupting her, I queried, "You called her a lady. Surely not—I mean," I hastily amended, "someone so poor and coming here with so little as you say—she must have been of the peasant class—the *am-har-arez,* as they're called in Israel."

"Well, so she was," she conceded, "but I always thought of her as a lady—to myself, you understand. She was not given to gossiping about her affairs like the other village wives. But the child was a joy to her—to both of them. Light of his father's eye. Often when Joseph was resting after his day's work, she would take the baby in her arms to the outskirts of the village. I would see them from my window—see her now in fact—sitting over there beneath those palms with the great pyramid behind and the purple sky all full of stars, and she turning up the baby's face to see them. And he would imitate her the way children do and point out the biggest, brightest ones. I think he wanted to give her them, for she would smile and shake her head and, drawing down his pointing hand, would kiss the little palm and hold it to her face. Well, you usually do think that way of your first-born. You don't have any children?" she suddenly asked.

"No," I whispered, the wound tearing wider as I recalled the house in Samaria and the little bundle lying on the chest beside my bed. "No, I have no child."

But she hardly listened.

"Well, time went on, and I was quite accustomed to having them as neighbors when one day Joseph, passing my house with his tools, suddenly turned to me and said, 'Herod is dead. The tetrarch of Galilee is dead.'

"I did not know who he meant, for the name was strange to me, but this event seemed of significance to Joseph. That evening I walked across to their house to give Mariam some sweet cakes I had baked in the ashes when I heard her call the child from play. When he came, she knelt down and, cupping his face in her hands, said, 'Little son, we can go home now.'

153

"'Home?' he echoed.

"'Yes—to Nazareth.'

"And when he asked if it was far away, she began to tell him of Galilee in the springtime after the latter rains, and they were both so absorbed that I was reluctant to disturb them and returned home. Soon after that they made preparations to leave, and I was sorry to see them go as if they had been members of my own family.

"'You will forget Egypt and all of us here,' I told the child Josue, 'and you will even forget me who baked you sweet cakes.'

"I was jesting, you see, though in truth my heart was heavy that morning. But . . .

"'No,' he said, 'I will not forget. Only think of me and I will think of thee.'

"And so I kissed him and they went off with the blessing of the whole village. He was but three years old, and I thought the world of him and more. And she was all her name implied: a lady—a lovely lady."

That was the end of my life in Egypt. I have said before that I felt a wave of nostalgia on hearing familiar names and places, but, added to that, was a sudden, overwhelming shame for my life as a prostitute. I had forgotten everything in Egypt, so well nourished was I and with so little hardship until recently, but now . . . To think of Mariam with her strong, loving influence, living in this village, in that house across the way—though heaven only knew why they came here so many years ago. I felt as if my presence now contaminated the place, including this woman's house. I had to move on anyway, for the resident Jewish community would be openly hostile once they discovered my combined nationality and trade.

Slowly I discovered how false was the peace of mind I had enjoyed these last few years. Now turmoil replaced it. All the old pain of my brother's rejection came back and the bitterness of losing everything I held dear. And yet—a faint hope stirred. I had not seen Israel for several years, and I was older now and had suffered enough. Perhaps if I returned Lazarus and Martha would forgive me. It would be foolish not to try.

Three days later I left the village and began the long journey back home.

CHAPTER
• NINE •

ND SO I RETURNED to Israel. But not to a new life—not to forgiveness and restoration to my home and family. Instead I found nothing but misery, sickness, loneliness and the desolate realization that my life seemed irrevocably fixed in the twilight zone in which I wandered. There was no milk and honey for me in Israel. Egypt had been my land of plenty, but I could not return there. That episode in my life was over.

The discovery that Martha and Lazarus now lived in Bethany was a great blow. I had hoped for some clemency in the more tolerant atmosphere of the north, but my heart quailed at the prospect of entering an austere Judean village only a short distance from the capital of orthodoxy. And how could I hope that my aunt and uncle would allow me to enter their house? I might well put my brother and sister in danger of forfeiting their own shelter beneath that roof.

But another reason also prevented me. No sooner had I set foot in Israel than I was immediately assailed, surrounded almost, by the same hideous, whispering voices that had so terrified me in the Samaritan woman's house. They had not troubled me in Egypt, and I had dismissed them long ago as hallucinations or the results of my illness in Shechem, but now they terrified and tormented me as the Egyptian gods had never done. No one else seemed to notice. Was I mad or possessed? I did not know. I was alone in a private world of noise that sometimes reverberated in my head and sometimes died away to a busy whispering in the background, only leaving me when I slept. Once or twice I tried to enter Bethany, but the voices came out of the village to meet me, blocking my way like a wall, terrifying me and driving me back. Such words will sound like madness—perhaps it was—but this in truth is what happened to me.

I had had money enough for my journey back to Israel, but after the first few days I was forced to revert to my old way of life and, from then on, ill luck dogged my footsteps. As my spirits sank lower, my health gradually failed over the years and, at the last, only the very dregs of our society would associate with me. Often and often I wept at the sheer degradation and hopelessness of my life, and yearned for some illness to carry me to the grave. But it seemed that I was not yet destined to die and that, even with wretched health, my life might be prolonged indefinitely.

For the better part of the year, I kept to the trade routes— one of the myriad of caravan followers—for some demon of restlessness kept me constantly on the move up and down the country east and west of the Jordan. During the feasts I took a room in Jerusalem. My family were always kept well informed of my whereabouts for, whether they would or not, news filtered back of the Magdalene woman who roamed the towns and cities of Judea and Samaria and the surrounding country. But so long as I did not actually see my relatives, I could learn to live with my reputation and nomadic existence. In the worst heat of summer, I haunted the ports—Dor, Caesarea and Apollonia on the Plain of Sharon or Joppa and Ascalon further south on the Plain of Shephalah. The shepherds soon became my friends, for they were also society's outcasts, and I often joined their campfires, bringing my food to share with them. It was somewhere to go at night when the wild dogs roamed in yelping packs across the plains. I saved all I could during the summer months and, as winter set in, returned to Jerusalem and a rented room in the lower quarter. When it grew bitterly cold, the middle-aged guard at the Antonia allowed a few of us to sit by the brazier under the shadow of the great fortress till his watch ended. Then we left promptly before his officer came and drove us from the premises.

So I reluctantly returned through the winding streets, up through the empty bazaar strewn with refuse and scurrying rats, and down under dimly lit archways into the vast network of courts and alleys where doors swung suddenly open and warmth, laughter and greetings spilled out on the frozen air as I passed with the snow falling as soft as feathers about me. A man with a child lolling asleep on his shoulder nearly stumbled against me as he left a neighbor's house and recoiled abruptly as he saw my painted face. Clutching his son, he spat in disgust before crossing swiftly to his home while I shrank back in the shadows—my usual reaction when I was rejected.

It was then that I recalled a wonderful moment when I had found a child outside my room one morning. Jerusalem was packed as usual for the Passover, and this tiny girl—she was not more than three years old—had somehow been separated from her mother, and I came upon her crouched, terrified and weeping, in the doorway. As I knelt beside her, she instinctively raised her arms to be lifted and, for the first time in years, I had a child in my lap. Her little body was as light and frail as a bird's as she clung to me, crying all the while for her mother, and for a moment she was mine.

But, looking up, I could already see a man and woman pushing back distractedly through the crowds and calling repeatedly, and I knew my solace was over. Unclasping her arms, I turned the child and pointed to them. With a cry of recognition and without a backward glance, she ran unsteadily toward them. Both saw her simultaneously, and relief flooded their faces as they rushed forward to snatch her up, scolding and kissing her simultaneously. Over her daughter's head the young wife smiled at her husband and, ignoring all our people's customs of public behavior, he reached out and lightly touched her cheek—a small gesture but by its very gentleness embodying all his affection. For an instant she held his hand to her face, and then they turned and vanished into the crowd while I shrank back in the doorway, ashamed to have witnessed something not meant for any eyes but theirs.

Standing now in the winter darkness in the backstreets of Jerusalem and watching from the shadows as the door swung shut on the man and his sleeping son, hearing his wife greeting him, all this came back to me with a redoubled pang. To know that I could never be invited into one home in this great city; no woman would open her door to me; no man would do anything but spit on me—a thing he would not do to a dog. Above all, the scene I had witnessed that Passover when the child was lost was something I would never know—the look between a wife and husband that clearly said that each was loved by the other. No man would ever speak such words to me—that he had chosen me for myself, as someone special and irreplaceable. I must forever endure the humiliating fact that I was less than nothing to the men I encountered. If not me, then someone else would suffice. I must never know tenderness or kindness, never hear a child's voice call me mother or trace and recognize loved features in another generation. "May you live to see your children's children . . ." What more bitter reproach might an Israelite woman endure than to see that prophecy unfulfilled in herself? But I deserved nothing less in the eyes of God. There

160

was but one blessing and I was thankful for it—my parents were not alive to see their daughter now.

So thinking, I turned away and went slowly back through the snow to my room. I, who once dreamed of being at peace in a room of my own, now dreaded the company which intermittently dogged my footsteps—murmuring, whispering voices that made me fearful of being alone, that forced me out into the streets to seek the company of anyone rather than remain solitary in my room. It was a long winter.

My life continued in this manner for the next few years. During this time my aunt died, and Lazarus and Martha continued living in our uncle's home. Various snippets of news came to me of our friends and relatives in the north and, increasingly, of one man in particular.

At first I did not connect the Josue the guards talked of that spring in Jerusalem with our old friend from Nazareth, for it was a common enough name. I simply listened as they gossiped of the stir he was creating in the synagogues up and down the country and the number of followers he had already amassed, and silently agreed with one soldier that "The time is ripe for such a man. There has been a dearth of them this last year or so."

This was true. There were too many would-be prophets and so-called mystics in Israel without yet another to swell the ranks, but none had appeared lately and such a diversion was always welcome. In fact it was quite amusing how there would suddenly appear, like an epidemic, a rash of "holy" men who foretold wonders and disasters—and then vanished completely. Even now when they referred to this Josue as the Nazarene and remarked that most of his followers were Galileans, it still did not impress me. I had not visited the north for years, and

Galileans anyway were always more susceptible to such people. So I laughed along with the guards and dismissed it from my mind.

But a few weeks later as I wandered about on the outskirts of Ephraim, wondering if I should stay there or move on to another place, my attention was drawn to a large crowd pushing and jostling at the end of the main street leading out from the town.

"What is happening down there?" I asked a woman friend who often accompanied me.

"I think it must be the Galilean they're all talking about," she replied. "He heals folk and the like but, of course, he's not very popular with the authorities down here. What is it they call him? Subversive. That's it—subversive. But then they never like the people listening to anyone but themselves. Why not go and see him before he leaves? I'm off to the well for a drink."

Any diversion was welcome, so, quite curious now, I followed the crowd, hoping to see this much talked of man in action. Perhaps he could cure the noises in my head. But even as I thought this, I dismissed it from my mind. He would see at a glance what I was. But perhaps he might work a few miracles. I was afraid that he might be gone by the time I reached the end of the street, but his departure was delayed by a group of women who had brought out their children so that he might bless them, stranger though he was. From where I stood I could see that his followers were vexed about it and were trying to turn the mothers away, but he would not hear of it, and so the little ones came flocking around him like so many brightly colored birds until he was almost hidden from sight. I wandered nearer, thinking that, prophet or not, he was a good and gentle man to spend so much time with a group of children.

As I passed a cluster of older women who were looking on, I heard one of them remark disapprovingly to her friend, "Oh, yes, that's true enough, but there is always another side to the coin. He simply walked out of the *naggar*'s shop one morning and asked his cousins to come and work there instead—and his mother a widow and he the only son! Imagine! I can only hope those relatives make a success of the business, or she will starve—and *he* not caring! The blasphemous folly of a man to turn the world upside down and neglect his own flesh and blood while doing it!"

Her voice went on, but I no longer heard. My heart had missed a beat before she finished her second sentence. Even as I stood rigidly there, the crowd, as quickly as it had gathered, now broke, eddied and swirled away from its central figure. He looked around to gather his followers, and after all those years I saw what I already knew I should see—the familiar features of Josue, my childhood friend, once a carpenter, now a preacher, a prophet! My heart leaped again with shock, and then with fear that he might notice and recognize me such a short distance away. But he did not have time to look in my direction, for his attention was suddenly arrested by a young man who, bursting through the scattered ranks of the dispersing crowd, went swiftly up to Josue and, dropping on one knee, kissed his hand in the customary salute to a rabbi.

I was rooted to the spot now with astonishment. Was *this* the Josue I knew of old? What charisma did he possess that this obviously wealthy man should seek him out? And what a contrast they made! The scarlet silk which lined the young man's cloak shimmered in the noonday heat, and as he raised his ringed hand agaist the sun's glare, the jewels flashed ruby and emerald in its rays. Josue looked like a beggar beside him. His *tallith* was thick with dust and dried mud caked the *tzitzith* —the ritual blue tassels— on the corners of his homespun *chalouk*. Dust covered his feet, almost obliterating his sandals; even his face was streaked with it. Perspiration beaded down the sides of his face and his eyes seemed drowned in weariness.

Creeping forward two paces, I strained my ears to hear their conversation, for suddenly, without warning, the buzzing and whispering in my head had begun again, rising in a clamorous crescendo that almost deafened me.

"Rabbi," I heard the young man ask, "tell me what I must do so as to merit eternal life."

And before I had time to be startled at the question, the familiar voice replied, "Sell all that you have—give it to the poor—and then follow me."

Josue's reply had been swift and decisive, and I could hardly believe I was hearing right. Neither, it seemed, could the young man. His face was a study in disappointment and bewilderment as he laboriously listed all his good works to Josue: how scrupulously he kept the commandments, fasted, gave alms, observed his religious duties, even released his slaves before their seven years' service was finished. There seemed no end to his virtues. At last he fell silent, yet his whole attitude was tense with the expectation that this prophet, this miracle worker would speak again. Josue's unorthodox answer had shaken him so much that he seemed not to possess the mental energy to challenge it. Instead he tried to circumvent it, but to no avail. Josue's eyes were fastened on him all the while, but he made no answer to the young man's protestations.

At last, still on his knees and eyeing the ground about him as though expecting to see a solution written there in the dust, he added a flourish to the list of his good works. "For three years now I have given a home to my wife's mother. She is a great trial to me, but for my wife's sake, I bear with her." He sighed and fell silent.

If there was a glimmer of humor to be seen in this last desperate remark, Josue did not seem to notice it. But I saw how lovingly he looked at this aspiring disciple who came to him with so much—too much, it seemed. After a pause he spoke to him for the second time. "You do well," he said, then added firmly, "but sell *all* that you have so that your wealth is stored in heaven for God's glory and not on earth for your own, and *then* follow after me."

My heart went out to the young man as he wrestled once again with this extraordinary answer, which I could not begin to understand myself. For the first time in his life, he had been told that despite his house and lands, his servants and his wealth, he was nevertheless unsuitable in his present condition. Again I wondered why he, an educated man, did not challenge Josue's words, which took away my breath with their audacity. What had happened to Josue these last few months that he should speak thus to one so far above him in rank? And why should such an ultimatum be necessary before anyone join him?

Utterly mystified, I looked back again at the young man, who had now risen to his feet and stood, clenching and unclenching his hands, as I had seen Lazarus do so many times when he was anxious and uncertain. Somehow, touched by this familiar gesture, I began to pity him in his dilemma, foreign though its nature was to me.

But at that moment he turned back to Josue, his whole attitude altered, as if he had once more gathered the dignity of his position around himself. He had never begged and would not do so now. Brushing the dust from his cloak and still not looking at Josue, he stated abruptly, "You need food for your journey north," and took a purse from his belt.

Since the man had first rushed up to him, Josue had not taken his eyes from his face. Even now he did not look at the money he proffered, and a disciple standing nearby came forward and took it from the young man's hand.

I thought then as I do now, that I was the only person who heard Josue say—demand almost—"Now give me what you have kept."

And both I and the young man knew that he did not mean the purse.

Twisting this same article in his hands and still looking at the ground, the young man wrestled with himself again, but it was a weak attempt. Finally he thrust back the purse into his belt and shook out the crimson folds of his cloak. This gesture seemed to reassure him, so that he could turn back and graciously incline his head to Josue before walking swiftly away, as if the other man no longer existed, as though their strange conversation had never taken place.

I heard Josue's men call to him, but he remained motionless in the middle of the road, with the hot breeze blowing the dust above his feet and his whole attitude—was it tense or expectant? I felt somehow that he was praying, could almost feel his eyes yearn after the man who was already far down the road. But even as I turned my eyes to his retreating figure, I saw the regal tread falter as his shoulders drooped, and his pace slackened until he was almost dragging his feet along. Suddenly I willed with all my strength that he would come back, for he had almost slowed to a halt. But, after a moment's hesitation, he struck his fists together with an exasperated, impotent gesture and quickly vanished into the bazaar. Seeing him gone at last and nothing realized—it was strange, but I could have wept with sadness and did not know why.

As Josue vanished along the road, the tumult in my head lessened. Exhausted and relieved, I sank down under a tree to ponder what I had just witnessed. For an instant I remembered my companion, but she was already gone too far ahead. No matter; I should see her again in another town. Then, with no clear plan in mind, I set out to trace Josue's footsteps up-country. From then on I found myself unconsciously following after him at a distance, although I never went too far north for fear of being recognized. Huddled in the background, I listened to his preaching. Ignorant and uneducated though I was, I could nevertheless experience for myself the profound effect he had on the crowds who had walked in a narrow path all their lives and chafed against it. Now here was Josue, turning the Law upside down, berating us for our blindness and enraging the Pharisees, who could not fault him no matter how cunningly they tried.

He was popular enough in his own part of the world, for Galileans, having no great love for the Law, found his teachings very palatable. But Nazareth disowned him. His relatives were scandalized at his making a public name for himself and acutely embarrassed by his miracles.

"Cousin, if you have any regard for us at all, then I beg you to go down to Judea where no one knows you. It is so shaming to be constantly asked, 'Surely he is not your cousin?' 'Surely not your nephew?' 'Surely that cannot be Josue-bar-Joseph?' I dread sometimes to walk abroad. Can you not settle down to normal life like Simon and Joseph, for your mother's sake?"

So Josue no longer visited Nazareth but stayed mostly at Peter's home in Caphernaum. But he did not return to "normality" and neither did he settle down. On the contrary, he was preaching everywhere—in the Temple, in the synagogues, in every city, town, village and hamlet up and down the country. He was constantly on the move. Then there were the miracles, which no one could explain. I myself had seen a blind man healed in an instant and, like the crowd, went away shaken and silent. Above all, there were the astounding claims as to who he was and whence he came—claims that were veiled and yet constantly held out to us so that the mystery of it was always present in our minds. Some said he made himself equal to God, but this I had not heard for myself and refused to give credence to. It seemed to detract from the sincerity of his mission. I could not begin to understand all he said but, fascinated, I believed him, though I was appalled at his daring.

I do not know when this change occurred in me—from astonishment and curiosity to acceptance and eagerness to hear more—but somehow it happened. Already I laid claim to personal knowledge of Josue and his family background, and could thus discount the accusations of "liar" and "blasphemer" that were hurled at him, including the doubts regarding his sanity. Men who spoke as logically as he were not insane. He had once been my friend, and I knew he was neither evil nor mad.

But if he were not these things, then only one answer remained—that he was speaking the truth. Because we could not understand the "kingdom" he spoke of or the constant reference to his "Father" was no sound reason to doubt that his was a divine mission. Had our ancestors understood the prophets any better or heeded them? But how carefully he must tread, for his enemies were watching him like hawks—enemies who wished for nothing less than to see him dead. What a dangerous path he daily chose to walk!

The more I thought about my erstwhile friend, the more I recalled things forgotten for years—snippets I had heard, fragments of conversation I now dredged up from my memory and tried to piece together. There was his cousin, John, six months older than he, and the stir when he was born to his aged parents. John, who vanished into the Judean desert after his mother died years ago, who emerged for a short while and was proclaimed a prophet—the first in Israel for four hundred years.

But now John was dead—beheaded at Machaerus—and Josue had seemed to step into his cousin's place as the focus of attention. Surely that was not simply a coincidence? Surely there was a link? Then there was something else about Josue I could not recall, something about his birth on the day of the Purification and Rededication of the Temple—the Feast of Lights, we called it. How I wished I had listened more carefully when mother and her friends were gossiping together years ago. There was some great mystery about that family that I could never resolve now.

Nevertheless it was good to see a familiar face again. Many believed in him and followed him. Why not I, albeit at a distance? Why I should have wished to do this—again, I do not know and, doubtless, neither did countless others. There was no compelling charisma about him, no personal presence (indeed, his cousins were a head taller than he and better clothed), and yet we flocked to him. Perhaps it was the gravity with which he spoke, never avoiding a question or making a display of his healing. He was displeased in fact to have it noised abroad, for this did not seem an important part of his mission at all. However, it was impossible to ignore him. He must either be accepted or rejected and, increasingly, I desired to seek him out and accept his teaching. Somehow he gave me hope that, though I had transgressed appallingly, my sins were not the worst. But how could I remedy this? My greatest sorrow was having to barter myself so as to eat and have a roof over myself in the worst weather. Often I wondered what would become of me—how long my health, worsening all the time, would allow me to continue this wandering, hopeless existence. During the last few weeks I had suffered almost unremittingly from the noises in my head—sometimes a constant whispering like hissing, malicious tongues which terrified me as I sat alone in my rented room, many times a hideous din beginning like a hive of angry bees and rising to a high-pitched crescendo which nearly drove me mad. But I always preferred to trace its source to my constant ill health.

My agony of mind was further increased by knowing that my brother and sister had realized none of their former ambitions in Judea. No word came back to me that either had married or that Lazarus had become a teacher. Small wonder they had disowned me. I had ruined their lives as well as my own. But although I was unaware of this at the time, I later knew that Josue often visited them when he was in Judea and told Martha to continue praying that I would one day be with them again.

But to return to my longing to alter my life. Sometimes when despair or illness overcame me, I felt I simply *must* harden my resolve to approach Josue and ask him what I might do to be accepted again into society. Even if he could not help me, at least he would answer mercifully, and I longed to be spoken to with kindness, for I saw how courteous he was to those women who helped in his ministry, how tender he was to those whom even the physicians could not heal. Yet as soon as I resolved on doing this, then indeed I felt as though I was tied to a leaden weight. The voices, too, increased in and around me, persecuting me so I could neither rest nor sleep until I thought I should go mad with the tumult and my own exhaustion. Then in desperation I cried out, "I won't go to him! I won't go!"

And only then could I sleep. I almost began accepting it as the pattern of my life. If only I knew that Josue would help me, then I might have resisted more strongly, but others who sought him out were not like me. They had a home and friends awaiting them. But would Lazarus receive me back simply because Josue forgave me? It was folly to think so. It was only later that I learned of their own faith in Josue and, but for living in our uncle's house and believing that I had chosen my life and rejected them in so doing, they would have sought me out long ago.

Only once did I progress far enough to actually speak to a disciple, and this was Peter. I knew him vaguely from the past, for he was born in Bethsaida and later, when he married, had crossed the lake to make his home at Caphernaum, near our cousins. On the day I encountered him, Josue and the other disciples had removed to a quiet place so as to have at least one meal undisturbed, and I felt so ill at the time that I had no energy to follow them. So I decided to wait on the outskirts of the village Josue had just passed through, hoping he might return that way, when Peter suddenly emerged from a nearby house. He had stayed behind to see a relative and now carried a bundle of food to add to their supplies. My depression lifted. Perhaps he would take a message to Josue begging him to come to me, as I could not go to him?

Rising, I stepped out into the road as Peter came hurrying down toward me, and even as I did so, the whispering began like a swarm of wasps inside my skull and I could feel myself faltering. But I *must* try! Peter had already seen me from a distance, and now, spitting in disgust, he circled me and passed on out of the village.

"The Rabbi Josue!" I cried. "I want to see him!"

There was no answer, and if there had been, I should scarcely have heard for the hammers pounding in my head. Normally I would have immediately surrendered, but I felt I *must* make a stronger effort with this disciple here before me. So, despite my weakness, I half-ran, half-dragged myself after him, repeating my demand until Peter, angered and embarrassed at my persistence, flung back over his shoulder, "The rabbi's exhausted. Have you not seen the crowds around him today? Now cease troubling me."

"But I must speak to him. He would come if you told him my name. He knows me," I added despairingly, for I was feeling overwhelmed with my physical weakness and mental burden.

Peter, who all this while had not slackened his pace, now halted abruptly and swung around. "Knows *you!*" His fierce eyes raked up and down me. "Knows *you!*" he repeated. "Take yourself off, you evil, lying whore!"

And so saying, he marched off muttering to himself, while I, battered and exhausted, sank down into the road.

"But you'll tell him . . ." I cried, but he was gone and I knew he would not speak of me. My head was racked with pain. I should have known better than to try, but I was so bitterly disappointed. It had taken me weeks to steel myself and now came this rejection. Weeping quietly, I rose and went on my way.

And so the days passed and my life continued as before, but with Josue receding more and more into the distance, for I no longer had the strength to follow him although I longed to do so. Never had I felt so weak and ill or so fearful of what would become of me.

CHAPTER
• TEN •

TIME PASSED AND THE summer lengthened. I never bore its heat well, and now, walking through Jerusalem, I wondered wearily if I could endure the city much longer or if I should make my way to Joppa. At least there were sea breezes there, and I should miss the scorching *khamsin* that swept in, sand-laden, from the eastern desert and made life even more intolerable. But while I was deciding this I suddenly heard Rhoda calling. She had gone into the lower bazaar to buy perfume, and now I saw her running toward me, waving excitedly. I waited listlessly, thinking not for the first time that occasionally I should prefer to choose my own companions. Rhoda and I had nothing in common but our way of life, yet, from time to time, I met her in some part of the country and for a while she would accompany me everywhere—for what reason I never knew, for I found it difficult even to sustain a conversation with her.

Now she came panting up to me. "Mary, come quickly!" she cried. "A woman has been sentenced to death for adultery—and you know her!"

And as I looked blankly at Rhoda, she added, "It's the one

who comes to the upper bazaar each week with her children and maidservant. The one who helped you last winter when you were so ill. Who ever would have thought it?"

My weariness vanished as I listened. I did indeed remember the woman. How could I forget her? Only a few months ago I had encountered her in the merchants' quarters of Bezetha, where I wandered feverish and ill yet desperate to acquire the handful of coins necessary to rent a room for a few days and gain some semblance of health. Coming from her house, she had given me money. Knowing what I was, she still took pity on me, and three times since then I had seen her in the bazaar. It warmed me to think that at least one woman, and not of my type, had shown me kindness. Those few drops of compassion gave me strength to live through that winter.

But now my heart gave a bound of fear. Rhoda said she had confessed to her crime and been condemned. Yet she must be shown mercy. If Josue were only here! I thought wildly. But a short while before he had saved another woman from a similar death, one who had led such a life for months before being discovered. But I could not believe that this charming and compassionate woman, this wife and mother, was capable of prolonged deceit. It must surely have been a sudden lapse, one incredible act of folly in an otherwise blameless life?

Whatever the reason for her downfall, there was no hope for her. Josue could not save her. He was long gone out of the capital, to some other part of Judea, and I had not possessed the strength to follow him. Nothing could save her now. Already the elders and the witnesses, followed by a great crowd, were dragging her "by the neck of her robe" as the Law decreed, through the upper town and out through the gate overlooking the ravine which bounded the city walls.

My heart was thudding with a dreadful fear as, with no thought but that I must be with her, I turned and ran up and down through the stepped streets, on and on, until I reached the upper quarter of Sion, already thronged with people. My breath came in labored gasps as, pushing wildly through them, I staggered on and finally reached the gate. For a few moments I leaned there, recovering, before pushing through the massing throng of men who crowded the cliff top, ignoring their insults and curses, for I was well accustomed to such things. But one of them, the worse for early drinking, suddenly cried out, "See, the Magdalene woman is with us again!"

And, catching my arm, he dragged me forward and thrust me beside the condemned woman, who stood with her back to the crowd. She looked out over the ravine to the olives massed on the slopes beyond, seemingly oblivious to the tumult behind, but as I almost fell against her, she gasped and spun around fearfully.

"See here," said the drunken man to her, "this is how you might have ended your days. Is she not a glorious sight?" he said, indicating my haggard, sallow features and unkempt appearance. "Thank God, woman, that you're dying a wealthy adultress and not a whore like this one."

And, pulling her shoulder, he twisted her around toward me. She looked up, white-faced, and for a moment our eyes met. I could see that behind the awful fear in them she recognized me. Then an elder, gathering his skirts about him as he passed my unclean presence, ordered the man away. As the throng surged forward I glimpsed my benefactor, huddled on the ground, turning a piteous look to the chief witness—her husband—who could have saved her if he wished, for the ultimate decision was his. But, stooping, he picked up a small rock and, with a token gesture, cast it into the ravine. Then, ignoring his wife, he turned and walked back through the gate and vanished into the city.

If only she had divulged the man's name (for he had escaped before they could take him), then her husband might have pardoned her. But this she had refused to do, for then he, too, would die. Her protection of this miserable wretch had cost her her life. Perhaps her husband wished to spare her. Doubtless his pride was hurt at her refusal. Afterward he may have bitterly regretted his action. I do not know. But surely he could not easily forget her? I could not read his face or his thoughts as he passed me at the gate. Then I, too, turned and ran.

Blindly and with no thought but to be as far as possible from the ravine, I ran down into the city again, out through one of the lower gates and down into the suburbs until I came at last to a panting halt among a grove of olive trees deep in the Kidron Valley.

That lovely, laughing woman who had passed through the bazaar with her two children, greeting and being greeted everywhere—already she was dead or dying. Such thoughts brought me weeping to my knees in grief. Exhausted, I lay motionless through the noonday heat, then, unwittingly, fell asleep.

When I opened my eyes again, it was almost night. Although I was cold and stiff, I felt reluctant to move, but there was naught else to do but stumble back into the city. Darkness had fallen. As I emerged from the trees, the vast bulk of the Temple loomed above me. With all my heart I longed to enter its gates and offer sacrifice for that woman—an oblation—but I knew I could never cross its threshold again. Such was my agony of mind, however, that I lingered there, filled with the knowledge of my own guilt compared to hers—yet she was dead while I lived on. Standing in the shadow of the Temple walls, I murmured the old prayers of my childhood—that her transgression might be erased by the terrible death she had suffered.

". . . Do not leave her soul among the dead . . ."

Then I shuddered as a vision of Sheol rose up in my mind—utter darkness, utter silence—and I, too, destined there. Could

I also pray for myself? It seemed impossible, for my head was throbbing again as, utterly spent, I sank down, murmuring mechanically,

> My guilt towers higher than my head,
>   It is a weight too heavy to bear—
> I am bowed and brought to my knees,
>   I go mourning all the day long . . .

Ah, my head! Would it never cease?

> I am like a deaf man who cannot hear . . .

Deaf indeed with this infernal noise. I must move away from the Temple. Feeling too broken to remain alone, I turned my steps toward the Antonia, for the night was cold and I knew the guards would have the brazier burning until the dawn watch. The usual man was on duty when I arrived. He ignored me, for which I was thankful. Sinking down before the brazier, I let my grief overwhelm me again, oblivious to everything for a while. Then suddenly I became aware of someone standing beside me and, looking up, I recognized the centurion, who had just completed his round of inspection. Not wishing that the guard should be censured for my presence, I hastily rose, but he signed me to remain. After a few moments he asked, "Why are you weeping?"

And as I remained silent, "You are very unhappy," he stated simply.

I did not mean to answer him, but I felt so burdened with misery that I heard myself say, "A woman was stoned here this morning. I knew her. She was good to me. Her husband could have saved her, but he refused. Now she is dead—for one lapse in her life—and I am alive who offends each day. I saw her face," I whispered, "before they killed her."

And the glowing brazier blurred as my weeping blinded me again.

There was a pause, and then the centurion said, "If it will comfort you—she died quickly. Her spine was broken when they cast her over the cliff. I understand that is the reason for throwing the condemned person backward. There is much mercy in your Law. My men were on duty at the gate and saw it all, for some came forward to control the crowds. She was dead before the first stone touched her."

For this I was thankful. I sat with bowed head, not noticing that he had left me, and only the sound of his sandaled feet returning made me look up in surprise. Silently I took the cup he proffered, too bemused to wonder at the gesture or the fact of his tolerating my presence and speaking to me as he had. The wine was hot and spiced, and I was grateful for it. After a while I felt strong enough to return to my room in the lower quarter of the city.

As I placed my cup on the ground, he said quietly, "I was listening to a remarkable man recently. He is gone now from Jerusalem, but the more I hear of him, the more I am impressed. Your people should be proud of having such a prophet among them."

I knew whom he meant, of course. He was not the first Roman to speak of Josue, but the first I had ever heard refer to him in tones of approbation, even of respect. I do not know what made me suddenly speak as I did. Perhaps his overt sympathy, my own misery or just the mention of a familiar name prompted me to say, "This man you speak of—he comes from Nazareth, near my own birthplace in Galilee."

He nodded. "I have already judged your home by your accent."

And as I smiled wanly, he said, "I know the district well. Before I was transferred I spent many months stationed over the border in Syria with my troops—mainly Gauls and Spaniards—and visited most of Galilee. Now I command the Samaritan auxiliaries here, but it is a barren place compared to your wooded countryside."

A wave of nostalgia broke over me as my inner eye conjured up the Waters of Merom, that quiet lagoon where the pigeons crooned contentedly from the green heart of the gall oak forests—"Abraham's oaks," we called them; where the herons sailed clumsily over the red and green of the bean fields; where the oleanders bloomed luxuriously, and mimosa and jasmine scented the air. Jordan! Jordan! Must I never see your northern banks again?

"You may find this hard to believe," I continued hastily to block out the loveliness that nearly broke my heart, "but our family knew his for years. He and my brother were always friends, as were his father and mine. And what he says is the truth. I know myself that he is no liar or charlatan."

Silence. Then he replied, "That is even more remarkable. I should like to hear all that you know of him—if you will tell me."

I made no answer, for I did not know if he was speaking sincerely. He was, after all, a Roman. But he did not press me further, only remarking as I rose, "That is enough for tonight. You are weary and I must return to my duties. Already it is the midnight watch."

I was fatigued and my head reverberated but, nevertheless, I found it hard to leave. Already I felt a vague undercurrent of warmth that he had asked me to return. And to speak of Josue was always a joy.

So for the next three weeks we continued our strange rendezvous—strange in that I could not understand why Cornelius deigned to converse with me of all creatures or why Josue, an Israelite, held such fascination for this Roman officer. But I did not wonder long. It was enough that I had found a friend. For the sake of these brief talks, I lingered on in

179

Jerusalem long after my usual sojourn in the capital. Soon I had told him not only all I knew of Josue, to which he listened intently, but also a little of my own home life before everything had altered for me. He never asked how I had arrived at my present state, and I never enlightened him about it or of my mental burden, which was daily oppressing me and growing worse. They made my conversations with Cornelius a torture, which I hoped he would not notice. This new-found friendship was too precious to surrender without a struggle. It seemed that I would be given neither rest nor peace until I ceased my visits to the Antonia and returned to my old nomadic existence, for, all the time, Cornelius was weaning me away from the streets with gifts of money, and chiding gently, "What would your old friend, Josue, say to see you thus?" Constantly he urged me to go to him. "I cannot believe that he would turn you away."

But I did not dare tell him that I had tried and failed to reach Josue. How could I say that I simply could not get near him— that I was not *allowed* to approach him! He would think me mad—perhaps I was—and I would lose his friendship. So I remained silent.

"I do not understand," he said at last. "You know he is the one person who can help you. He may have some influence with your brother, and you might be able to return to your home again."

But I simply shook my head speechlessly.

He, hoping to give me the courage he presumed I lacked to approach Josue, asked suddenly, "Do you know what he said of you?"

"Of me!" I looked up, startled and alarmed.

"That the harlots would be entering his kingdom before the Pharisees, those meticulous upholders of your Law."

I looked down again. I could not believe it. It made no sense. Cornelius must be mocking me. Feeling a momentary hurt, I rose quickly, and he watched me go without a word.

For several days after this I lay ill in my room with a return of my old fever, and but for the money given me by Cornelius, I could not have paid the rent. I felt remorse that I had left him so abruptly, and determined to visit the Antonia the next evening, for I was fearful of losing my only friend.

Fortunately I arrived as Cornelius was completing his round of inspection. Seeing me hovering in the shadows, he beckoned me over to the fire.

"Forgive me for not coming recently," I burst out anxiously, "but I have been ill. I hope you did not think I had left Jerusalem?"

"No," he replied, "I did not." Then, "You are well now?"

"Yes," I lied.

An uneasy silence, then he said abruptly, "I have received new orders today. I and several other officers have been recalled to Rome. Replacements will be arriving within a few days, and then we shall leave Jerusalem."

I was aware of nothing but black misery. Even the tumult in my head had ceased. There was no need for them. They had won again. My small cup of comfort was dashed from my lips after the first few drops. It was always the same when I found a friend. Somehow he was taken from me. It had happened before several times.

"Will you be back?" I asked dully.

"Yes, but not for a year at least, possibly two. My father-in-law has some influence with my superiors and I may be given new duties in my own country. Besides, my little son will forget me unless I return to Mantua this summer, for he is but four years old and the light of my eyes. His mother is dead and I hope to find him a new one, for he is too much with nurses, and that is not good training for a future general."

Seeing no answering smile, he changed the subject. "But I

shall continue to receive news of your countryman, Josue. Perhaps one day his teaching will reach Rome." He added somberly, "By the time I return he will either be King of Israel or dead."

I could think of nothing to say but, "You have been good to me and I thank you."

Leaning forward, he said earnestly, "Find your friend, Josue. He *will* help you—I know it."

And to please him I replied, "I will try and go to him."

He nodded and, rising, threw back the short scarlet cloak from his shoulders and donned the plumed helmet. "I will pray for you that you might be given the strength you need."

Strength! If only he knew what I endured night and day with my physical weakness and my mental burden!

"Do!" I replied, suddenly bitter at his going and my own helplessness. "Your gods are kinder and will listen to you."

"I was not referring to those entities," he said quietly. "I was speaking of the one true God—the God of your fathers, Abraham, Isaac and Jacob. Do not stop believing in his mercy."

Nonplussed, I remained silent as he continued, "I could give you money, but I hope its very lack will spur you on to seek out Josue, for I know your reluctance to return to your old life after such a lapse—and you are still unwell."

I had hoped to detain him awhile longer, but I could not think how to answer him. From high on the watchtower came the cry of the sentinels in the gathering darkness. All, apparently, was well.

"I earnestly entreat you to go to your friend and not lose heart. Remember his words—when has he ever turned someone away?"

Suddenly I longed to tell him everything and implore him to take me to Josue himself. Why had I not thought of that before?

He would protect me. But already he was standing before me, his cuirass gleaming in the firelight.

"Farewell," he said, not prolonging his departure. "I will often pray for you."

Turning, he walked briskly away with erect military bearing and vanished under the great gateway.

"I shall miss you," I had said. Miss! I thought my heart would break.

"I, too, shall miss our talks," he had replied.

Only our talks. He would not miss me.

I trudged back across the worn flags of the deserted court-yard. Once I was in my room again, despair seized me. How was it that I poisoned everything I touched? Nothing went well for me. Every friendship was doomed, for before it began it ended. Sitting there in the darkness, too dispirited even to light my lamp, I knew suddenly and overwhelmingly that I loved Cornelius—the only man to offer me friendship, compassion and understanding. Oh, why had he entered my life only to be taken from me? We had talked of Josue and that was our main bond, but he had heartened me in other ways—not only by giving me food and money, but through his courteous treatment I had regained a remnant of the self-respect I had lost years ago. In speaking of Josue and his greatness, he reminded me of my own heritage. "You should be proud," he said, "to be an Israelite woman living at this hour." I, who had never regarded myself as aught but an outcast from my own people. Lastly he told me of his home, his son; he had involved me in his life and made me yearn for the same. He said he might return, but when? And where would I be then?

I rose and went over to light the lamp. How could I go back to the streets after this interlude? But I must. I had no energy to be bitter, but a deep sadness overwhelmed me.

"Cornelius," I whispered then, moaning in my grief. "Cornelius! Cornelius!"

A sudden whispering around me. Jubilant whispers emanating from the shadows and converging upon me. A soft laugh. The room was full of horror, and in my weakened state I could not bear it. Panic-stricken, I jumped up and whirled to the door, knocking against the chest in my haste. The oil engulfed the wick and extinguished the feeble lamp, leaving me in darkness. Overcome with fear and the weakness engendered by fever, I sank fainting to the floor.

For three days I lay huddled in my room, with only sufficient strength to collect a little water each evening after sunset. But on the third morning the landlord came up at daybreak and, straddling the doorway, uttered the grim question, "You owe me rent. When do you propose paying?"

"As soon as I'm well," I whispered. "Only give me a little more time."

He gazed at me for a moment and then pronounced, "You're finished. You'll never earn another drachma."

Striding into the room, he went over to my small bundle of possessions and systematically rifled through it, extracting a bracelet of my mother's, ivory combs and other small trinkets, which he wrapped in my good shawl. Rising, I tried weakly to stop him, but he thrust me aside, saying, "I'm taking these in lieu of rent. When I return from serving my customers, I expect to find this room empty."

And he strode out and down the stairs.

There was no redress, for I had only received justice, albeit untempered with mercy. All I had now were the clothes I wore and a tiny bundle of oddments hidden beneath my pallet, and the handful of asses and other small coins Cornelius had given me days ago. These I would use for my journey north for, faced with this man's ultimatum, I suddenly knew what I would do. I resolved to abandon my way of life. I would never walk the streets again. I *could* not after such a lapse. Without money, I should soon be starving, but by the time my coins were spent, I should have reached Galilee—and there my journey ended. For I was weary of my life. I was tired of living. I was going home to die.

CHAPTER
· ELEVEN ·

IT WAS MIDSUMMER WHEN I finally left Samaritan country and wandered into Nain. I had returned to Galilee at last. All the way up north, my mental torment had increased daily and my bodily feebleness worsened until I was walking the last few miles in a fever of delirium. Somehow I made my way to the well, which was deserted at that time of day, and drank my fill of water. My last coin had been spent two days previously, but in my weakened state it seemed as if a week had passed since I ate a piece of bread or a handful of dates. As the day grew cooler, I wandered back into the town and made my bed in a corner of the empty bazaar among the rubbish and scurrying rats. I dozed fitfully through the night and awoke well after dawn, aching all over and sick with fever and hunger. My head, too, was still throbbing and buzzing.

Pushing back the weight of my hair—even my combs had been stolen—I surveyed my wretched state and touched the depths of despair. So this was to be my end. Sick and starving, I now knew that I would never reach Magdala or see Gennesaret again. Even Nazareth, just four miles away, was too much for me. I was to die here in Nain, for I would not break my resolve.

Money only brought me food and food served only to prolong my life.

But as the day progressed, fear set in. To choose to starve was nothing less than suicide, and perhaps I did not want to die just yet. But alive or dead, my life was hell. Oh, what was I to do? As the heat intensified, I wandered on through the crowded bazaar seeing everywhere the ugliness of life—the beggars and cripples, poor, maimed creatures with all manner of deformities, and children too, covered with running sores. Was death any worse?

I had thought that it would be easy to die, but it was not. My fever gave me a raging thirst, and passing the heaped pyramids of grapes and oranges and pomegranates was an added torture. It was useless. I *must* eat and drink. For the next hour or so, I tried to beg a few alms from the passers-by, but with no success, for they knew me for what I was. Perhaps if I could walk that far, the houses of the wealthier residents beyond the center of the town would yield something. There might be food thrown out for the beggars or fruit trees in the gardens from which I would be allowed to take a handful. I had nothing to lose by trying, and I would find it easier to die if I could only eat something first.

With my head reeling and buzzing, I turned off the main street and dragged myself to the outskirts of town, where the wealthier folk—merchants and suchlike—had their homes. I walked slowly past them until I saw one house, built in the Roman style, that was obviously being used as a meeting place for a large gathering. The owner was a Pharisee, Simon by name, and well known for his patronage of new people and new ideas and for being lavish in entertainment. Indeed, as I approached the house, a meal was already in progress in the great room lying open to the garden, and I could see the long, low tables spread with meat and fruits and wine. Standing there in the blazing heat, I almost sickened at the sight, but I forced myself to go forward. I *must* eat—and there might be someone among the guests to throw me a few alms, if only to be rid of me. It was my only hope and a slender one. The buzzing in my head became a hideous inferno of noise as I followed the side path around the garden, trembling at my coming ordeal, for I now had nothing but my pitiable state to recommend me. My dragging feet felt weighted with lead as I fearfully crossed the cool shade of the pillared terrace and stepped down into the room.

Galilee, like Judea, is a small place, and one soon hears of the famous in it—and the infamous. Magdala knew me. So also did Bethsaida, Caphernaum, Cana, Sepphoris and Nazareth. But not one of these places had seen me, for I never dared venture too near my old home. This house in Nain had not seen me before, but it knew of me. My name had already gone ahead and paved the way for my reception. The conversation faltered and died away; a low murmur of surprise; a whispering; and then—more damning than any spoken insult—utter silence. My degradation was now complete.

Shaking, and with my face burning, I stood with bowed head, seeing only the patterned tiles of the floor through the veiling screen of my hair. The tumult in my head was unbearable now—an unceasing clamor—as I waited for someone to acknowledge me, to see my pitiable condition and give me food or a little money. No Pharisee would be seen publicly refusing alms to a beggar, which was the state in which I now appeared before them. I did not wish to embarrass him. If he would but toss me a few coins, I would leave.

Clutching my bundle and swaying with exhaustion, I raised my head again. The room swam mistily about me and the faces blurred as I looked around. Although I could scarcely see, I could already feel the tide of hostility creeping across the floor to lap about my feet. It was hopeless. In their eyes I was but one thing, and that I should always be so long as memory remained in them. I could not also qualify as a beggar. Better to go now than be forcibly removed.

Wearily, and wondering if I had the strength left to do so, I turned away and moved toward the step, my body bowed with the physical anguish of my mental burden. Suddenly, it stopped. All was peace and I could hear a bird fluting outside in the garden, the chink of a plate as a guest recommenced the meal I had interrupted. I put my hand against the pillar to help myself mount the shallow step and, suddenly, the thought came into my tormented mind: Why had those whispering voices, that hellish noise ceased now? The only time they left me in peace was when I felt utter despair, but if ever I resolved to relinquish my wanderings, return to Bethany and beg to be taken back, then they tormented me until I circled the village and went away.

Once when I tried to obtain some employment as a servant, they prevented me from speaking and I could not hear the innkeeper's wife for the noise they made, so she turned me away. "Are you deaf as well as dumb, woman," she asked, "that you don't answer me?" I had hoped so much that I might be allowed to live decently; I would clean dishes, sweep floors—anything—in return for food and a place to sleep. I had hoped, too, that word of this would reach Lazarus, and, seeing that I had abandoned my old life, he might allow me near them again. But having spent what little money I possessed to buy cloth for a new tunic so that I might appear respectably dressed before the innkeeper's wife, I was then left with not a single coin for food.

I could not escape the voices, however hard I tried. I was a prisoner in their power, with no hope of freedom. Each Passover I stood outside the Temple gates longing to go up into the Court of Women to receive the high priest's blessing—but I could not. Each sabbath I lit the candles and tried to pray again, but they forced me up from my knees, and the flames threw

190

shadows that frightened me, so I went out to seek company that I might not be alone. Then, the cruelest blow, they rejoiced when Cornelius was recalled to Rome. They knew he was my friend and they did not wish me to have any but themselves for company.

Cornelius! The name went through me like a dart, making me moan in misery, all my love and grief welling up anew. They did not want me to love anyone. I was only left in peace so long as I abandoned the places and the people I knew were good and worthy of being loved, as well as the prayers that brought me closer to them.

Someone must be here whom they did not want me to see—someone good—or they would not torment me until I yielded and turned to go and only then give me peace. I knew only one such person to be in Galilee. Was he here in Nain—in this house? If this were so, then they were driving me away from a man whose every word I knew to be the essence of truth. If all he preached was a lie, they would not block my way to him; they would leave me in peace as they had in the past, when men lied to me and I had believed them.

Peace! A *false* peace! A *lying* peace! The thought flashed in my mind like lightning and in one exultant moment I glimpsed, recognized, then finally grasped that at last I had the measure of what had possessed me all these years. They *wanted* to see me wretched, for misery rejoices to see others in like condition; it eases their own private hell. They hated the truth, for truth was alien to them; they were liars from the father of lies himself, and like all persecutors, they were cowards also. God in heaven! Why had I not seen this before! They were not only angry when I tried to defy them—they were *afraid!*

Weak and starving, filthy and degraded though I was, yet, for the first time in years, my spirit, which had almost guttered out, flickered into life. Death awaited me outside in the street, and in the voices' hateful zeal to bring me, in utter despair, to that end, they revealed their weakness, for now I had nothing to lose by defying them. If they had not brought me so low, I should never have had the courage to turn at bay and fight them. Now that I knew them for what they were, my knowledge gave me strength to lift my will against theirs and make my last bid to escape. That was what had terrified, cowed and chained me to them all these years—the weight of their persecution, the horror of their malignant hatred and my ignorance of the kind of beings from whom it emanated. It was as though I had looked into the depths of their minds and seen reflected there the unplumbed well of misery that was almost my own. But only once had I hated as they did, and even that I set aside long ago. But they had not. They had not forgotten. Their hatred embraced everyone and everything.

Why did they oppose so overwhelmingly my love for those once dear to me? The answer exploded like a sunburst in my mind. *Because love—even such love as mine—could overcome them! Love vanquished them utterly!*

Now my path lay clear before me. If that was the meaning, then I would go on loving—because they could not bear it. It weakened them and strengthened me. I would never stop loving. I would go to my grave loving—but I was not going to die; not yet. I was going to fight them and wrestle back my soul with the only weapons I had and which they could not match— love and truth. Martha, Lazarus and Cornelius—I would not relinquish them or cease loving them. And as the voices retreated from truth, so I would seek after truth and follow those who preached it—and, as yet, there was but one man doing this—Josue.

Josue! The name, like a magnet, dragged my head to look back over my shoulder and, from far across the room, his eyes looked straight back into mine. At that moment I not only believed, I knew with inner certainty who he was. Our Messiah has come, I repeated to myself with utter conviction as I turned and faced the assembly again.

Such a medley of thoughts passed through my mind in those few moments as I stood at the foot of the stairs. In the past I had not minded so much that Josue knew of me, so long as I did not have to *see* him face to face. Then, strangely, the reverse occurred, and for months now I had been trying to get near him, only to be deflected by an inner assault far worse than physical blows, which had cowed me utterly. Now, by some strange coincidence I found myself in the same room with him, meeting him again after a lapse of years that had wrought such changes in both of us—for him all gain and for me, all loss.

Even as I thought this, all the memories of those early days rushed back: walking by the lakeside with the breeze rustling through the olives and lifting the vines; the flowers covering the hillsides each spring reminding us to make ready for Passover, going with Martha to gather the crocuses to make saffron dye for our new tunics; the wet earth, so fragrant after the latter rains; sunshine glinting on the water and the little boats rocking gently on the swell; the rough accents of the fishermen as they mended their nets in the shelter of the rocks, and the bare, brown feet splashing in the shallows; the *hazzan*'s goats nudging up the hill and through the narrow streets; our old home with the evening shadows lengthening across its walls and mother's voice calling me through the sabbath evening as the sunset flushed the hills, dyed the tamarisks a deeper pink and turned Gennesaret to a lake of gold. All dear things past and gone. All innocent joys lost, never prized until taken from me.

I felt no bitterness, only a deep sadness—but a sadness not untinged with hope. For he who had loved and shared the same way of life would give me back a part of what I had lost. In this same town he had given back a son to a widowed mother—a son who was dead. Then he would surely give back to me the peace of soul for which I longed. He *could* do it, I knew, and this thought alone made a little spring of joy bubble up inside me. I did not know what it was, for I had long forgotten how happiness felt, but balm poured over wounds could not be more healing. Despair melted as hope increased and strengthened like the first notes of our joyful songs I had sung years ago of the ascent going up to Jerusalem—weak notes as yet, for they had not been sung now for a long time . . .

Coming back from my reverie, I found my eyes still fastened to his. The whole room waited. He was watching me—willing me to fight—willing me to go over to him—and I must if I was to be safe. Even now *they* were with me, silent so long as I hovered uncertainly on the step, silent while they awaited my retreat from the room. Many times before I had feebly attempted to defy them and been overcome, but now, instead of advancing with defeat already writ large upon me, I must make my first (and last) positive effort to overcome them with the knowledge I now possessed. But my physical strength had long since ebbed away, and I had nothing now to aid me but my faith in the healing help of the man who sat so far away on the other side of the room. He alone could help me to be rid of my persecutors. For years I had not been able to pray for more than a few moments, but now I knew that my belief in its efficacy was the one thing that would take me to my goal, the one thing that would block out the voices. Feebly I clasped my hands and only I (and they) heard the whispered plea that issued from my lips as I began to pray—

> God of hosts, bring me back;
> Let your face shine on me and I shall be saved . . .

Immediately, as though totally unprepared for such a response from one "in extremis," the voices rose like a scream of rage, unsurpassed in vehemence, and something almost like a physical blow struck me between the shoulders and toppled me, gasping, from the step down into the room again. Strange that this last hateful gesture was my blessing, for they unwittingly started me on my journey across the room—away from them.

It was like wading through deep water. My feet were leaden, as though I walked in a dream; the room was blurred and I could hardly see. I could only fix my eyes on the spot where I knew Josue to be and stumble in that direction.

Somehow, although I was physically impeded, I came to the first table, and already my head was a trough of anguish and noise. The old familiar panic flew into my breast as the hammers started beating in my brain. It was worse than being locked inside a bell tower. They knew how I hated noise and would drive me mad with it until I accepted the "peace" they offered. My head was jarring and reeling, and there was a roaring in my ears. Beneath my feet the floor seemed to be undulating. It was as though I looked down through moving water at the sea bed. It was getting deeper and deeper—no wonder I could hardly walk—and I felt suddenly suffocated with fear. I could not do it; I must move back to the safety of the steps. I felt myself sinking; I could not breathe anymore—I was drowning in it; and from the depths of the mortal fear that enveloped me, I choked out my last supplication—

> Save me, O God,
> for the waters have risen to my neck.
> I have sunk into the mud of the deep
> and there is no foothold.
> I have entered the waters of the deep
> and the waves overwhelm me.

The old words were coming back to me, reprieving me a little. Oh, let me keep on . . . don't let me forget . . . not now . . .

> I am wearied with all my crying,
> my throat is parched.
> My eyes are wasted away
> from looking for my God.

To the onlookers, I was simply an outcast woman wearily crossing the floor, step by step. They could not know the inward battle as, inch by inch, almost deaf and sightless, I fought my way through the enemy's ground to safety, murmuring disjointedly—

Those who attack me with lies
Are too much for my strength . . .
O God, you know my sinful folly;
My sins you can see.

The floor was steadying, but I was not yet halfway there. I must not stop for an instant. They must not find a chink in my mind through which to penetrate . . .

I suffer taunts. Shame covers my face.
I have become a stranger to my brother,
An alien to my own mother's son.
They make me a byword—the gossip of men at the gates,
The subject of drunkards' songs.

I was passing through the assembled guests and they were still following me, trying to get back in. Help me keep them out . . . I must not let them gain possession once more . . .

This is my prayer to you,
In your great love, answer me, O God,
With your help that never fails . . .
Save me from my foes . . .

They were near me again, blocking my path, and the old, sickening sensation flooded over me as I tried frantically to reassure myself. I was *not* drowning. I was *not* suffocating. It was all deceit . . .

Lord, answer, for your love is kind;
in your compassion, turn toward me.
Do not hide your face from your servant.

Lurching forward a few more steps, I cried once more in panic—

> Answer quickly for I am in distress.
> Come close to my soul and redeem me;
> Ransom pressed by my foes . . .
> . . . I have reached the end of my strength . . .

The room was reshaping in front of my eyes, and my passage across the floor was easier. The inner tumult was fading and the external harrassment seemed further behind me now. They could no longer draw close enough. Their first and last mistake was to leave a vacuum in my mind, believing they had already won as I had turned to leave the room but a short while since. But in that brief interval I had filled their place with determined prayer, which crowded out the fear and weakness that allowed them such easy entrance. With my journey almost over, they could no longer stop me. My will was growing stronger, and I was determined not only to resist them but to vanquish them utterly. I would not just defend; I would attack. Cowards that they were, they could tell by my measured tread that they had finally lost, could hear by my whispered utterances that I no longer noticed them. I was drawing near to my goal now, and if they were to stay with me, then they too, must come closer. I suddenly knew with triumphant certainty that they dared neither follow me nor go before me to impede my progress—before *his* eyes, which I could clearly see still fastened upon me.

Then, all at once, I was moving freely and in utter silence across a solid floor, between the reclining figures, past tables laden with untouched food, past Simon the host and—a miracle—they were going, receding behind me. At the far end of the room, there was a buzzing like a cloud of flies, angered and entrapped, and then it faded out over the garden and vanished forever.

Slowly the realization of what had happened surfaced in my mind. Victory was given me. For years I thought that God had delivered me over to the Evil One, and, believing this, I had turned away in despair. Now I knew with compunction that He had never abandoned me or willed any such punishment. Josue's teaching alone had taught me something of this. I could have resisted this evil, which had led me away into Egypt, away from his healing influence, only renewing the attack when I returned with memories of Josue and his mother in my mind and longing to abandon my old life. I need not have surrendered, but my own fear, wretchedness and natural timidity had enslaved me to them for years. Why had I not remembered until now that "He does not treat us according to our sins nor repay us according to our faults"?

I had judged myself, not Him, and it was strange that this realization should come just as, passing the couches of Peter and John, I came at last to his and sank down exhausted before it. I had sought and fought to reach him for so many months, but now I could not utter a word. He must supply everything now, for I could do no more.

Slowly I opened my eyes. Sunbeams slanted across the floor, dappling the patterned tiles, and from the garden trees came the sound of bird song so sweet in the stillness that lapped around. Somehow it took me back to the old days in Galilee.

Dropping down through the silence came the familiar voice from those past years, "*Shalom-tekl-alekeim*—Peace be with you, Mary."

During all my years of wandering, I had been accosted in many ways, but no man had ever saluted me with the traditional greeting of our country, as one Israelite to another. But now, so gravely, so courteously, he wished me peace—the one thing I craved. By his words he acknowledged that he knew me. He greeted me as a friend. Such goodness broke my heart. I could not answer but, filled with gratitude, I raised my head and his full-eyed love simply looked me out of pain and I was healed at last.

Then, slowly, as my eyes took in his whole appearance, a sense of unease stole over me. There was something different . . . something wrong. . . . Suddenly I knew what it was.

Simon, his host, was a strict Pharisee and therefore insisted that each guest who entered his house carry out the cleansing ritual required before the commencement of the meal. But no one had attended to Josue. His hair was unkempt and the blue *tzitzith* on his *chalouk* were smothered with dust. From the marks on the *couffieh* which fell over his shoulders, I could see he had wiped his face and hands before eating, but as my bewildered gaze traveled to the end of the couch, my eyes fell finally on his feet, still covered with the dust and grit of the road.

Slowly the significance of these things filtered into my mind. In my country it is a great discourtesy to omit offering the traditional comforts and tributes to an invited guest—the kiss of welcome; the bathing of the head, hands and feet after the heat of the journey, even the gift of a clean tunic if one were required. No man would have dreamed of approaching a Pharisee's table without first receiving these ministrations from the servants waiting in the anteroom with water, oil, combs, brushes and towels. But no one had attended Josue. Knowing his host, I could now guess why.

The Pharisee's invitation was not out of kindness but curiosity, so that Josue might be used as a tidbit of gossip for future occasions. If he also provided diversion and amusement to the guests, then this would further add to Simon's overweening pride that his house was indeed the center of all the latest activities and current sensations. Such an invitation from a wealthy official to a carpenter-turned-preacher was sufficient patronage; let no one think that he took the Nazarene seriously! Hence the lack of any preliminary attentions as Josue entered the house, for these were obviously not required by a Galilean peasant who claimed that ritual cleanliness was not enough— not even essential! Then let him sit there in his own sweat and dust; it would keep him in his place among his superiors, and he would soon grow uncomfortable breaking his bread with blackened fingernails.

I looked down again, grieved beyond measure. I had deserved the abuse heaped on me over the years, but he did not— Josue, so homely and familiar, so gentle and courteous, treating all men alike. They despised him for the seeming weakness in his acceptance of such treatment; yet he seemed not to have noticed it. But I could not bear to see him so insulted or ignore this callous neglect. He was my friend, and they had not so much as washed his feet.

Strange, but this unkindness broke me. I lifted my hand to brush away the dust, but my tears arrived first, flowing silent and unchecked, and there was healing and cleansing in them for me. At last I grieved for someone other than myself. With my head pillowed on my arm, I knelt, weeping, beside the couch— and still he said nothing. Time passed while the assembled company watched—and still he said not a word. His very silence was consoling, bringing such balm in its wake and such solace that I would have sought sanctuary there forever.

But the other guests were already murmuring among themselves, and I knew I must not remain there any longer. I could not leave without giving some token of my gratitude, though, and a happy thought occurred to me.

Unwrapping the small bundle I carried, I took from it a rounded alabaster jar with a long, narrow neck. It had belonged to my mother, and I had filled it with a precious ointment bought in the bazaar at Jerusalem a year ago. It had comforted me to have it, but now, as I bethought how the money was earned to buy it, my tears flowed afresh, mingling with the ointment as I broke the neck and poured it out over his feet.

Why I did this I perceived only dimly at the time. They had omitted the courtesy of washing his feet; then I would supply it. Such a small token of love and consolation, and yet it was all I could offer. Into it went my sorrow at what I was and my hope of what I might yet become if he would help me. Kneeling beside the couch, I smoothed liquid coolness of the ointment over the sore and calloused feet, wiping off the grit and dust with a handful of my loosened hair and kissing well again each graze and bruise.

Suddenly Simon burst out with a stream of invectives. He could restrain himself no longer. Assenting voices rose from the surrounding tables now that the host had spoken. What was such a woman doing in his house, her unclean presence polluting his room? Everyone knew the Magdalene for what she was—everyone but the Galilean! If he was such a prophet, then he should have ordered the servants to take me out the instant I entered the room.

I had expected such words before—indeed, I deserved worse. As I retied my bundle, Josue motioned me to stay and then turned to Simon. To my utter amazement, I heard him defending me against the Pharisee—I, who had brought shame on him by openly claiming him as one I knew—Josue was defending me. In the silence which followed, I heard him tell some story of two debtors owing money that they could not repay. Their problems were resolved when their creditor remitted both debts in full.

"Who would feel more gratitude, Simon—the man who owed the larger or smaller sum?"

The Pharisee remarked with an ungracious shrug that it would be the former—"but that is obvious. I fail to see the relevance of your story, Rabbi. I am more concerned that this woman leave my house. She is an outrage to myself and my guests—a feeling which I fear you cannot share."

But Josue ignored this speech and, before the whole room,

openly rebuked his host for the deliberate omission of the customary courtesies shown everywhere to an invited guest. Instead, it was left to me to supply them. He condemned Simon's patronizing attitude and warned the whole company against judging others.

Crouched on the floor and, like the guests, scarcely believing what I heard, I trembled now for him and not myself. Thinking it might help if I went, I half-rose to leave, but rounding off his address, he turned finally to Simon again. ". . . and so I tell you, if great sins have been forgiven her, she has also greatly loved. He loves little who has little forgiven him."

Then, speaking directly to me, he said, "Your faith has saved you. Your sins are forgiven."

Until these words were uttered the guests had been silently digesting his fierce rebuke, but now there came a gasp of astonishment and a hubbub of outraged protest erupted around the tables. Who was he to forgive sins? Only God could do that! This was blasphemy of the worst kind. The man must be mad . . .

But Josue's words had already washed over me and I knew that they were true. Under the cover of the noise and argument, he leaned toward me and said, "Go to the widow's house and wait there for Lazarus. And go in peace."

So, ignored amid the general clamor, I went. Later, on Calvary, I was to learn how much it cost him to forgive me.

With all hunger and exhaustion temporarily forgotten, I went swiftly back into the town and made my way to the house of the widow whose son Josue had brought back from the dead. Strange, but I had no fear or apprehension of approaching her. He had told me to go there, so all would be well. The town was asleep in the blazing heat as I walked up to the doorway and peered inside. An old woman, white-haired and angular, glanced up from her meal and then, seeing my appearance, looked me slowly up and down. For an instant my courage wavered and I could only greet her in a whisper. Then, taking a deep breath to strengthen my voice, I said, "My name is Mary. The Rabbi Josue sent me to you. I am to stay here until my brother comes up from Judea to fetch me."

Without a single question or remark she nodded and, hobbling forward, took my arm as I stood there in the doorway. "My son was dead and now he is alive again," she announced with great satisfaction and drew me into the house. ⸺

It was years since I had been invited—nay, welcomed—into another woman's home, and I could hardly believe that such things were happening to me again. I sank down, marveling that everything was being resolved with no apparent effort at all on my part and looked wonderingly as the old woman thrust a piece of bread and a handful of dates at me saying, "Eat this while I prepare you some food. There is water over there in the gourd."

Later when the meal was ready, I fell upon it ravenously while she sat watching me, nodding and smiling. "You will see him tomorrow," she burst out suddenly as if unable to contain herself.

"Who?" I mumbled with my mouth full of vegetables and rice.

"My *son!*" she pronounced happily. "Tomorrow you will see him for yourself. But now," she said, taking the dish from me, "you will sleep."

And so I slept for the rest of that day and all through the night and into the noon of the next. When I awoke, I was greeted with a smile—yet another wonder. The sun was shining as I put on the clean tunic she had washed for me, but first we scrubbed off all the dust and dirt, all the tarnished paint on my face and the yellow dye that clung so obstinately to my palms. Finally the old woman plaited my hair under a fresh, white veil and then handed me a little mirror so I might view the result.

Peering into it, I saw my face so haggard, thin and world-weary; but ill health I could bear now that my soul sickness was taken from me. With that thought I suddenly heard myself laughing—laughing for joy that the Magdalene woman had vanished forever and soon I would be Mary of Bethany. I did not doubt it. Then my laughter turned to tears, so the woman gave me bread and fruit and sent me out to the garden, saying that I must look well for my brother. I ate my meal wandering outside in the sunlight, delighting in a commonplace flowering cactus and the gaudy scarlet hibiscus. By the time I returned to the house, I felt as though I had climbed up from a pit and was at last living and communicating on the same level with others.

Later that day I met the son of the household, who had been out laboring in the fields beyond Nain. I felt a little apprehensive of my reception, but on being told who had sent me to them, he greeted me and then went about his own tasks. During my stay there, he kept his own counsel, and neither of us asked questions of the other. I was content, for his silence bespoke no contempt of my presence in his home. This in itself was another miracle—no one seemed curious about me at all. Nevertheless, this did not prevent my wondering how Lazarus had received the message to fetch me. Would he come? Then I chided myself. How could I doubt it?

Then, about a week later, the old woman hobbled in from collecting the water and announced, "Your brother is here in the town, enquiring for the widow's house. It won't take him long to find it," she said, and chuckled. "It's the best-known house in Nain."

Despite my faith in Josue, my heart gave a bound of fear. Yet why would Lazarus come all this way if not to forgive me? Trembling, for I had not seen my brother for several years, I waited in the room while the woman deposited the water and went out again. Time passed, and then I heard the familiar voice in the garden, and the old woman replying. Then Lazarus stood in the doorway, older and thinner but the same as ever.

For a few moments he looked at me, taking in my altered appearance. Then he said at last, "Little sister, come home."

And so I went home with my brother. Home.

A few days later we reached the outskirts of Bethany. It was early evening and the women were returning from the spring. A short, sturdy figure was the last to climb the wet steps and toil up the street, and my heart leapt. Unknown to both of us, Martha had been keeping watch on the rooftop most of the day and had only left her post to collect the water. Now, feeling both eager and timid, I left my brother's side and hurried forward to the foot of the hill.

"Martha," I called softly.

My sister turned and saw Lazarus waving from the distance, and then me standing like a statue in the middle of the road. One moment she was above clutching the pitcher and the next it came bouncing down the hill, scattering the water and finally smashing into pieces beside me. Fast behind came my sister, and the next instant I was in her arms, being crooned over as though I were a child again. Such a welcome was beyond what I deserved, and my tears welled up afresh as we clung together in the middle of the road. Again, as with Lazarus, not a word of reproach except concern that I looked so tired and ill—and she looking older and more work-worn than ever. What they had endured because of me!

But there was no time to brood over this dark thought. It was a happy trio that wandered back into Bethany that evening. Uncle was not effusive in his welcome—I could not expect it— but he was courteous, asking me to look upon his house as my home, for that was what Josue had wished. Whether it was as uncle wished I never knew, but I was grateful to him for his forbearance.

Two or three days later it was as though I had always lived

there. Again and again I marveled at how everything had been resolved so quietly and naturally for me. Once more I was leading a normal, domestic life, and I could scarcely believe it.

But Lazarus enlightened me one day by saying, "You believed that Josue would arrange everything for you—and faith *makes* things happen."

Whether this was true or not I could not tell, but I felt I could bear anything now that I was back with my family once more. There was plenty of gossip, of course, and several people completely ostracized us, but there was no active hostility, and after the marvel of my "conversion," Bethany returned to normal. It was right that I should suffer, but I was grieved for Martha and Lazarus.

On the first sabbath of my return, we sat down together and I told them of my lost years away from them. All the misunderstandings on both sides were accounted for, and then we never spoke of it again. My brother said it was useless to look back with bitterness and regret. The past was irrevocable. But we were united again and that was all that mattered.

Martha nodded emphatically, adding, "When the message arrived that you were coming home . . . Well! It seemed . . . it seemed . . ."

"Like a dream!" Lazarus sang the line from the psalm and we all laughed, which ended, as had all recent laughter, with my weeping. I wept when Martha asked me to make the bread—so natural a request, as though I had been gone but awhile—and laughed through my tears when Lazarus chided me for not mending the rent in his cloak. It was years since I had been scolded. Time after time I realized afresh my brother and sister's goodness, but they would not hear of such sentiments. I could only say a heartfelt, "It *is* so good to be home again!"

"Amen to that!" confirmed Lazarus, and so another chapter in my life closed and the next began.

*   *   *

For many months now the lives of my family had been filled by Josue, whom they were firmly convinced had a God-given mission. During the journey down to Bethany, Lazarus had related to me what I had not known of Josue's sudden emergence into public life, the disturbing effect he had on people and the hostility he aroused among the religious authorities. No man had ever spoken as he. He knew what he was saying, and he neither argued nor speculated. He stated facts—astonishing facts—and said we must believe them. If we rejected his message, then the onus must be borne by ourselves.

It was strange that, despite this uncompromising attitude and our own lack of understanding, our belief in him was not diminished but heightened. He somehow filled our minds until there was room for nothing else. How this happened I do not know, but it is sufficient to say that he had traveled far in our estimation from the Josue of old, whom we respected for his learning and loved as a friend. We called him *Rabboni* to acknowledge his grasp of the Law and his mastery of all its facets, but in our hearts we knew he was also the Christ whom Peter had been inspired to recognize and proclaim—the Messiah for whom we had waited centuries, the Holy One of Israel who would restore us to our former greatness.

CHAPTER
• TWELVE •

H OW PROVIDENTIAL IT WAS that we lived in Judea, for Josue, preaching in Jerusalem and throughout the province, became a frequent guest at our uncle's house. I recall so well a visit he made at the time of the Feast of Tabernacles. It was a golden autumnal morning, and we were sitting outside preparing the vegetables when suddenly the familiar voice greeted us. Looking up, we saw him standing by the gap in the hedge. Immediately a great flurry ensued as my delighted sister rushed to bring towels and water, while Josue came and sat down under the canopy of green boughs that Lazarus had erected in honor of the feast.

"What think you of that bench?" queried Martha as she brought out a cooling sherbet drink. "Lazarus made it during the summer."

Josue obligingly stood up and, casting the appraising eye of a fellow craftsman over it, nodded and resumed his seat. We three chatted awhile, exchanging our news, then Martha hurried within to prepare the meal. I continued chopping beans while the talk veered around to Josue's work and all it meant to him. It was not a conversation but a monologue, for I could only listen and try to understand. Strive as I would, I failed to gain a clear idea of his objectives. The whole picture seemed veiled to me and only the odd facet was revealed, focused on and then put aside. I *should* have understood more, for Josue couched his talk in the simplest terms and rendered it even more acceptable with his homely accent of the north—the slurred vowels of the Galilean. But then, I was very ignorant. Yet he said these things not to Lazarus or my elder sister but to me as the pigeons pecked and strutted out in the sunlight. Even the distant rattling of stew pots blended into the background. Not surprisingly, we were both startled when Martha's red, perspiring face looked around the canopy at us.

"Mary, for shame!" my sister cried in exasperation. "You've not even finished the beans yet and I need them now if I'm to—"

"Oh, Martha! Martha!" Josue broke in with mingled affection and amusement. "*So* busy about so *many* things—and in this heat too! Come and sit with us instead. Mary is right to keep me company when I'm here so short a time." Stooping, he picked up my bowl of vegetables. "Add some rice to this and there's enough for all."

My sister looked aghast. "Just rice and beans—on a *feast!*"

Josue smiled. "The feasts are for you to enjoy, Martha—a celebration, not a penance. Yom Kippur is over. One dish will serve as well as ten, so lend us your company for a while—and give yourself a little recreation, too. Come, Martha," he said, using our local expression, "Come and sit under your own fig tree and vine."

My sister laughed and, plumping down beside me, sighed with relief. "Well, it *is* good to leave that fire for a while," she said, sifting through the lentils as she spoke. "I know it's wrong, but a feast always means food to me. Once Tabernacles and the Dedication are over, I can be easy for a while, but it seems no length at all before Purim's upon us and the Feast of Weeks.

Then in the twinkling of an eye there's the *shalosh regalim*—Passover, Pentecost and Yom Kippur—here before I know it! Still," she chattered on, "it's pleasant to sit down with one's friends to a good meal. Now let me not interrupt your talk. You know how I run on. I was saying to Mary but yesterday that I really must learn to—"

Breaking off in mid-sentence, Martha suddenly screamed with horror and we both started. "The water for the rice! It will have boiled away to nothing! There'll be no bottom left to the pot!" Throwing aside the bowl, she went running back to the house.

Laughing, I set about retrieving the lentils. "Dear Martha," I said.

"Yes," answered Josue.

Later that day we went down with him to the outskirts of the village, where Lazarus awaited him with Matthew and some of the other disciples. The olive groves and vineyards were stripped of their fruits, and now children played around the huts and tents that had been built all over the countryside during the week of celebrations.

"They know nothing yet of the meaning behind the feast," my sister observed, "only that the harvests are in and it's time for play. Thank God they'll never spend a lifetime wandering homeless in the desert. Ah," she said, breathing in the air, "can't you almost smell the rains coming?"

Then her mind swung away to another topic. "We mustn't miss the processions tonight, Mary—or the torch dance in the Court of Women," and, clapping her hands, she sang the rhythmic refrain.

> Here our fathers adored the sun,
> But we turn our eyes to the one, true God.

"Lazarus," she appealed to my brother, "you've remembered

your promise to take us up tonight? I love to hear the musicians and see the torches flung high in the air when the cymbals clash. Did you know they hear them twenty miles away in Jericho?" She turned to Josue. "Will you be there too, Rabboni? How I envy you men in the upper court. You have a far better view. You can look down and see the great candles flaring in the dark like pillars of fire!"

"We shall be there, Martha," he replied. "But I tell all of you now," gesturing his disciples forward and gazing intently around to fix our attention, "as I shall tell the people tonight— that neither torches nor candles will light your way for long. But I would be to all men an everlasting light and if any man follows me he will never walk in darkness but will have the light of eternal life. For I am the true Light of Israel. I am the Light of the Gentiles. I am the Light of the World."

Uncomprehending, we remained silent, but already a cloud was gathering over the celebrations in the Temple that night. Oh, why must Josue draw attention to himself here in Judea, where his enemies abounded? Let him tell the whole of Galilee and Samaria what he pleased, but not here in Jerusalem, in the Temple itself. It was deliberately courting danger, openly inviting retribution. He would not say such things if they were not true—but what did he mean by linking the Gentiles with us? That was a sure way to lose followers. Glancing over at Lazarus, I could tell by his expression that such references were anathema to him. Matthew was grim faced, too.

In a subdued frame of mind, we returned to the house.

"Do you think he'll go tonight, Mary, and say those things to the people?"

"You know that he will, Martha," I replied. "When has he ever *not* meant what he said? He will be there in the Temple and he will tell the people what he has just told us."

And so it happened. On the first day of the Feast of Tabernacles, Josue told the pilgrims gathered in the thousands that by following him they would be led through the homeless-ness of the desert and out into the light of eternal life.

Six months later he was dead. But in the meantime he had a task to finish, and time was running out. The authorities were united in their hatred of this man whom the people wanted as their King, and if their will prevailed, the Romans would exact a terrible revenge on the whole country. The numbers of his followers had swollen into hundreds, and many had been sent out to heal the sick and exorcise evil spirits. The authority of the Sanhedrim was falling into ridicule. Among this same breed were many who closed their minds and utterly refused to believe events they had witnessed themselves. This persistent, willful blindness, this deliberate hardening of the heart was a source of grief and anger to Josue. What hope was there for such men, who would turn away from a blatant truth simply because it was not in their interests to believe it? Even with his closest disciples there were times when he was amazed at their slowness in grasping what he said, their taking only the literal sense of his words and not attempting to look beneath for a subtler meaning.

"You have all listened to what I've said. Then why do you ask such foolish questions?" And as they remained silent, he added, "So late in the day and yet still you act like slumbering men! Are you blind and deaf—and witless, too!—that you cannot recall what you have seen and heard since you have been with me? How is it that you *still* don't understand?"

Looking urgently around at them, he awaited some response, however faint, but none was forthcoming.

"And these are the chosen men," he stated ironically, "who are to understand my words and impart them to others that they might also benefit."

James and John gazed with burning concentration at a point just beyond the rabbi's shoulder, while Peter seemed absorbed in shaking the dust from his sandals. I could imagine Josue's frustration—so little time left and still so much to be learned—but how to reach them! It was always the same: five steps on, then ten paces back. Disappointed anew, Josue turned away.

"How much longer must I be with you?" he murmured wearily. "How much longer must I *bear* with you?"

If only it were all finished; accomplished. But he knew himself how much longer that would be.

Whenever he was in Jerusalem, Josue's resting place each night was at my uncle's house, and when he taught in the surrounding countryside, Martha and I went out, taking food with us. Several women followed him in his ministry—two or three widows and some whom he had healed of various infirmities—and they usually bought the food and cooked it. Judas was in charge of the group's small store of money, although Matthew, as a former publican, was better qualified to handle it. But he refused outright, and the task went to the only Judean among them.

"You should have volunteered," Peter rebuked an unrepentant Matthew. "At least we Galileans don't cheat each other," he added tactlessly.

Matthew flushed abruptly but, aware that Peter meant no sarcasm, hastily urged, "Let us give him a trial. I have nought against the man."

"He's a southerner," growled Peter, "and that suffices me. Have *you* ever met one that wouldn't take advantage of a Galilean, despite their being born with the Tablets of the Law in their hands?"

"Yes," answered Matthew stubbornly, "I've met more than one—a goodly number, in fact."

And Peter turned away in disgust.

Not surprisingly, I too received disapproving looks when the disciples saw me arrive with Martha—looks which plainly said,

"There is that Magdalene woman again." But none of them dared say anything openly before Josue. It was an agreeable surprise, therefore, when Peter tried, with rough kindness, to make amends for his treatment of me that day I had begged him to take me to Josue and he had refused. The fact that I was not turned away at Nain and that my family had also received me had obviously disconcerted him, and now he looked angry and embarrassed each time I appeared. Although he was good-hearted, he resented being made to feel in the wrong by the presence of a mere woman.

"*Shalom!*" Josue greeted us as we approached, but Peter turned away, pretending we did not exist. However, this did not prevent his eating his share of the food I prepared. For, like the rest of his companions, he was unsure when his next meal would be taken. So he swallowed his pride with my rice and vegetables, which, according to audible mutterings, could not compare with the food he ate at home in Galilee.

"Would you leave me for a mess of pottage, Peter?" asked Josue.

Whether something was eventually said or whether his own good nature prevailed I never knew, but one day I found Peter preparing a fire for us so that we need not search for kindling before we reheated the food. Flat on his face by the ring of stones, he puffed away until the sparks fanned into flames. Then, climbing heavily to his feet, he grunted to no one in particular, "That's the hardest task done. Now make haste with the food, for we leave Judea today."

He never spoke directly to me again, but after this most singular act I knew he now accepted me on an equal par with the other women, and I was content, no longer feeling uneasy when we took out food to them.

It was during these times that I realized more and more how Josue kept a handful of his followers closer to him than the rest, creating an inner nucleus which, not surprisingly, created some

215

jealousy and mutterings among the others. All rabbis took note of their more gifted pupils, but there seemed no reason why Peter, Andrew, James and John should be chosen in preference to, say, Josue's own cousins, James and Jude—or even Nathaniel, whom he praised so highly. All this quartet had in common was the fact of their growing up within a stone's throw of each other and all being fishermen on Lake Gennesaret. But now their families only saw them when Josue went preaching in the north, or when he sent them back to their old jobs for a brief spell while he went off alone for a day or two. But it was never long before they were resummoned.

"Your cousin is waiting outside the village," came the call through the doorway of the *naggar*'s shop, and Jude handed over the tools to his brother. "Complete that task for me, Joseph," he would say, and, removing his leather apron, he would go off to find his brother, James.

Susan came down to the shore to bring the message to her husband and brother-in-law, "James, he is waiting at Nazareth for you. Yona has just told me that Peter and Andrew have already gone down. John, come back to the house and take some food with you."

James clambered over the tangled heap of nets and, swinging the fat toddler, Judith, onto his shoulder, set off up the beach.

Most of the disciples' wives had long known Josue as a friend and had, on the whole, given their blessing to their husbands' following him on his ministry. Most of them had relatives or sons old enough to continue the work in their absence. Nevertheless, there were many complaints when their menfolk were away in other parts of the country for five or six weeks at a time. But as Yona once said, "It is best to let him go if that is what he wants. After all, if Anna lets Simon go, then I can't justify keeping Andrew at home—and he would be as sullen as soaked flax if I did!"

James and John, a raw, aggressive couple, also had a place in the inner circle around Josue. John followed his elder brother in most ways, but, unlike him and like Josue, he was silent if he had nothing relevant to say. Perhaps that was why John was the Rabbi's favorite—perhaps not. We could not tell the reason. The mind may proffer the most profound and logical arguments in favor of another, but the heart has its reasons which reason knows nothing of—and Josue's heart favored John.

John was also the only man who did not have a wife and family to consider and, consequently, never had to ask as did the others:

"Rabboni, do you need me for the next week or so, because I think I should go back now and see how my sons are working in the boat . . ." ". . . if my daughter's child is born yet . . ." ". . . if my wife is coping alone now that her mother has returned home."

This last was from Philip, who remarried after his first wife died. Although Josue usually refused such requests unless they were in Galilee, this time he let Philip go. In fact they had all gone to the wedding earlier that year, and the disciples had two or three days' celebration before they set off again. Peter mixed too much of the red wine and the local *schechar* and was glad to set out once more after Anna had scolded him rigorously.

"A disciple's load," he observed dismally and with an aching head, "is a heavy one."

"Mine is heavier," commented Josue briefly and unsympathetically, and quickened his pace.

It caused no small amount of talk among the disciples and their families that Josue never visited his old workshop in Nazareth, where his cousin Joseph now worked. It was as though he had forgotten that he was once a carpenter. Apart from a reference or two in his parables, he neither mentioned his former trade nor practiced it to finance himself, as all rabbis did with some trade. Still, they excused him; it would be rather difficult to carry about the tools of a carpenter's trade. A tent maker or shoemaker would have an easier task. The one thing they found hard to overlook was his omission to visit his mother when he was in Galilee. Mariam had long since gone to live with her sister-in-law, for they were both widows now, but, although she was surrounded by her nieces and nephews and their children, it was still a scandal to her relatives that her own son scarcely saw her. Indeed, if she wished to speak to him, she had to first find him, and often she had to wait until he was alone before approaching him. Mary, widow of Cleophas, defended her nephew, but no one else had anything but harsh words for this most undutiful of sons. What use lay in preaching love for one's enemies when the most basic family affection was lacking in the preacher?

"We know you say nothing, Mariam, but we know how wounded you feel."

But they did not. The sacrifice made by mother and son was not done grudgingly but gladly. Mariam was not like other women.

If the others missed their families, John certainly did not, for since his father, Zebedee, died, Salome had waxed most tyrannical over her sons and it was a relief to be away from her stranglehold for a few weeks. He was happy fishing but equally happy roaming the countryside, so John stayed with Josue and, as a result, imbibed far more of his teachings than the others. Needless to say, Peter resented John for a while, although he had no reason to be jealous of him. Right from the start it was Peter whom Josue singled out and Peter whom he promised, in mysterious phrases, a key position in the future. When Josue spoke, he always looked to see if Peter was listening, always questioned Peter to see if he fully understood. And when his disciple failed abysmally, Josue took great pains to go through everything again. But it was to Peter, too, that Josue spoke most harshly and Peter whom he rebuked again and again. Peter, who loved his Master in his own inarticulate way, would be as miserably cast down as a few moments previously he was elated. At such times we could almost see him wishing himself back at his nets in his beloved little boat, the *Deborah*, named after his favorite daughter, skimming over the waves to his old home in Bethsaida. But such moods always passed, and he soon revived again. Such was the price for training in leadership, for Josue saw qualities as yet untapped in Peter that we could not detect ourselves and which John, favored though he was, did not possess.

"*Peter!* A *Rock!*" exclaimed one of Josue's cousins incredulously when the former modestly informed him of his new name. "You're about as solid and stable as the wind! You blow hot and—"

But here he was almost eaten alive by Anna, who, though privately agreeing with Jude, was not going to stand by and see her husband criticized. So Jude retreated, wondering, not for the first time, if he had been wise to leave a good trade in Nazareth and go along with his cousin.

I recall, too, that sometimes as Martha and I prepared the meal and the men rested, tired and silent, Josue would leave us and climb up into the rocks to a quiet place. Often someone would have to fetch him when the food was ready.

"He looked around with a desolate air when I called him," remembered John. "Like a man waking and finding reality too much to bear."

"I wish he wouldn't go off like that," grumbled Andrew. "Once when we were spending the night in some cave, Peter woke suddenly and found he'd vanished. Discovered him a hundred yards away—or, rather, fell over him. It was still dark—and icy cold!"

"Peter was very angry," Philip observed. "Any wild animal could have killed him—and we still asleep!"

But Josue, more than anyone, needed to be alone from time to time, far away from the crowds that followed him relentlessly, as those needing help often do—flocking out into the desert after him, hunting him down, and, when he crossed the lake, pursuing him around the shore and wading out to drag in the boat long before it grounded. Then he could not help but pity them.

When he had eaten he always rested awhile with the others under the shade of an overhanging rock. Knowing that, despite his stillness, he was not asleep, I sometimes wondered what he thought, what he saw behind those closed lids, for these respites seemed to strengthen him more than any food we could offer. I felt compassion for this weary man, hunted down by the crowds and even by his friends should he leave them for but an hour to be alone. Concerned for his safety, they stalked him; jealous for his company, they flushed him out even in the cock-crow watch. They needed his presence to reassure them that, homeless and jobless and with the present as uncertain as the future, nevertheless all was well. They never considered his needs when, starting awake, they found him gone. But it is in the deep darkness, when dawn is still drowned in night, that the exhausted mind and body reach their lowest ebb and must have recourse to some source of strength. If he was from God, as we believed, then God must be with him. Lazarus told me several times that this was so—that he was the Messiah foretold centuries ago by our greatest prophets.

"Listen carefully, Mary, to aught that you may hear him say about himself, and remember it. Later we shall understand everything, but, as yet, we are none of us ready for the whole truth to be revealed. That day will come—and soon, I believe."

I had never heard my brother speak so solemnly before, and neither could I fully understand all he implied. He himself had only vague, wild thoughts that he hardly dared frame into words, but he guessed that whatever he surmised would be surpassed by the eventual reality. A Messiah was one thing (although history had prepared us for a glorious, warriorlike figure who would rid us of our occupiers and vengefully smite every nation where we had been exiled and enslaved throughout the centuries), but Josue had also said, "Before Abraham was, I am"—as if he had simply stepped into time from eternity. And yet there was but one God—pure Spirit—and Josue was a man like us, human and finite. And yet—"Before Abraham was, I am."

The mystery was beyond our plumbing, but, on the whole, Martha and I were pleased to put aside the riddle, content in knowing that we had found the perfect friend who met us on our own level in everything. Sometimes I almost envied the women who followed him about the country, though, just for the joy of it, I went with them several times into Galilee to see the old, loved places again. But Josue made it clear that my duty lay at home now, helping Martha and attending to Lazarus and our uncle, and that my wandering days were done.

The Feast of Dedication ended and then, to our relief, Josue left Jerusalem and went out to Perea, east of the Jordan—a safer place altogether. We hoped he would not return into Judea for a while, but as the weeks slipped past into spring and Purim came and went, Lazarus suddenly fell ill of the fever that usually afflicted him in the rainy season with its fluctuating temperatures.

At first we were not unduly worried, but after a few days its increasing virulence alarmed us. Growing steadily worse, Lazarus could no longer retain the food and diluted wine we fed him in an effort to preserve his failing strength. Our brother had never been strong, and his health was always our first concern. Seeing him now, delirious and failing rapidly, dread seized us as we saw his illness take the same course it had in our parents. It was plain to both uncle and ourselves that no physician could help him. Immediately we sent word to Josue of our brother's decline. But it was too late. The next day Lazarus died, having lain unconscious the previous twelve hours.

Our only consolation lay in Josue's pending arrival, knowing that he would share and ease our grief. We would leave the burial until the following day. He would be with us by then. But the next day came—and the next—and the next—and still he did not come. Lazarus had lain four days in his grave before word arrived that Josue was approaching Bethany. At that time the house was still full of mourners.

Martha, apprehensive of Josue's returning into Judea, took me aside as we went out for more wine, and whispered, "Mary, I think one of us should go and tell him not to come into the village. He'll be in great danger if he lingers here, with the authorities watching for him all the time. We know he would have come before if he could, but Lazarus is dead now and there is no reason for Josue to endanger himself for our sakes."

I nodded acquiescence. "I won't be at peace, either, until he's back in Perea or Samaria—anywhere but here. You slip out now while I take in the wine. He can rest in the olive groves, and we'll bring out food to him this evening, when everyone's gone."

So my sister went out unnoticed and ran toward the edge of the village, hoping that he was still on the road approaching it. But when she saw him already on the outskirts, her resolution faded in her gladness that he was with us once again. Even that, though, was clouded by the sad knowledge of our little family being more depleted than ever, and that Josue was too late to see Lazarus. If only he had come sooner!

"Rabboni," she cried as she ran toward him, "I know that if you had been here, my brother would not have died."

She could not help a note of reproach mingling with her belief in Josue's powers.

"Your brother will rise again," Josue replied, walking on into

Bethany, with Martha running in her eagerness to stay beside him and hear what he had to say.

"I know there will be a general resurrection at the last day and that my brother will rise again," she replied, "and this comforts us."

Then, coming to a panting halt, she wiped her eyes on her veil and said as she wept, "But that day is a long time hence, and we grieve for him now."

Josue stopped in his tracks and, turning to her, replied in measured tones, "I am the Resurrection and the Life. He who believes in me, though he is dead, will live on, and whoever has life and has faith in me, to all eternity cannot die."

He paused; then he asked, "Do you believe this, Martha?"

If my sister's understanding was not equal to the occasion, her faith was. "My Lord," she replied, addressing him with the title we always used when he spoke as more than a man, more than a rabbi, and reminded us forcibly of the mystery of his presence among us, "My Lord, I have learned to believe that you are the Christ, the Son of the living God. It is for your coming that the whole world has waited. I believe whatsoever you tell me."

"Come," said Josue.

As he neared the house, my uncle and I and many of the mourners came out to greet him. Despite myself I could not help feeling relieved that Martha was too late in preventing his coming.

We took Josue out to our brother's grave. Leaving behind the keening crowd, he went forward alone and stood beside his friend's resting place. I went over to stand by Martha, and when I turned to look again, I saw Josue weeping silently. This grieved me far more than all the ritual, noisy lamentations around us, for I would not see him sorrowful for the world. Then, with a deep sigh as though accepting the inevitability of death, he turned to my uncle.

"Move away the stone."

My heart gave a sudden bound. I heard Martha protesting, but Josue turned to her, saying, "Did I not say that if you believe you will see God glorified?"

And as he said this, I recalled my brother's words when I had first returned to Bethany, marveling at how everything had been resolved so easily for me. "You believed, Mary, that what Josue had begun he would finish—and faith *makes* things happen. Even now there are parts of the country where he can neither heal nor help *because the people will not believe*."

Such thoughts went whirling through my mind as the men went down to unseal the tomb. Why should he give them such an order? Not for a sudden whim to see Lazarus again—Josue was not given to sentiment—and certainly not after the body had lain four days in the airless cave. But already an expectant feeling had permeated the whole crowd as they waited, tense and silent now, while the stone crunched back, revealing the black mouth of the grave below us.

To those who will believe I can only say that the impossible happened. I had heard of it occurring in other places, but now I witnessed it with my own eyes. But it cost Josue immensely to obtain this miracle. We watched him as he prayed on his knees—and an Israelite does not pray thus unless earnestly beseeching some great favor—for the intensity of his standing prayer swiftly bowed him and brought him down. The groans that seemed forced up from the depths of his being issued from him in heavy sighs. It was as if his very life force was gathered up and poured into his petition that this immense grace might be obtained. At last he rose and, going forward to the top of the steps, looked down into the darkness below.

"Lazarus," he commanded. "Come out here to me."

Silence. And then—I heard Martha catch her breath as a muffled sound came from within the cave—a dragging step on the sanded floor. Then as we clung together in an agony of dread and hope, a shadow fell across the entrance and our brother came slowly walking up the shallow steps toward Josue, the loosely wrapped shroud trailing from his limbs and holding in his hand the *soudarion* that had covered his face. The penetrating scent of nard hung heavily on the air. As if in a dream, I watched him and Josue talking together, and then Josue indicated that Lazarus should be taken into the house to be washed and fed. While I stood there like a statue, Martha and my uncle went forward and, taking my brother gingerly by the arms, they led him away.

There had been several times in the past few days when I had wondered why Josue had not healed Lazarus. He did not need to be in Bethany to save his life. But the very thought had seemed disloyal, and I had suppressed it. Now I knew why he had let Lazarus die before coming to us. This overwhelming miracle was to be wrought in the heart of enemy country, and wrought publically before a great crowd so as to convince and convert others.

What does one do—how does one thank a man who has brought back a brother's spirit from beyond the grave? As Josue passed me on his way back to the house, I fell involuntarily to my knees. No less a gesture might I show—and yet, was he not still our best-loved friend, weeping with us in our grief and rejoicing (when did I ever see him rejoice before?) that his prayers for Lazarus were answered?

"Father!" he cried. "I thank you for hearing my prayer."

Nothing more can be said of such an immense grace, and yet there were many witnesses who refused to believe what they had seen; who accused my uncle, Martha and myself of falsifying Lazarus's death and carrying out a mock burial so as to give greater credit to Josue's so-called resurrection of the body. Martha was even "seen" taking food out to Lazarus each night— and all this when they had witnessed him lying dead in our house but a few days before! They were almost enraged that such a thing had happened and went out of their way to lie to others and deceive even themselves. It was the same "hardening of the heart" again that had angered Josue so much before.

As for my brother, he returned to ordinary life, quieter than ever but the same Lazarus. At first we viewed him from a distance, expecting him to be somehow unapproachable now, but Lazarus rallied us during our first meal together. Martha nervously helped him to some food, dribbling a tiny portion into the dish as though unsure he should be eating bean stew along with us, or even eating at all.

"Now, Martha," my brother chided gently, "it is me, you know, and I've not eaten for several days, so be more generous with those vegetables."

I was longing to ask him so many things, but as he volunteered no information, I did not seek enlightenment for a while. But one morning when we were alone together, I could not resist suddenly saying, "You were dead for four days, Lazarus."

"Yes, Mary, I was dead," he replied.

"But, Lazarus," I questioned eagerly, "During all that time . . ."

But he shook his head and made a gesture of silence. A few moments later I asked tentatively, "But at least you will tell me what Josue said to you when he called you from the grave?"

"No, Mary, I cannot," he replied.

And that was the end of the subject forever.

After this he was rarely at home, and it was uncle who willingly supported us while Lazarus went out into Jerusalem and all around Judea telling the people of the miracle that had been worked for him. Lazarus, who dreamed of becoming a teacher—a rabbi—was now seeing his dream realized, although not quite in the way he had anticipated. Indeed, he was so successful that the Pharisees' hostility was turned toward him as yet another follower of the Galilean and yet another threat, and all the greater in that he claimed the ultimate in miracles had happened to him. It was not long before we feared for his safety as much as we did for Josue's.

Adar passed into Nisan, and we now knew that Josue had every intention of being in Jerusalem for the coming feast. The danger that stalked him was almost tangible now, and if our religious authorities could only discover him alone and undefended, then he would instantly be taken. They dared not openly arrest him, for his popularity with the people was so great that a riot would ensue. Although the Roman soldiers were adept at quelling such disturbances, the religious authorities would not emerge unscathed. Blood would be shed and an accusing finger pointed at the Sanhedrim for causing the bloodshed. Herod would be enraged, and he was more to be feared than the procurator. Tetrarch of Galilee Herod might be, but his influence—and his spies—were realities in Judea.

Despite the increasing danger Josue came back into Bethany with his disciples and was the guest of honor at a meal given by our neighbor, Simon, whom he had healed of the leprosy. As the disease had slowly disfigured him, the Law decreed that Simon had to leave his home and go out into the desert or some other lonely place to live. In our country this terrible affliction is considered the result of sin. When the first white patches appeared on his skin, Simon knew he was condemned to misery and loneliness and his family to penury for the rest of their days. Rejecting the desert, he chose instead to live with a handful of other lepers in the Hinnom ravine, below Jerusalem. It was an unsavory place, with all the refuse of the city thrown into it, but it was home to Simon and his friends, who hoped that through acceptance of their suffering, they might yet atone for their own unrepented sins or sins committed by long-dead relatives who were unable to merit mercy for themselves. Simon's wife brought him food and wine, but others there had no family and each day clustered at a safe distance from the city gates to beg alms from those entering or leaving Jerusalem.

"*Amê! Amê!*" came the piteous cry if an unsuspecting person ventured near them, for if the lepers did not cry "Unclean!" and move away, they disobeyed the Law and would be punished. But even if one could not see their disfigurement, it was sufficient to note that these beggars in the distance were different, with their uncovered heads. The lepers were not allowed to wear *couffiehs*, and this singular omission made them instantly conspicuous.

On a visit to our home, Josue had missed Simon and, on being told of his affliction, Josue immediately went out to the ravine to seek our neighbor and his friends. After reassuring them that the leprosy was a bodily sickness only and not the result of sin, he healed them all. Then Simon, with his restored family beside him, went into the city to show himself to the high priest and offer a sacrifice in thanksgiving. The feelings of Caiphas on being told Josue's words can be imagined.

Glad as we were to have our neighbor with us again, we felt secretly dismayed that such an invitation had been sent out to Josue, whom we had thought to be somewhere in the Ephraim region and as safe as he could be at that time. We almost hoped that he would not accept or that the message would not reach him, but it did, and when had we ever found Josue ungracious? By the time we arrived at Simon's house, but twenty yards from ours, the guest of honor was already there, with Lazarus and the other disciples. Joanna and Simon's wife, Rachel, were already serving the food, so Martha and I hastened to greet and help them while uncle joined the men at the table.

It seemed a happy enough occasion, but all through the previous week and intensifying every day I had felt a sick apprehension, a heavy foreboding that Josue's work was soon to be consummated. We were used to his living in constant danger, being threatened, reviled and stoned, but my heart told me that this time it would be different. Yet even now his mother and relatives were traveling down-country as though it were just another Passover. A few days hence we, too, would be setting out for Jerusalem, less than an hour's walk away.

There seemed no reason or foreknowledge for me to have taken with me to Simon's house the jar of spikenard ointment which lay hidden in the adjoining room. As I said, my heart, not my head, told me that the time had come to perform this final act of service before he left us to go up for the feast. Now, as we removed the dishes and the other women went out with Rachel for their own meal, I knew I must carry out my intention before Martha returned, looking for me. Putting down my dish of oranges, I went out and retrieved the vessel from where it lay beneath my cloak. In the dim light I gazed at it, and my heart was heavy. In our country this extract of myrrh is used for anointing a body before burial. It was not an appropriate gift to bring to a feast, and yet I took it with me that day, knowing somehow that it would not be out of place.

The room was quiet as I returned. The men were somnolent after their rich meal, and only desultory remarks were passed as they lingered over their wine. I was hardly noticed as I came up noiselessly behind the couch where Josue lay. As he turned his head, I poured out a few drops of the ointment into my palm, so that he might see what I had brought.

I was praying that he would query such an offering—that he would tell me to go away and not be foolish—but instead he reacted as I somehow knew he would. With no hint of surprise, without word or sign, he showed acceptance. He simply put down his cup and waited.

An immense sadness filled me, for he waited, silent and unmoving, as the lamb which feels the slaughterer's knife against its throat. Such acceptance chilled me. Why must this anointing be so inevitable? Yet still he waited, and now the whole room waited with him. If this was necessary, then it must be done—and now.

The unmistakable odor of oil of spikenard filled the house as, bending over, I first anointed his head and then once more knelt and poured the remainder over his feet.

To those who watched there must have seemed neither use nor meaning in such an act, but sensing that he faced even greater suffering than that he had already experienced, I felt that if I sorrowfully anointed him as one already passing from us, he would understand through this gesture all that he meant to his friends. But scarcely had I risen to my feet than Judas inveighed furiously against my wanton extravagance.

"Why do you let her waste that ointment, Rabbi, when you know the price it would fetch in Jerusalem? There are poor aplenty who would profit by it. Simon here could tell you of the lepers he used to—"

"*Let her alone!*" cut across Judas's tirade and halted him in mid-sentence. Josue had already looked up sharply when Judas accused me of waste, and now his disciple's zealous concern for the poor served only to further exacerbate him.

"Opportunities will always abound for you to help them, but I shall not always be with you."

And there followed the quiet words I had somehow anticipated and dreaded, "She has anointed my body beforehand to prepare it for the grave."

A shocked silence filled the room. Then his voice, hard as iron, rapped out again, "Why then do you interfere?"

A pause; but the man of Kerioth declined to answer.

Then once more Josue said, "*Let her alone!*"

I knew it then. His very tone convinced me that he would not allow Judas or indeed, anyone, to thwart such actions, however unconscious, that prepared him for the road leading onward and upward to Calvary. All I knew that day in Simon's house was that we loved him and he was going from us. All I dimly realized was the necessity of marking his departure from our midst, but my very action had unwittingly sealed his fate—and he had suffered me to seal it. Now his face was set toward Jerusalem, and I knew he would not return.

CHAPTER
· THIRTEEN ·

THE EVENTS OF THAT week are history now, but when I look back, I see those last days as in a dream—the unreal atmosphere of tangible fear and pending disaster closing in around us, and moving inexorably through it the central figure of this greatest of historical dramas, which had now reached its last act. All I saw, all I was later told, is engraved forever on my mind.

The last preaching in the crowded Judean synagogue and the silence as his audience listened intently to the text he had chosen from the Scriptures, too absorbed in the words of this marked man to smile at his northern accent, which had earlier diverted their attention. His last visit to our synagogue in Bethany—indeed, his last to any synagogue—as one of the seven lectors, along with Lazarus. Then Josue sitting down to give the *midrash* on his particular set of verses; Josue performing *maphtir*—reading the last lesson from the prophets; telling us about himself; Josue reciting the closing prayer and the blessing before the *tebah;* Josue delivering the scrolls back to the *hazzan*. He would not read them again; instead he would replace them—with himself.

Then the last journey up to Jerusalem, with Josue going ahead as if eager to arrive and yet strangely distressed, his self-control wavering—for his will, like that of any man, had a breaking point. This a stricken Peter later told us when he unwittingly tried to turn his Master back from the path he had nearly traced to its end. The disciple's unthinking, chiding remark that Josue's fate was not inevitable was received with mingled anguish and anger.

"*Now* as I near my goal; *now* when I need your aid—you block my path! It is the *friend* who understands and supports—but *you!* You tempt me to abandon everything! Get from my sight, you son of Satan!"

We still could not believe that he meant what he said.

Then the Pharisees' fury at Josue's reception as he rode into Jerusalem from the Mount of Olives. "Has the whole world gone after him?" they said. But it must be, or the very stones on the road would cry out in protest. The last meal he took with us in Bethany: a warm spring evening with the wild hyacinths stained crimson in the sunset. The last visit to the Temple on the day before Parasceve. Going up with his disciples through the Golden Gate and into the Court of the Israelites. Putting on the fringed and tasseled *tallith* with its blue-embroidered pomegranates, as blue as the flax flowers back in Galilee where the linen was woven. Putting it on for the last time. Tying onto his forehead and left hand the *tefillin*—the phylacteries containing portions of the Scriptures—which Joseph had given him twenty years ago at his bar mitzvah. The leather was worn now, but they were old friends and would not be replaced. Tying them on for the last time. It was the ninth hour as he turned with upraised arms to the *qadosh haqedoshim* to recite aloud the great blessings of the *Shemoneh Esreh*.

Later that day came the early celebration of the last Passover meal he was to eat with his friends, for they were no longer disciples. He had already taught them all they were able to grasp, and the rest must now be left for the Paraclete to impart after he was gone from them. As host at the meal, he rose and served the meat to his guests. Then looking around at this last assembly of his friends, he revealed, "I have longed with all my heart to share this Pasch with you."

Yet mingled with this longing was the bitter sadness he could not disguise at the sight of the man opposite him, whom he would have as his friend—if that man would but allow it. But nothing must spoil what was to follow.

They had eaten the Passover lamb, but now he was replacing it with another sacrifice—his own flesh and blood—represented by the unleavened bread and purple wine he now held. A sacrifice to be constantly repeated until the end of time. A sign to them of what was to happen before the next sunset, and in the future a sign to all people not only of his death but his resurrection and ascension also. He showed them what they must do. He broke the bread, giving a strange new meaning to this commonplace gesture. As an Israelite, he knew the Law forbade the cutting of bread; it must always be broken. Now, before the soldier's spear cut into his flesh, he showed them what he had already chosen—a death that would wrench his body asunder like that which now lay disparted in his hands. It was unlawful, too, that fragments of bread, the staff of life, should be left to rot on the ground. They must always be collected and eaten, not wasted. When he had fed the thousands, he had reminded the disciples of their obligation to walk back down the grassy aisles between the people and gather into baskets all that was left lying on the ground. So, too, his body would not know the corruption of the grave. The flesh containing his pierced heart would be raised from the earth and given back to them in the outward form of fragments of bread. As ordinary bread gives health and strength to the body, so, too, the eating of the body and blood of the risen Christ would be the one thing necessary to nourish and prepare his followers for the life they would share with him in eternity. For "My flesh is *real* food. My blood is *real* drink and unless you eat my body and blood you shall not have life in you." As the yeast leavens each individual grain of wheat, so he, too, would raise them up into the Godhead and absorb them into his heart. He would change the darkness of death into sunrise.

Now at this first breaking of bread, as a sign of friendship, he dipped a fragment into the dish of *hasereth* and offered it to Judas, but the man of Kerioth, churlish in his haste, had already risen to attend to a more pressing matter. So Josue turned back to the guest of honor on his right—and saw his second betrayer. Already deeply distressed at his rejection by Judas, the foreseen treachery of Peter's threefold denial was an added bitterness. But Peter, he also knew, had no malice in him. Already his disciple was anxiously watching him, jealous lest he offer the fragment to John instead. One day true fidelity would replace this jealous devotion, but at the moment the man was transparent. Sorrow was lost in compassion and the first piece was given to Peter.

It was time now for the third cup of wine to be passed around among the guests in the most solemn toast of all, the Cup of Benediction. But, lifting the goblet, he again gave the wine and the ceremony a new meaning. It was now the cup of his blood, and like his flesh it was offered to them by one who was both high priest and victim. The psalms of the *Hallel* were not then sung, for he had other words to say to them. All sorrow, impatience and disappointment were banished and only tender, earnest love remained. Peter was listening but it seemed more anxiously wondering where his Master was going and why he could not accompany him. Pouring more wine, he resolved to tell Anna they would be staying on in Jerusalem for a while after the feast. There could be no returning home while there was so much mystery and uncertainty surrounding them. But here the ever-watchful Matthew touched his arm, reminding him that it was unlawful to drink more than four cups of wine and this was his fifth. Disgruntled, Peter put aside his cup and tried to fix his attention on what the man beside him was saying. John on the other side was already engraving on his mind the lovely truths of the relationship between Josue, his Father—and themselves. So much to be said, so little time to say it, and yet these truths were the crown and glory of his life, and his love made him yearn that they might share in them also.

Then, walking in procession, they went out into the night singing the psalms of the *Hallel*. Peter's baritone led them.

> Not to us, Lord, not to us,
>> But to your name give the glory.
> For the sake of your love and your truth,
>> Lest the heathen say—Where is their God?

Then Josue's voice singing—singing his last song on earth as they crossed the Kidron Brook and took the familiar path up through the olive groves to the Garden of the Wine Press.

> Give thanks to the Lord for He is good
>> For His love has no end.
>> Let the sons of Israel say—

"His love has no end," the disciples replied as they followed up the winding track. Soon they had reached the garden, and the final verses of the victory song rang out on the night air—

> The Lord's right hand has triumphed;
>> I shall not die—I shall live and recount His deeds . . .
> The stone which the builders rejected has become the
>> cornerstone . . .
>> O Lord, grant us salvation; O Lord, grant success. . . .

Josue's voice died away and his upraised arms dropped slowly to his sides. Like clouds that cover the moon, the heavens were closing to him. The Father with whom he shared eternal unity was now turning away, and for the first time in his life on earth, I saw that Josue was utterly alone. "O Lord, grant success," he had prayed and experienced for the first time the stunning misery of utter silence. Caught unawares, he was bewildered; then dismay slowly mounted within him. He had never thought it would be like this. He had known—and yet he had not known . . . How could he, having never experienced it before? But now, stripped of his one consolation and suddenly plunged into a most dreadful solitude, he saw in an instant, with a shock of fear and with appalling clarity, the full horror of his last hours—and he instinctively recoiled with dread. But not only that. Worse, far worse even than his approaching death was the strange agony that was already seeping into every fiber of his being, every cell in his blood and brain. By taking on the guilt of mankind and offering to pay for it, he was now shouldering the full, crushing weight of God's justice — experiencing in the most heightened sense (as only he could) not only each sin from first to last as if it were his own but also the punishment due for each transgression, repenting and atoning for them all. And like all who transgressed mortally, he was now cut off from the source of forgiveness. A sweat of anguish broke out on him as he sank down under his burden. It was a living death, a taste of hell—and coupled with this agony was ever the knowledge of his own death, now only hours away—but such a death and to what purpose?

Surely the world would love a God who so craved a share in the human condition, with all its weakness, misery and pain, to the extent of a hideous and undeserved death? They would see him full of promise, cut off in his prime for their sakes—and they would turn to him. Not that he had need of their poor love, infinitely and eternally loved as he was, but he desired it, for in his hands, preciously kept, it was safe forever from the machinations of Satan. For love presupposes the surrender too of the will. But—and he groaned aloud with the knowledge of it—in each man there was a free will, and love does not know coercion.

The Passover moon rode high in the heavens as he clenched his hands on the rock slab before him and acknowledged his helplessness in the face of this fact. Love was his life, and man's refusal to love nearly killed him. The sure knowledge of the uselessness of his sacrifice for so many was a sea of bitterness to him. There was Judas already gone, his disciples soon to betray him, his countrymen to disown him. The failures of future centuries rose up before him—the whole pageant of history, with all its horrific events caused by the perverted will of man and the prince of this world he was now leaving—and to leave it he must die. Again his mind returned to the inexorable fact. His heart beat suffocatingly and his *chalouk* clung wetly as he gazed unseeing before him, begging for courage and strength to combat his fear and wavering resolve. He had never dreamed that his will would be so shaken as to almost break him. But the exiled spirit walled in by flesh could not return to the life of the Trinity unless the body died—and he could do it all if only his Father were with him! The grain of wheat would willingly fall and die and yield its fruit—*but stay with me! Let me not be alone!*

But he was and would be to the end. His was utter dereliction, so that no man might ever say, "He knows nothing of my misery for he is God and cannot suffer." No one need ever die without God, but *he* must in order to appease divine justice. It was this unparalleled, unknowable agony that had brought him to his knees, that had felled him face to the ground, crying, "*Abba! Abba!*"—an all-pervading agony of such fear and stunning misery, of such bone-deep, soul-saturated loneliness that body and spirit were almost disparted; an agony that, unable to bear alone any longer, sent him stumbling over the stones to his friends to reaffirm the ties of kinship he had forged when he had first joined himself to the human race.

Peter, leaning against a tree, looked around at his approach, then looked again in sudden concern. Josue's whole frame was bowed down, and his clasped arms seemed to contain some great grief. Peter was alarmed.

"What ails you, man? Are you sick? Are you in pain? *Speak!*" he ordered as his Master swayed speechlessly before him.

Slowly Josue raised his head. In the moonlight his eyes were black and dolorous and his face haggard like a man bereaved. Twice his lips shaped the words before the whisper finally came. "I'm dying . . ." and his hand strayed to his breast. "I am dying of it."

Peter sighed with relief. "What mean you now, Rabbi?" he questioned resignedly and with the same hint of condescension he had earlier shown when chiding Josue for persisting in his talk of death. This latest outburst seemed but the culmination of a whole week of distress.

"I am dying," Josue persisted, unhearing. "Understand me, Peter. I am *alone*, and for me there can be no greater grief."

Uncomprehending, the disciples stared at him, disturbed to see the rabbi whom they had followed for three years now so completely broken down. Peter broke the awkward silence.

"I think we should all return home," he pronounced diffidently. "It's been a long and fatiguing day." He turned to Josue. "Come back to our lodging and rest. There's ample room."

For a moment Josue gazed unseeing at the ground, painfully adjusting to the new fact that from his friends he was to receive neither understanding, compassion nor support. Then he looked up and nodded.

"We shall go soon," he confirmed. "But do you remain here for a while—close—and keep watch. And while you keep watch pray for me—and for yourselves that human frailty may not overcome you."

He left them and, still sick at heart, returned to the shelter of the rocks. Time was passing rapidly, and he must hasten too. But he prayed more calmly now, in a hopeless, inward murmur, as if acceptance had almost been sealed.

Abba, this suffering is more than I can bear. Take it away, *Abba,* I wait on your will. Let it not happen. But if acceptance turns you to me, then so be it. Only answer me. Say but once, "My Son, My Beloved," and all can be accomplished.

Silence. Nothing. Only added strength to bear what must be borne.

The pain of loss. This slow, inward dying that never ended. He had told Peter there was no agony like it. Yet without his sacrifice, this same pain would be the eternal lot of countless souls. Never to see his Father. Never to come into their inheritance. A loss immeasurable. It must and would be bought back for them, however great the price.

I will not leave you desolate, he had promised. So be it. That promise would be kept. He would not abandon the task. *One day you will see me again and then you will rejoice.* So be it. He had come among them so they might know and share in the life of the Godhead—for love is sharing. That joy *would* be theirs, his gift which no one might take from them. So be it. But—

Bring me through it, he prayed. *For the glory of your name. For the sake of this world we love. Abba, sustain me and bring me through and out of this suffering.*

It was nearing the midnight watch as he returned to the huddled forms of his friends. James, who saw him glorified on Thabor with Israel's greatest prophets, was sleeping soundly. John—his very name meant "favored of God"—neither watched nor prayed. Peter had tried to stay awake by drowsily thinking of Josue's words at supper. He was willing to believe what he was told, but though he had studied it closely and chewed his piece thoroughly, it still looked and tasted like unleavened bread. He could not fathom it, but if Josue said otherwise then it must be so . . . Lord, he was tired! The next moment he too was asleep.

Josue looked down at his chief disciple, his Rock who had sworn his own life away but a short while since to protect him. Peter, who had never wielded aught larger than a fish-gutting knife, had bought an old, rusted sword lying unclaimed in the local smith's and girded himself with it.

"No man will challenge or arrest you while I have this," he had prophesied. But Josue only looked at him, and suddenly Peter was lost as unaccountable misery swept over him. Then his jaw set in a determined line, and slapping his hand on the sword hilt, he strode off down the road.

"Lord," he said quietly after a while. "Sometimes I'm a fool. Sometimes a drunken fool. But I will always defend you."

Gazing down at his disciple, Josue no longer saw the resolute Peter. Instead it was Simon the fisherman—Simon the impulsive, quarrelsome, prejudiced, tactless man who feared his wife's tongue and spoiled his daughters; Simon the drinker of beer and lover of strong wine who slumbered so heavily after the unaccustomed richness of the Passover meal.

Standing above his friends, Josue watched alone—and waited—tensed, full of dread and longing. Then his heart leaped. Far below, where the track merged with the bushes, there was a movement. *Abba*, he prayed instinctively, *bring me through it*. And all those you have entrusted to me. The little owls were calling as he blessed them, and James stirred and muttered irritably. Then the measured tramp of Roman infantry, and lights flickered below in the trees. It was not only the birds of prey who were abroad that night.

"John—Simon—awaken! We must leave now."

But as the disciples stirred and opened their eyes, Judas stepped forward from the shadows and, going up to Josue, kissed his hand. A centurion stood at a respectful distance but with his sword prudently drawn. Peremptory questions and direct answers—and Peter coming heavily forward, befuddled with sleep and wine.

"What is he doing here?" nodding toward Judas. "Where has he been all this time?"

Then suddenly he came to—saw Josue and his friends on one side of the clearing and Judas and the soldiers on the other, and as understanding dawned, a red mist rose before his eyes and rage nearly choked him.

"*You!*" he roared at last. "I *knew* it! You southern cur! You treacherous . . . I'll *kill* you! I'll *kill* you!"

Josue was quick, but Peter, charging like a bull, was quicker still and almost hurled himself across at the luckless Judas. As the men of the twelfth legion spread out defensively and Roman steel flashed in the moonlight, Peter panicked. With something between a snarl and a sob, he raised his sword in a two-handed grip and lunged forward. The weapon executed a clumsy arc and, missing Judas, who leapt back, struck the high priest's servant and gashed him from ear to chin.

"*Simon!*"

Josue's voice jerked him back and Peter retreated, suddenly appalled at the blood coursing down the face of the man before him. His sword dropped from his hand as he backed away toward Josue. Then, turning, he saw his Master standing alone. The others had vanished completely. Gasping at their defenseless state, Peter swung around again, only to face an advancing line of infantry with raised shields and drawn swords and, on left and right, a phalanx moving in to block them on three sides. Caiphas was taking no risks.

Peter looked wildly about him. As a fisherman, he had faced death several times when the *qadim*, like a terrible whirlwind, blew in suddenly from the east, lashing Gennesaret to a boiling fury and threatening to smash his frail boat to pieces. But that was grappling with the elements. There was a challenge there. But not here. To resist, to fight back, meant death.

"*Run!*" he shouted as panic seized him again. Crashing through the straggling line of torch-bearers and hangers-on, he leapt down through the rocks and bushes to the safety of the ravine. He would hide among the tombs that covered the valley from end to end. He would be safe there until morning, for neither Roman nor Israelite would dare search a cemetery by night.

So the peaceful gathering for Passover ended in noise, confusion and fear. Torches flared; shadows loomed in the garden; figures fled away into the concealing darkness, obeying only the inherent urge to survive. And Josue was alone again—alone for the remainder of his life on earth.

Back down the hill once more and across the brook. The measured tramp of sandaled feet, the cry of the guard high up in the watchtower, and the Sheep Gate slowly opening. Back into the city to the high priest's house, where the lamps still burned and robed figures flitted to the door to watch for the soldiers' return. Then accusations and lies on one side—and silence on the other. Then a pertinent statement by the prisoner and a sudden eruption of anger, and the first blow struck.

"You of the *am-ha-arez* to address the high priest thus! Answer directly! No more evasion now!"

Night with a keen wind scattering the sparks from the glowing brazier across the courtyard, where a handful of soldiers crouched at their eternal dice. Night with the moon shining coldly on the white marble of Caiphas's house. Then once again, as midnight slipped into the cock-crow watch, the regular slap, slap of the sandaled feet of the escort across the flags and the stumbling steps of the prisoner. Back through the passageway and down the steep ramp to the underground cell.

Freezing stone and walls running with damp. Rotting straw and the scampering of rats. Darkness as black as pitch. A torch flared as the bound prisoner was thrust across the threshold and fell heavily into the room. The guards were now off duty, so they bore him company till sunrise. At last the heavy door grated shut, the key turned and the bolts shot home. Retreating footsteps . . . laughter . . . then silence. Exhausted, numbed with cold, parched, bruised and aching in his bonds—and still it had scarcely begun.

Abba, bring me out through this suffering. Bring me through it.

Waiting. Waiting. Would the morning never come, we thought, when the news was brought to us while it was still dark. "They have taken him." Stark and brief came the worst tidings in the world. Then at last the first streaks of dawn tinting the blossoming sprays of the almond trees. Dawn with the sleepy twitter of sparrows and Peter sobbing brokenhearted in his wife's arms.

"He looked at me, Anna. He turned and looked at me. He knew what I'd said. He *knew!*" he whispered repeatedly till Anna grew frightened and called Deborah to comfort him. But Peter had the death wish on him.

"I should have stayed there in the cemetery. I shouldn't have gone after him. I should have stayed there and hanged myself. I swore before God that I didn't know him—and he knew, Deborah, he *knew!*"

Then everything accelerated as the news flew around and the crowds flocked to the Antonia, where Pilate had set up his Praetorium on the Gabbatha, the great flagged inner courtyard where the trial was to be held. The Roman governor was most displeased to be brought into the affair at all, suspecting that this might be the first of many flare-ups common during a great

245

feast like the Passover. Arriving earlier from his coastal head-quarters at Caesarea, he had prudently brought along extra men against the eruption of the celebrations into violence, for the Passover provided an ideal political arena for the warring factions in the city. By the time the bulk of pilgrims had arrived, the entire cohort of the twelfth legion was garrisoned in Jerusalem. One could hardly move for troops.

We ourselves had hurried up from Bethany the instant the dawn broke and now struggled through the crowd to reach our friends. I recall looking about and seeing myself surrounded by women. Mary, sister-in-law of Mariam, with her sons' wives, Esther and Akbor; Susan, Salome, Joanna, Yona; dear Martha holding tight to my hand; Miriam, Anna and her daughters and, yes, there was Matthew's wife, Tabitha, standing beside us. Had all our menfolk been arrested as conspirators? My heart lurched with fear, but then Lazarus came pushing to our side. After that there was no time to think of anything but that it was the eve of Passover. Not much could happen to him with the feast so near, I thought. I was wrong.

Several times during the trial we glimpsed Pilate coming out to confer with the religious leaders. He was at their beck and call in this, for they would not incur defilement by crossing the threshold of the Praetorium. Besides, they had no wish to see again face to face and in broad daylight the man they had taken by stealth and illegally tried and condemned during the concealing darkness of the midnight watch.

Haggard and perplexed at this early call and scenting danger for himself, Pilate said he wanted only to be rid of the whole affair. That we could believe, knowing him as we did. But the chief priests, like wolves encircling their prey, hounded him back into the court, back into the Judgment Seat. They wanted the prisoner dead. Let his blood be upon them, but the man must die. They feared him because he spoke the truth *to* them and *of* them. He sounded their death knell. If the people continued listening, there would soon be insurrection and a resulting massacre by the Romans. The Sanhedrim could not be seen to countenance any ruler but Caesar.

And so the trial went on. The procurator, despite being four or five years in Judea, knew neither Hebrew nor Aramaic, and Josue had no Latin. So the interrogation proceeded in Greek, somewhat slowly at first for the prisoner's Greek was rusty. Koine after all, was the language of the businessman and the wealthy. Then the thought occurred to Pilate—Was not the man a Galilean? Blessed reprieve! Send him to Herod! Josue was the tetrarch's responsibility, not Pilate's. But neither word nor sign did the emperor's puppet draw from the King of the Jews—not even a minor miracle to tickle his jaded palate—and before Herod had finished his nostalgic dream of a little villa tucked away in the foothills of the Appenines, the prisoner was back.

Outside we waited—and waited. Then the rumor went around that a maidservant had rushed into the Praetorium with a message to Pilate from his wife that the man was innocent and that he should take no part against him; but the girl was taken out and the trial went on. A man with the eyes of Rome upon him—and the eyes of Tiberius were harsh indeed—cannot put his career in jeopardy for the sake of a woman's dream. Why should he please Claudia, anyway? She never considered him. The dream of the little villa faded as he recalled his wife's love of Rome, with all its fashion and gossip. Well, at least it was better than here, he conceded. Immortal gods, would he never get away from Judea! Of all the places in the empire, it was the most difficult to govern—and he would never have been posted here but for his father-in-law's influence. What was that he had learned as a child? *"O mihi praeteritos referat si Iuppiter annos."* To turn back the shadow creeping across the dial. He should have been a farmer. He would have liked a little farm tucked away below the mountains, but when your father and three brothers chose the military life, it takes moral courage to be different without being accused of cowardice—and marrying Claudia hadn't helped.

He sighed and turned back to the prisoner. He was tired of being used, and yet he could not ward off a decision much longer. The sham respect the religious leaders showed him was now overlaid with menace. If this man were simply a pious fanatic, they would have ignored him or dealt with him themselves, but he was obviously too influential to be dismissed like that. Caiphas had his own reasons, and, innocent or guilty, he wanted the Nazarene dead and he, Pilate, was to have the blood on his hands. Yet if he released the prisoner he would stand accused of freeing a traitor to Rome, which would be a blunder not likely to be overlooked by the emperor—particularly if it were placed alongside his past record as governor of Judea. Someone must lose in this charade of a trial. Mentally consigning the whole of Israel to Hades and Caiphas in particular to its lowest regions and worst torments, he suddenly disclaimed all responsibility and retreated from the Judgment Seat. Bringing out Josue along with another prisoner, he placed the burden of guilt on the crowd by asking *them* to decide whom he should release, as was the Passover custom. Each feast a free pardon was given to one man.

They chose Barabbas, who was guilty of sedition—an ironic choice—and in the same breath rejected their Messiah. The rabble rousers and the paid men of the Sanhedrim had been at their work among the throng, fanning that mass emotion that warps judgment till "Crucify him!" ran the insidious whisper from mouth to mouth. The words spread like a contagion through the crowd, increasing in volume till they swelled up into a great, vibrating shout that rolled like thunder toward the archway, where the prisoner stood bowed and trembling in agony from the scourging Pilate had ordered in the hope of appeasing the crowd.

With all the force of an onrushing wave the shouts struck, broke over and swirled around him. I looked around at my countrymen in horror and disbelief. Less than a week ago they had hailed him as their King, yet now, forgetting everything, they abandoned him—for their will prevailed and he was led out to die along with two others, petty thieves, who were to share the same fate. These were brought out of the Antonia by a group of Samaritan auxiliaries, for they were stronger than Josue, who was still being loaded when they were already on the road and beginning their last journey.

It was about the fifth hour. A pale sun gleamed on the Temple roof and a cold spring breeze scudded across the worn flags as the last prisoner came slowly under the gateway. A purple robe—ghastly mockery of kingship—trailed from his shoulders to the ground, impeding his agonizingly slow progress, so bowed down was he with his burden. Worse horror—two thorny branches from the jujube tree that grew in a corner of the fortress had been formed into a cap and thrust on his head. I felt myself sinking at the sight and the knowledge that it was to be as he said. But Lazarus gripped my arm and steadied me.

"Let us go on ahead," he whispered, and I nodded, still looking vainly around for Mariam, whom no one had seen that morning.

Until then we had been hemmed in by the crowd, but now we struggled out and pushed our way up through the stepped streets toward the Ephraim Gate. How strange that the busy life of the city should go on around us as though nothing of great note were happening! The pilgrims buying, the sellers haggling and everywhere the bleating and lowing of the sacrificial animals crushed into makeshift pens. It all seemed grossly unreal as we passed through and arrived at the western gate. And there we waited . . . and waited.

The soldiers arrived with the first two prisoners—and still we waited. Then at last he came into view. Salome, who was below the gate, saw him first, and her cry of horror was drowned almost immediately in the moan of pity that rose from the assembled women and was lost in the hubbub of the milling crowds on their way to the upper bazaar. Some were mildly curious, but most were indifferent. It was a gloomy sight when one had come all the way to Jerusalem to enjoy oneself.

We had only glimpsed him previously at a distance, but now we saw him clearly. He was almost unrecognizable. His face was scratched and bruised, and his eyes blackened and filled with blood. Blood matted his hair and trickled down from the plaited thorns forced down so hard upon his brow that they rested just above his eyes, piercing and stinging. One great spike had penetrated and lifted the flesh by his right temple so it stood out like a grotesque, swollen vein. A Roman scourge is a terrible weapon. Its many thongs, knotted and tipped with lead, flay the skin, and now rags of flesh hung down from his shoulders, chest and arms. His *chalouk*, torn open at the throat, revealed these lacerating wounds as he moved slowly toward us, a raw, bleeding mass, scarcely human, with the rough, splintered wood of his great burden—the horizontal cross-beam— falling across and chafing the gaping wound on his right shoulder. Blood was everywhere. Could a man lose so much and yet still live!

The sight was unspeakable, and more than one of us prayed that he might die there below the gate as he reeled, staggered and fell and was dragged to his feet with a blow to set him on his way again (and what agony for him to be touched!). Almost immediately he sank down once more in the filth of the road.

"Hasten, man!" shouted the centurion above us as he stood idly swinging his hammer and a handful of iron nails. "It will soon be Passover and your people want you dead by sunset."

Slowly raising himself on one arm, Josue turned his swollen eyes up toward the gate, as if measuring its distance against his ebbing life. Cursing impatiently, one of the auxiliaries caught hold of a passerby, a Cyrenean, and ordered him to help carry the cross-beam, which had fallen across the prostrate figure on the ground. But the man argued violently. He still had his beast to purchase and his two sons were waiting for him in the Temple. Besides, he had not come all the way from another continent to help a common criminal. But eventually he was forced out into the road and with ill grace lifted one end of the beam—and gasped in sudden surprise.

"This is far too heavy for one man to bear!" he exclaimed to the onlookers. "It's well that he'll soon be resting on it rather than the contrary."

The soldiers chuckled, but the Cyrenean, looking down at the man on the ground, suddenly grunted, "Poor wretch! This is no way to die."

While the argument was continuing, another auxiliary dragged Josue into a kneeling position so as to reload him. In that short interval a woman stepped forward and swiftly wiped away as much dust and blood from his face as she could before being roughly pushed back into the crowd. This compassionate gesture enabled him to look up and see his mother standing before him. I had not seen her till then or noticed her go forward. At her feet lay the prisoner's board, still wet with fresh white lead. The red and black characters of the official notice were clearly legible—*Hic est Rex Iudaeorum*—and below, in our own language—This is Josue, King of the Jews. Stopping, Mariam retrieved it from the dust. Reknotting the cord, she hung it around her son's neck. Then she lifted his matted hair from his face, and for a moment her hand rested lightly on his tortured head in a last blessing. Then, turning abruptly, she walked out through the gate. With one supreme effort, her son rose and staggered after her and reached the threshold at last.

Oh, save yourself, I was praying, save yourself. You *can* do it. But as if reading my thoughts, he turned slightly, and in a voice

251

scarcely above a whisper, told us to conserve such pity, for the day was coming when we should have terrible cause to weep for ourselves and our children. We still did not understand that it was essential that he die.

And so he passed out of the city he loved and mourned over—out to where the vertical posts reared stark against the sky awaiting their cross-beams. It was about the sixth hour as the hammers sounded in the still air. And then for three hours we watched him die. It was a long time. There was a cold wind blowing up on that place they called Golgotha, and yet we never moved. We simply sat there on the great boulders—the townspeople, the religious leaders, passersby, the mocking and the silent—fixing our eyes on the central cross. We waited for something to happen. Perhaps we expected a miracle, for somehow we did not really believe that he would simply die, like the other two crucified along with him. Yet it was plain that he could not last much longer. His limbs, stretched and pinioned on the beams, had been dislocated and the nerves severed in wrists and feet. His sunken eyes were half-closed, his mouth was blue tinged and twisted and the now dried blood coated his body like mud. All the time that icy wind was blowing, drying out the remaining moisture in his skin till it resembled nothing more than tanned leather. In the silence we could hear the slow, painful in-breathing as he pressed his feet, crossed and pinioned with one great nail, against the upright beam to prevent his sinking beneath his own weight and, with this achieved, the rattle and gasp as he breathed out again. Each filling and emptying of his lungs was achieved in agony.

Mariam remained beside him, but his eyes were now so dulled that I could not tell if he saw her. Grief froze her like a statue, and yet it was as if with every fiber of her being she summoned up all her strength and will and directed them upward to give him added aid to suffer. A bond was forged between them by her wholehearted acquiescence and cooperation. If a reprieve came at that moment, I believe she would have ignored it. If her son willed to die branded with blasphemy and sedition, then she would not try to dissuade him, for they were of one heart and mind and his will was also hers.

Time and again he had said, "I have come to do my Father's will"—and to the last moment of his life he conformed to it. Yet even as I recalled this, another picture came into my mind of the child Josue and Lazarus playing in the *naggar's* shop long ago, and their curiosity making them heedless of Joseph's warning not to touch the sharp knives on the bench—until Josue cut his fingers on them, and then he learned to be obedient. Josue, our dying friend, still learning to the end of his life to be obedient through suffering. He resembled nothing more than the atoning scapegoat driven out of Jerusalem at Yom Kippur, driven outside the city walls and into the wilderness loaded with the sins of the people. This was Josue's Day of Atonement.

"He's dying . . . He's dying . . ." came the repeated whisper throughout the long hours. But he was dying when they first nailed him to the cross. Yet still the words went around—"He's dying . . . dying . . ." How long could a man be dying and yet not die?

Since the sixth hour the sky had been lowering, but now the heavens grew darker and darker and soon it was almost as black as night. Fearful of this sudden eclipse, many went away. The soldiers ceased their squabbling nearby and looked up.

"A bad omen," one remarked. "Such a Passover!" and tipping a little *posca* onto a sponge, he impaled it on a hyssop wand and lifted it to the cracked lips of the dying man. But Josue only tasted the diluted vinegar that had been mingled with the obligatory myrrh to deaden pain, and it was given to the other two instead.

As the ninth hour wore on, we all with one accord moved

253

closer, knowing that this must surely be the end. From somewhere there came a faint rumbling like thunder, and a man in the crowd jested nervously, "Such a Passover indeed! A sudden eclipse and now an earthquake!" But no one smiled. Then from the Temple came the faint notes of the silver trumpets as the sacrificial lamb was killed and its blood poured out over the altar.

But we scarcely noticed, for suddenly Josue raised his head, as if the signal for which he had lingered was come at last. Looking above and beyond the Temple roof, his voice rang out strong and exultant:

"Father, it is achieved!"

The last word echoed and reechoed in the darkness. This was no death rattle but a great shout of triumph.

For a moment I, like the rest, was stunned by the power in his voice. Then I leaped to my feet sure, so sure that here was the miracle we had longed for—and it was to happen now! But in that same instant his head fell forward, his body slumped and the holes in his wrists gashed wider as his arms suddenly bore his full weight. He was dead.

"Not too soon," remarked a soldier throwing down his dice. "And I get the coat!"

But a white-faced centurion gestured him into silence and thrust him back from the spoils.

In my shock and anguish I did not recall his saying that no man would take his life. He would lay it down of his own volition and in his own chosen hour. That hour had come, and though he had suffered torments, his death was not through weakness but an act of his own will. But nothing of this did I remember as, sinking down, I rent my garments in grief and sobbed aloud.

A soldier climbed up and drew out the nails while John and our friends Joseph and Nicodemus held the body. Then they lifted him down and gave him back to his mother. The other two prisoners had already been thrown into a hastily dug, unmarked grave in the Hinnom ravine, but Pilate had agreed to Joseph's request that Josue's body might be given back to his relatives. Joseph had already offered his own tomb as a resting place. So with John and Nicodemus bearing his body, Mariam his head and I his feet, we carried him to the nearby garden. Joseph had already gone ahead with Lazarus to open the cave entrance. He had not realized it would be used so soon.

The sabbath was almost upon us as we laid him on the rock shelf, wrapped in the linen which Joseph had provided, and sprinkled around the myrrh and spices that Nicodemus had brought. Then it was time to leave, for soon the *shofar* would sound from the Temple that Passover had begun. After the sabbath we would return and finish our task, but already my heart was breaking at leaving him there so hastily shrouded and in a borrowed grave. At that moment Mariam came out and, seeing my distress, led me away as she had done years ago when mother died. We had all marveled at her self-control, for in our country we are not stoic at even the most ordinary death.

Now the women, including Martha, wanted her to return with them. But she turned to John instead. "We will go home now," she said.

And he took her back with him to the suburbs where he was lodging with his brother and sister-in-law.

"Why does she go with him?" Jude protested to his mother. "We're her relatives, not John and James."

"Son, let the matter rest," Mary replied wearily.

"But she's your *sister!*" he exploded. "And Akbor expects that she stay with us!"

"On such a day as this you argue about trifles! Mariam has chosen to lodge elsewhere, and if *I* feel no neglect then why should you? Now—for my sake—for your cousin's sake— *Peace!*"

And she walked away.

CHAPTER
• FOURTEEN •

I RECALL LITTLE OF the following day—only that we
huddled desolate in our homes, unmindful of the Passover
feast being celebrated around us. Our only comfort lay in
preparing the spices to anoint his body for its solemn burial.
Everything else seemed irrelevant, useless. We had already
forgotten all he said.

The day dragged on. Immediately after sunset Lazarus and
our uncle set out for the house where James and John were
staying. Peter and Andrew came in with their families from the
adjoining lodgings, and soon the room was full to overflowing.
Indeed, John slept in the next house so that Mariam might have
the company of Susan and Salome. But Mariam had gone early
that afternoon to the Temple with her sister-in-law and intended passing the night at Mary's lodgings in the city. The others
chose to remain at home. Their despondency dismayed Lazarus
as he looked around at them. After three years of definite
direction they now seemed aimless and lost, vaguely wondering
if they should stay on in the capital or return to Galilee and
resume their old trades again. Anna was already urging her
husband back to Caphernaum, and her will could prevail, for

Peter seemed incapable just then of making any decision for himself. Salome, too, persuaded by Anna's example, was scolding her eldest son in the opposite corner of the room.

"Only think what your father would say if he could see you now! Three years following that man and see the results! Him dead and buried—God rest his soul!—and you left faring no better than when you started!"

Salome had been ambitious for her sons, and this crumbling of all her hopes now exasperated her to the extent that she boxed her first-born's ears. But now John intervened, followed by an anxious Susan, who already had trouble enough with a teething, fretful infant.

"Peace, mother, peace!" John urged, coming between them. "We are all too cast down to make any hasty decision on returning to Galilee. We must put aside such an issue for the next few days until we see what may happen."

"What may happen!" Salome rounded on her youngest. "Now hearken to me, John. No matter what the others decide, I will not have my sons made fools of any longer. You surely don't propose to carry on that man's work, and"—this with grim satisfaction—"you know the consequences! Now you do as your mother bids you. It's your duty—you owe it to me. And Susan, be sure you tell James the same! Now give me the child, daughter, and fetch the gourds."

Muttering to herself, she sat down with her grandson while John wandered miserably off with three-year-old Judith and Susan looked wistfully at James. If only they might go home now. Esther, she knew, was longing to return to Nazareth with her husband, and it would be good to see her own James back in the boats again. And the climate here was not good for the baby. Yes, she must take them all home—but only if James came with her. Across the room Yona was saying nothing to Andrew but looking ominously significant.

This was the scene of misery and confusion that Lazarus

encountered. After the women were dispatched to fetch the water, some sober discussion took place, and for no clear reason it was agreed that they would all stay on for the rest of the Passover week and then leave for their various homes. There was always the hope of something else happening, for John recalled Josue's words that another would come to them if he went away. John could recall little else at the moment, but it would not be right to depart so soon. They must wait anyway to attend to the body. Mariam would be grieved to leave her son buried in Judea.

"I don't recall anything like that being said," grumbled Peter with a flash of his old jealousy. "There is nothing a stranger could tell us. After all, we were closest to him . . ."

Then his voice trailed off and inside the folds of his *couffieh* he wept a little with remorse—and envy of the one who might come and supplant him.

Lazarus returned to Bethany more depressed than ever, having failed in persuading them to stay beyond the week. I believe my brother had more faith than they at that time for, having been restored from the dead, he was already daring to think—He gave me back new life; then why not . . .? Then he sighed. Josue, living, worked such miracles, but Josue, dead—a corpse could do nothing but rot. Yet still Lazarus went on hoping all through that sabbath day.

Midnight passed and it was already far into the cock-crow watch when, being careful not to wake Martha, who was sleeping soundly at last, I rose from my bed. It was useless trying to rest any longer. I would go and keep vigil in the garden until Mariam and the other women arrived after daybreak. Then, once we were all assembled, we would ask the men placed there by the Sanhedrim to remove the stone for us. In the meantime Josue would not be guarded entirely by strangers. When Martha woke, she would quickly guess my errand and follow me.

Taking up the bundle of spices, I stole from the house and walked slowly in the darkness toward the capital. Usually it was dangerous to be abroad so early, but I did not expect to encounter anyone after the feasting of the previous day. My mission, anyway, made me impatient of delaying an hour or so longer. The sabbath had seemed interminable. There was no sign of movement on the Antonia as I passed under its walls. The Temple loomed massively into the darkness, and I inhaled the mingled odors of incense and rancid fat which hung for days over the city after Passover. Then, as I neared the garden, a figure stepped forward to greet me and I recognized the voice of our friend Miriam. She, too, was unable to sleep and came to await the dawn with me.

"Joanna promised to meet me," she whispered, "so I shall wait here until she comes, but go on if you wish. Mariam will be here the moment it lightens."

This suggestion well suited me so I set off alone along the track that ran behind Joseph's house and through a grove of screening olives into the garden. But as I emerged from the trees, there was a crunching of sandaled feet over the stones and two men suddenly loomed out of the darkness, almost knocking me down in their haste. Before I could recover and retrieve my bundle of spices, they had vanished. I could only imagine that they were the guards hastening back to the city now their term of duty was ended. But surely it was still too early for the watch to be changed? However, I had more important matters to occupy me than Caiphas's paid men.

Thrusting aside the incident, I hurried on into the garden— and saw immediately that the tomb was already opened and not a guard to be seen anywhere. Running up to the cave, I stooped and looked inside. It was empty. The linen shroud lay undisturbed on the rock slab, but of the body it had contained there was no sign. Shocked and dismayed, I rose and looked about the garden. The worst had happened. He was stolen from us—but by whom? Not his friends. Not the Sanhedrim, which was only too anxious to prove that he was but a man and a dead one, too. A vanished corpse would only endorse the general belief in his resurrection. Not for nothing had Caiphas posted his own guards by the grave. But only recently they had been attacked and overcome, and the body taken—for what reason I could not begin to fathom—hence their headlong flight to raise the alarm. I, too, must do the same. I must tell our menfolk what had happened.

It was almost the dawn watch as I flew back down the road to Joanna and Miriam. With one accord we turned and ran out to the suburbs to Peter's lodging. Despite the early hour he and Andrew were already at their meal when we rushed in. Our agitated babel did not impress Peter. Indeed, he only put down his crust to inform me that I should do better to return home and rest like Anna and Yona, who were still asleep.

"Be sure that Mariam doesn't hear of this when she returns today. She's had grief aplenty without listening to such hysterical babble. Besides," he added, "you've no business to be abroad at night. I'll warrant Lazarus knows nothing of it."

As I remained silent, he went on. "I thought not," he grunted, and looked across at Andrew as if to say, "You see, I was right about that woman."

Taking a deep breath to instill patience, Joanna stepped forward and began the tale again. As my testimony was suspect, I remained silent in the background. It was the wisest course with Peter present, but I knew he would listen to Joanna, a sober woman who was not given to fantasies. Her husband, Chusa, was an official at Herod's court and an admirer of Josue.

But before she was half-finished, John, impressed by our persistence, threw his cloak over his shoulder and ran out into the road—which immediately sent Peter after him, jealous that John should be first. Andrew shrugged his shoulders and opted to remain at the house while Joanna and I followed close behind the two men. Before we reached the olive grove, we met a grim-faced John returning.

"It's true," he said briefly to Peter, who, speechless from running, could only stare at him in amazement, which swiftly turned to anxiety.

"We must go back at once for Andrew and James, and then decide what to do—where to start looking. You women come with us. If the guards return and find you here, they'll suspect us of elaborating some plan to spread rumors of a resurrection."

But as we began retracing our steps, John suddenly exclaimed, "Mariam! Who'll tell Mariam?"

We all halted, aghast.

"Well, we can't let her discover it alone," said Peter briskly. "One of you women must stay behind and break the news—and tell her we're moving heaven and earth to find him!"

"Mary, you must stay," said Joanna turning to me. "Chusa will miss me if I don't return soon, and Miriam needs to rest. I'll take her home."

And indeed the aging widow, who had already borne great hardship in following Josue, looked drawn and fatigued.

"Yes, you stay," confirmed Peter. "It could harm Chusa's position if Joanna was seen, but if the guards find you here, it won't matter. Simply say you're awaiting the mother and you know nothing of the body vanishing. No need to even mention you've been in the garden. Do you understand?"

"When Mariam comes, I'll take her back to Susan's lodging and we will await news from you there," I confirmed.

Peter turned back to John.

"The gates will be opened soon, so I'll go into the city and rouse Matthew and the others. You go back and fetch Andrew and James—and *run!*" he bellowed unnecessarily as they parted at the crossroad.

It was as well that I should wait for Mariam, for, like Miriam, I no longer possessed the energy to go looking for Josue's body.

He was gone, and searching would not bring him back. Those who took him obviously did not mean us to find him. But how to tell his mother!

Desolate now and sick with misery, I wandered back up the road, still clutching the bundle of spices. Twice before I had anointed him, and I had hoped for the comfort of serving him again in like fashion. Who was so heartless as to desecrate a tomb and steal him away at dead of night? Passing through the gap in the wall, I entered Joseph's garden again and looked hopelessly around.

Not a soul was about, for it was still very early, but the light was strengthening now, blurring the sharp outline of branch and twig and softening the garden so it shone gray and silver like a pearl. The sodden grass was rimed with dew and a white mist hung over the trees. Silence. An expectant hush as slowly, almost imperceptibly, a pink glow like fire stole across the Kidron Valley and glimmered over the garden. The first pigeon called softly into a Nisan dawn, and high up in the cypress came the rustle of wings as a dove "croo-crooed" drowsily in reply. On the trellised wall the first flower unfolded and lifted its chalice to the sky. A faint breeze stirred the vines, whispered a secret to the wind flowers and, rustling down the white aisles of the lilies, scattered their incense on the air. Points of fire glinted and shimmered in the wet grass about my feet. The dawn-lit garden shone with a quiet radiance. Seeing it, my vision blurred and my throat ached. It seemed such a mockery. He was stolen from us and now we should not even have the poor comfort of giving him the last tokens of our love or looking on his face again. Many of us had scarcely eaten or slept since he was arrested, and in my weakened state I could bear no more. Turning away, I leaned against the lichen-stained wall and, burying my face in my hands, sobbed aloud at this final blow.

"Woman, why are you weeping?"

Looking up with swollen, half-blinded eyes, I dimly noticed the figure of a man standing a short distance away, and a faint hope stirred. Perhaps this gardener was a witness to the happenings of the previous night? He may even have acted on some order from Joseph and removed the body himself. Why had I not thought of that before?

Trying to compose myself, I stumbled eagerly across to where he stood. Behind him the first rays of the rising sun shone palely through the mist, blinding me even more as I replied, "I weep, sir, because the body of our Master whom we laid here but two days since is gone. I cannot think who has taken him or where he has been carried . . ."

But my voice broke at the thought of Josue's body falling into his enemies' hands. Uncaring that this man was but a servant, I fell on my knees and begged, "Where have you lain him, sir? If it is you, or if you have any knowledge, then tell me that I might go swiftly and carry him to a place of safety. That I might have good news for his mother when she comes."

And as he remained silent, I cried, impatient and fearful, "Tell me, sir, I implore you! You may trust me. I am his friend."

One quiet word only came in reply, and yet in that same instant it fell on my ears—oh, it must surely also have thundered through the universe, shattering the rocks, sounding on the sea bed and splitting the heavens apart, such was its power to move.

"Mary."

The garden blurred and reeled. A cockerel crowed faintly in the distance, and in that same moment I looked down and saw the great wounds on his feet. One word only might I whisper and then I could no more for the stunning joy that flooded through me.

"Rabbi."

I call my sheep by name. They hear my voice and they follow me. And fain would I have followed and clung to him, but he moved away. Already there was work to be done and messages to carry. "Go back to the city and tell my brothers—and Peter— whom you have seen. Tell them that I am returning to my Father who is now their Father also and whom they too will see."

Somehow I arrived again at the gap in the wall and then looked back, hardly daring to think he would still be there, but he remained under the trees where I had first seen him, as if to reassure me that it was indeed he.

I recall little of the journey back, but a strange sight I must have looked to the early risers as, with hunger and exhaustion forgotten, I sped back through the stirring suburbs to the city. A blackbird fluttered, scolding, across my path, then, flying up into a juniper tree, caroled his own morning *Shema*. High above came the thunderous rumble as the Nicanor Gate opened its bronze jaws to the first worshippers, but the Temple itself might have fallen into ruins for all I noticed that morning. All the disbelief and uncertainty of the past few days vanished like mist before the sun. Our Messiah had returned from the dead! From the *dead!*

Now with his rebirth, life was given back to the mourning earth and nature, eclipsed by his death, now shone with his life. Dressed in their own livery, the flowers lined the roadside— blue hyacinths, silver-leaved olives, the scarlet wide-eyed anemone and the white and gold narcissi—royally dressed to greet their King. "Lift up your hearts—He is come!" sang the olives like water in flood after the rains as I ran past the blossoming gardens and up through the green suburbs. "Lift up your hearts—He is here!" they shouted for joy to me and to the whole world as, laughing and weeping like a mad woman, I flew on through the gates and into the city.

On and on I ran through the narrow streets, stumbling over the old men laying out their wares, whirling past a clutch of squawking hens only to collide with a tethered donkey. The fruit panniers overturned but the owner's cry fell on deaf ears. Was that all he could think about? Fleeting amazement that the whole of Jerusalem, these proud descendants of Benjamin and Judah, had not heard the news! Then, as I turned the last corner, an old woman standing in her doorway suddenly held out a basket of flowers in a gesture of delight at their loveliness, as if to say, "Were there ever such beauties on the hills before?"

It seemed a fitting end to my journey. Never were crocuses more lovely than the purple and saffron of those she held with the dew still wet upon them. All the sunlight of springtime seemed gathered into their gold. *Everything* was pure joy that morning. Almost speechless from my headlong flight, I accepted her silent invitation and flung out my arms as if to embrace them.

"They are glorious, mother, glorious! Oh, was there ever such a day as this?"

"Aye," she said, slanting a seasoned eye up at the blue. "But we've waited a long enough time for it."

"A long time," I panted as I turned up toward the house. "Centuries and centuries—and we are here to see it!"

Everything had come true. All he said, all I had read in the Scriptures—it had all been fulfilled. Soon the whole of Israel would know their Messiah. Soon we would be a great nation again. And once more the refrain went beating through my mind—He is alive! He is alive! He is *alive!* I could not take in the full wonder of it. I had yet to realize what this resurrection meant for us as well. But one thing I instinctively knew as I staggered to the door of Matthew's lodgings—I was not the first woman to see him. No need to run and seek out Mariam. The mother already knew her son was alive. Small wonder she was not at the tomb with the rest of us.

Then, clutching the railing of the stairs, I recalled just in time that if I burst in looking as I did—wild-eyed, muddied, tear-stained and exultant—no one would credit my words, and Peter

266

least of all. So gathering my last remnants of strength, I rearranged my veil and drew my cloak about me to hide the grass stains on my tunic. Then I walked in quietly among them and waited until every eye in the room was fixed on me in puzzled attention, for in our country it is not the custom that a woman should make a cynosure of herself. Her place is always in the background.

When absolute silence prevailed, I spoke in as low and steady a tone as I could muster. "I have seen him. When I returned to the garden, he was there and spoke to me. He is alive and come back to us"—and here my voice trembled slightly—"as he said he would."

Having stated the news which had been consuming me all the way back to the city, I now wished for nothing more but to burst into tears of joy, but my credibility depended on my calm, so I stood rigidly there awaiting their reaction.

This time they believed me. Minor though I was according to our Law, yet I knew what I was saying. But if I had anticipated a joyous spate of questions, then I was disappointed. Tabitha, clutching a wheaten loaf, gaped at me from the shadows and a knife clattered in the silence. But the men continued staring at me in astonishment, their minds and bodies too tired to fully grasp my words. Such a vacuum could not persist, so, realizing that for the first time in my life, I was in control of a situation, I sealed my statement with words I knew would bring home the news to at least one of them.

"He called you his brothers," I announced turning to the figure at the end of the room. "'Tell Peter,' he said. 'Tell my brothers—and Peter.'"

There was a pause, and then Peter rose and came slowly toward me. Like the rest, he looked haggard and exhausted, and his eyes were almost closed for he had wept himself half-blind with the shock and grief of his denial. He had gone into mourning more thoroughly than the rest by clumsily shaving off his beard. Now, with cuts among the two-day-old stubble, he looked a sorry sight. He asked hoarsely, "He spoke of me? You are certain, woman, he said my name?"

His look was piteous. This was a different Peter from the man who had lectured me but an hour since.

"None but yours," I confirmed gently. "The name he gave you."

I am no joy giver. I have brought scant happiness to few people in my life, but that was a feast day for me—the day when I became the messenger through whom new life was put back into Peter, who looked neither incredulous nor amazed at my words. On the contrary, it was as if a sign, long sought for in misery, had been given and this giving, so sudden and strange, nearly broke his heart again. For a few moments he gazed through me. Then his mouth twisted and, turning, he went and looked out over the city for a while.

When he returned to the room and faced us again, his eyes, though still swollen and bloodshot, had once more the old look of doglike devotion.

"We will go to Joseph's garden," he announced quietly, "and if he is no longer there, no matter. We shall see him soon. He will show himself to us."

Then, wheeling back to the door, he laughed delightedly. "Look, here comes John at last, with Andrew and James. They think there's nothing to hasten for—only more bad news—and I told that lad to run!"

Sparks of the old Peter flared up as he swung back impatiently into the room. "Well, what ails you? Come! We'll tell the others and then we'll go to the garden, the Temple, Galilee—anywhere!" he exploded, "until we find him again."

Oh, you will see him soon, I thought as the room suddenly burst into life. If I have, then you surely will. Then I was swept aside amid a clatter of sandals and the familiar jabbering of

Galilean tongues. *Couffiehs* were securely adjusted and cloaks swept over shoulders that seemed to have squared themselves again as they surged out onto the steps.

Standing in the doorway with Tabitha, I watched them set off down the street in the sunlight. Already Peter was recounting his past experiences, and the old boastful strain flared up. "Remember how I walked on Gennesaret with him? He called me and immediately I went out onto the water. You all thought it was a ghost!"

"And then you sank," Thomas commented dryly. "Cephas!"

For an instant Peter looked discomfited, but Matthew brought them back again to the main subject. "You shaved off your beard too soon, Peter," he remarked kindly. "You should have waited two or three days."

And if the laughter that followed was rather inordinate, then the passersby would only assume that these men had been celebrating the Pasch too well.

As John, James and Andrew came toiling miserably up the street, Peter rushed down to meet them with the others close behind. They converged in a jubilant, gabbling throng around these latest arrivals, and from my vantage point I saw the good news begin its long round. But at that moment its messengers reminded me more than anything of boys new-released from school in Magdala—laughing, shouting, punching each other delightedly and exulting like children that they were forgiven. How brave and happy they were now their Messiah was back, somehow defying the laws of nature, as a Messiah should. Soon his kingdom would flourish and power be placed in their hands! That was all they understood that day, but more was required than this joy to re-create them. His Spirit must needs come to touch and alter, turning them overnight into different men and endowing them with a wider vision.

But now, ignoring the early pilgrims flowing up through the

269

Golden Gate into the Temple, the four brothers performed a celebratory circle dance—very popular around Gennesaret but not in the Holy City—with arms linked as they whirled clumsily around to right and left, faster and faster—until they were called to a sheepish halt by Anna, scandalized at her husband's caperings.

"Are you all *mad!*"

Following behind with Susan, Yona and Salome, she had not yet heard the news, and I did not wait to see the womens' reception of it. But as I came down the steps, I saw Susan make a gesture to her mother-in-law clearly indicative of wine being poured lavishly down a throat, and Salome, nodding grimly, advanced on James and John.

"Do you think they will ever be sober again?" Tabitha called down to me while the twins, David and Yeshue, gaped through the railings at their father. "Even Matt has gone mad today. Only look at him!"

"Yes," I answered with conviction. "They will—and soon— but today they must dance for joy. *Shalom!*"

Leaving her, I crossed the street as sounds of a shriller commotion reached my ears and I knew that Salome, at least, had heard the news. Looking back once more, I saw Peter's striped cloak whisk around the corner with John's brown one following, and then they were gone. Frail vessels as yet but, nevertheless, my countrymen and a gallant little band of Galileans.

Still holding the bundle of spices, I walked down the sunlit street, hearing all around the chatter of the Judean women as they returned in clusters from the well.

"Did you have a good *Pesah?*" they called in holiday mood to one another, and "A blessed *Pesahim!*" came the happy cry from doorways, steps and balconies as they passed by.

I had almost forgotten it was still Paschal week. How much

had happened since I set out in the dark on my mournful errand—and to think that I went to keep vigil, and all the time *he* was waiting for me!

Smiling to myself, I turned out through the Fountain Gate and followed the road home to Bethany to bring my brother and sister the sweetest news in the world.

ENVOI

THE REST, AS I have said, is history.

He was with us forty days, and hundreds saw and bore testimony of it. When he left us, we were desolate but continued in prayer in Jerusalem as Peter insisted we should, until the final seal was set on his work by the coming of the Paraclete among us. And so the great task began. We could no longer see his face, but he had left us a precious deposit of faith, which we guarded jealously. For already minor "Christs" were springing up throughout Israel.

We expected hostility from our countrymen and were not long in receiving it, but despite active persecution, his words were fulfilled:

"And I, if I am lifted up, will draw all men to me."

The preaching of the Christ who was crucified and died a manifest failure became an instant success.

Peter, as foretold, became our spokesman in the Church, and before long he had declared that the Mosaic Law must not be imposed on the Gentile converts. It was a stumbling block to them and must now be set aside.

Slowly the doors of our minds swung open, and for the first time in our history we looked out beyond our own narrow frontiers and saw the Gentiles in a new light—the Gentiles who mattered, whose salvation was desired by God as much as our own. So the good news swept like a fire throughout Israel and the neighboring countries. Ignoring language, custom and culture and leaping across such barriers as seas and mountain ranges, it fanned out to Italy, Greece, Africa and Asia Minor, Spain—and far away into lands that were but a name and a mystery to me. "I came to spread fire on the earth and what do I desire but that it be kindled?"

Long after we had left Israel, the great convert, Paul, set out on his missionary journeys, taking as his special task the conversion of the Gentiles. Now Paul is dead, and Peter also. Peter, who was commanded for love's sake to feed and tend the flocks of Christ, has amply proved his love. Many others have also been put to death, and now only John remains—and even his safety is precarious, for his pen confounds the heresies that spring up around us.

Mariam, too, is no longer with us. The world has yet to realize her greatness. Now, at the end of my life, my plea to her is that which she heard from the crowds outside her home in Nazareth—"Mother, we would see your son." And soon she will answer with the same words as when she took him from exile in Egypt: "Child, we will go home now."

Finally the prophecy made to us as he passed through the Ephraim Gate has been fulfilled. Jerusalem is razed to the ground. The news was brought to me but a week since. The old order has finally passed away—as he said it would.

We women helped as much as we could in the public ministry and were greatly assisted by the larger number of Gentile women who came to us seeking instruction. They, in turn, opened their homes and gave financial aid to those

Christians in need. One whom we were particularly pleased to welcome was Sarah, wife of Judas. Stricken at the betrayal of Josue and her husband's subsequent suicide, poor Sarah fled back to her home in Kerioth. But Mariam sought her out and, convincing the timid woman of her friendship, brought her back to Joanna in Jerusalem, who treated her so kindly that Sarah followed her about like a grateful, adoring child. We hoped she would eventually help us in our work, but soon afterward her parents urged her to remarry so they might be cared for in their old age. Sarah, weak-willed and eager to please, was persuaded to return to them.

During this time Martha and I remained at home in Bethany helping the Judean Christians adjust to their new faith in a hostile community still awaiting a Messiah. Lazarus went everywhere, preaching and healing, and we only saw him when he came to Jerusalem to attend the meetings there with Peter and the others. Our brother was particularly hated by the religious authorities, for having returned from the dead, his influence was immense with the ordinary people. Indeed, but for the riots that might ensue, he would have been imprisoned more than once.

Finally an ultimatum was given him. Either he cease his work or leave the country. Lazarus chose the latter, for if he could not preach in Israel, then some other country might be his mission field.

The news was given to us in Bethany, and within hours we were escorted aboard a foreign cargo ship bound for one of the distant trade routes. We had left our homeland forever. "Next year in Jerusalem," we said to our friends in a last farewell, but now the old saying had a different meaning for us all.

During the many months we were at sea, we endured the extremes of any long voyage, storm-tossed for hours amid a panic-stricken crew or becalmed for days with the water rationed and tempers frayed with impatience. We made no conversions aboard the *Phoenician Star*.

Israel lay several hundred miles behind when we finally crept along the coast of Gaul and slid into the harbor. There we were put ashore as the captain had been instructed and paid to do. Tanned by sun and wind, we disembarked with nothing but our clothes and a few keepsakes given us by our friends. But several inhabitants of the little coastal town, on hearing we were Israelites, came forward to help us. Already they knew of our Messiah and were disposed to learn more.

So almost immediately the work began again. Had he not said—"To the uttermost ends of the earth?" Then to its most distant corners we would go if we were needed, but in the meantime there was a harvest to be reaped in Gaul.

My story is almost ended.

Our task was not easy, but after two or three years the numbers of those received into the Church swelled, and finally the ruler of the country, following the example of his convert wife, ordered the pagan temples to be destroyed. What thanksgiving we felt to see those idols crash into the dust! Today a great cross stands at the entrance to the harbor, telling all approaching vessels that this is a Christian country. It is as he said—"My Word shall prevail."

Martha, as hardworking as ever, died ten years after our arrival here. Right from the start she went wherever she was needed, especially among the children, who even now, with grandchildren of their own, still tend the place where she lies.

Lazarus, at our ruler's express wish, organized the building of our first church and laid down the tenets by which its people were to live and minister. For my brother was appointed bishop of our country, by command of its ruler and consent of Peter and the others in Jerusalem. Lazarus, whose school friends had called him Rabbi and whose greatest wish was to become a teacher; Lazarus, who lacked the energy and initiative to run a family business—to him fell the task of firmly establishing the Christian faith in Gaul. He toiled but a few years—long enough to see it expanding and flourishing—then, as his health failed rapidly, appointed his successor, whom he had marked and trained from the start. And so my brother died—for the second time. Only now there was no bleak limbo awaiting him, for "No man can see God and live." And I believe that, at the last, Lazarus saw his friend and Master again—saw, and died of it.

During this time I had taken as my special task the education of those girls left orphaned or abandoned by their parents and who, unless cared for, would soon run wild in the streets, begging and living as they could. But now there were many capable women far better equipped than I to succeed me. So, after my brother's death, I felt free to leave the house where we lived with the girls and choose the solitary life I love here on the fringe of the desert. Many visit me as they pass through on their way to more distant mission fields, and often, too, my girls come, bearing gifts of fruit and news of the others, which I delight to hear. But usually I am alone and content to remain so. To live out my days in peace is beyond what I deserve, but this blessing, it seems, is not to be taken from me. So, thankful, I wait.

And for what do I wait? For nothing less than the return of the God-Man who walked through the land of Israel for a few short years and then was gone. He has promised to return—the whole Christian world awaits it—but the years roll by and still he tarries. Yet sometimes I glimpse him at the heart of things—in the desert flowers—in the song of the birds at sunset—and more especially in the silence when I suddenly start around, so sure that I will see him there and hear his greeting. But it is only the rustle of the breeze and not his cloak as he draws it across his shoulder, only the sky's reflection and not the blue and white *tallith* that covered him as he turned toward Jerusalem to pray.

Often I recall his words: "He loves little who has little forgiven him."

Much has been forgiven me, and therefore I love still more. Therefore my lamp is trimmed. For I am ready. I am waiting. Outside, the burning sun beats down on the sands, and through the silent heat of the day and the long watches of the night, my ears are strained for the sudden joyful shout:

"Behold, the bridegroom comes!"

Then indeed shall I start up and with a great cry of longing and love run out to meet you. Then indeed "this wilderness and this solitary place shall be glad, and this desert shall rejoice and blossom as the rose. It shall blossom abundantly and rejoice even with joy and singing," as the words fall again on my ears as in Bethany of old:

"Mary, the Master is here and tells you—*Come!*"